ONE BLACK EAR

Sheldon Baverstock

CRANTHORPE
—MILLNER—

A CIP catalogue record for this title is available from the British Library.

ISBN 978-1-912964-29-1 (Paperback)

www.cranthorpemillner.com

First Published (2019)

Cranthorpe Millner Publishers
18 Soho Square
London
W1D 3QL

"One Black Ear" would probably still be just a thought process were it not for my wife Dagmar and son and daughter, Kel and Kim, who challenged me to 'put my money where my mouth was' and write it. Joined by my son-in-law Tom, they are a team that have given up hours of their time to read, edit, offer suggestions and provide guidance on many drafts. My harshest critics and most sincere supporters, without them I would not have been able to pick myself up and dust myself off through the arduous process of bringing this book to fruition, and get it published.

A special thanks to Kim whose input and guidance was invaluable when I struggled with how to handle some of the sensitive descriptive passages relating to my characters. She reminded me of the power of allusion.

Also a special thanks to Dagmar whose tireless attention to detail meant my publisher received a pretty clean manuscript.

Which brings me to the team at Cranthorpe Milner. They have been everything they promised to be, extremely supportive and professional. Polishers of rough diamonds.

Finally I would like to acknowledge LIV Village, just north of Durban on the Kwazulu-Natal coast, from where I drew ideas for my book's community. Established by two dedicated individuals this community has saved the lives of countless orphans, giving them love and hope of a fruitful and rewarding life.

About the Author

Born and raised in South Africa, Sheldon began writing towards the end of a long and successful career in IT. Tenures with various global companies saw him and his family set up homes in England, New Zealand and Australia where he currently resides. He has two daughters and two sons. "One Black Ear" is his first novel.

Prologue: *Ka Malakabe*

'Out of fire' (Sotho)

From where the old man is lying in the cave's dark interior the cat's back and muscular shoulders are clearly outlined, a menacing silhouette against the light outside the entrance she's guarding. The tufts lining the tops of her ears twitch as they rotate, listening, able to pinpoint with deadly accuracy any object that makes a sound. She's big for a caracal, the dominant predator in these hills. This cave is her lair and she's arrived back from a fruitless night's hunt, still hungry. When she turns from her position at the entrance and finally enters, she knows she will find it occupied. Something outside is distracting her though, she peers out into the distance.

Inside the old man shivers in the darkness. He's been here since yesterday evening, brought by the elders of his tribe, to die. As was the custom for people of his years, infirm, near their end. His breathing is short, it rattles his skeletal frame. Dawn. Even in the cave he can smell it, the crisp freshness of the new day. Air clean and cool. Free of dust, it has settled with the cooling night air. Darkness retreating before the emerging light on the horizon. Gradually birdsong starting, just one or two calls at first but growing in volume as a new day is delivered to them from the darkness. Now, first signs of a red horizon. Sky streaked with the remains of yesterday's clouds waiting to be coloured with the glow of the rising sun. A sudden dark flutter in the canopy, the first flight.

The silhouette at the entrance to the cave, the old man knows, also observes the new day. Past the black outline of her he can see the hills he had roamed for nearly a century. He thinks he saw her glance back. He knows she will finish his time on this earth. As the elders intended. A death fitting for a onetime warrior such as he.

The white shroud rolling over the mountains surrounding the distant foothills might be swirling morning mist. It *does* roll gently like a mist, but it has a signature, a smell, hanging ominously in the air it moves through. The smell of burning grass, heavy and pungent, accompanies the smoke as it falls lazily into the valley below. A white, moving tablecloth being drawn over the golden veld. Gentle white swirls, no hint of the violence that has given birth to it.

In South Africa, fire is often the forerunner to a new birth. The lush green of newly emerging veld grass after a fire, rolling into the distance like fresh green paint on a fire-blackened canvas. The kaleidoscope of colour presented by flowering proteas bursting from blackened hillsides of *suikerbos* devastated by fires on the slopes of Table Mountain. More recently, smoke not white, black, acrid, from burning tyres ignited by rioting young people in protest, looking for change, freedom, the birth of a new nation. Fire is the seed and the pain of this land's rebirthing process.

Now, in the dimness of the dawn light, as if drawn over the ridge by the smoke, a thin line of red creeps above the highest rim of the mountains. Red like the last of a setting sun over a dark ocean. But this horizon is growing. More like a sunrise. Flames peeking over the ridges now, seeking out more veld grass to devour, fuel for an insatiable natural combustion engine. The first explosive cracks pierce the air as the fire gathers momentum downward, gathering speed as it moves from the rocky slopes of the mountain into the dry grassy hillside. Rabbits pop up and down like fleas leaving a dying animal, seeking ways to outrun the monster descending towards them.

The caracal slowly begins to edge back from the entrance into the cave. Unsure whether to retreat to the cool darkness or make a run for the river below.

In the distance, across the river, on the other side of the valley a wide sweep of grassland awaits its inevitable fate. The tall grass waves slightly in the up-draught created by the now huge, roaring fire spreading across the downward slopes as far as the eye can see. Sky dark and orange tinted. This monster's roar grows louder as it thunders towards the animals below it, frantic to escape. They know, gathered together, they have a decision to make. The river. It is fast-flowing and has the potential to offer its own dangers. The fire has no thought for what lies ahead, only its desire to consume.

It will not be the first time the river has played a role in a fiery grassfire. This land is prone to drought and a bolt of lightning can ignite bone dry grass easily. Releasing an inferno that will not be stopped by a miserly few drops of rain from a stillborn storm unable to deliver salvation from its huge pregnant clouds.

One by one they plunge into the water. Survival has made strange bedfellows. Game swimming alongside wild dogs and predator cats. The food chain on hold. Although the current takes them downstream, it is not strong enough to sweep them away and their somewhat diagonal crossing is successful.

By mid-morning it's quiet. A black, hissing hillside slope rising into the smoke hanging listlessly above the devastation, unmoving with no wind to ride. On the other side of the valley and the river that cuts it off from the fire, the veld is unchanged. Dotted with animals still damp from their swim, beginning to graze, looking up at the blackness from time to time. They have unexpectedly become residents on the side of the river they only ever gazed at from a distance in the past, wondering.

In the cave high on the hillside, suffocating smoke sucked in by the cool space of the cavern claimed only one life.

PART ONE

Chapter 1

Caracal Ridge

Standing apart from the tour group gathered around the bus, Roger peered across the dark icy waters of Table Bay to the city seven kilometres away, wrapping itself around the base of the mountain. A gust of wind blew strands of grey across his forehead and he retrieved a hand from the warmth of his pocket to tuck them under his beanie. Off to one side between the city and the island, a low rain cloud swept slowly across the ocean, slanting rain falling behind it like an old galleon, wind billowing its grey sails, leaving a shower of sea spray in its wake.

It was his second trip to Robben Island, and he knew better than to bother with the fare offered by the tiny kiosk they had stopped at halfway around the island. There was a rush of people off the bus, through the cold wind to the toilets nearby, and the line ensured he had time to wander off and take in the view. It was a bleak day. *Much like the mood some South Africans felt growing within them,* Roger thought. *Those that had expected overnight wealth following the release of Nelson Mandela from this windswept island. Not just jobs, electricity and education. A huge challenge in itself, the African National Congress having to catch up years lost through apartheid. After the initial euphoria, the need for everyone to be realistic.*

A large piece of driftwood had made it past the onshore waves, rocking and rolling in the almost black water, on its way, escaping the island. Being some distance from it, with its shiny dark shape appearing and disappearing as it rose and fell in the choppy sea, Roger imagined he was watching the back of a swimmer. An escaping prisoner. One of those that had felt so desperate, left forever on this desolate island, they would try anything to get off it, as had happened about two hundred years ago when African leader Makhanda Nxele tried but didn't make it after falling from his boat and earlier Jan Rykman who did, swimming all the way to the mainland.

Roger's first visit to the island had been a few years earlier, also a business trip to Cape Town. That day was sunny and still. It was not long after the first free election and everyone was positive, proud of the 'rainbow nation' and its new multi-coloured flag. He remembered standing in the disused quarry, already a shrine, the sun reflecting off the white limestone walls with such intensity he had to squint though his Ray-Bans like they were made of plain glass. This was where Nelson Mandela and his friends had spent eight hours a day doing backbreaking work. No sunglasses. His eyes were damaged forever.

***

In the years following Nelson Mandela's release from incarceration on the island and in later years on the mainland, the Lenbruikte family, like many South Africans, were experiencing mixed emotions. Mostly excited anticipation after Madiba was freed but also apprehension, common for many white people. The family, colourful threads in this emerging tapestry of the new South Africa, were the most recent owners of Caracal Ridge, a farm nestling in the foothills of the Drakensberg mountains. With ancestors born in these foothills hundreds of years ago, their workers would have to be considered the farm's legal owners.

The Lenbruiktes, a complex set of characters, over time come together and move apart, like pieces in a game of dominoes, sometimes connected sometimes not, seldom providing an expected outcome.

When it came to their country's past and present issues, the family's thought processes spanned two generations. In the eyes of their 'silent generation' father, Tom, it was what it was. How could anybody change what the government decreed. "It's what people voted for, I'm happy to just get on with it. What can just *one* person do anyway?"

With the start of reform in South Africa his children, brothers Clive and Dirk, fraternal twins Pat and Lerryn and, oldest of the girls, Eve, like many white 'baby boomers', found themselves becoming reflective. They had known since they were old enough to know, about the injustices handed out to the indigenous people of the country. Why had they done so little to try and change the situation? Now, knowing what just a few had achieved, even if it *had* cost them half their lives in prison, they could not say they, themselves, had been a powerless minority within the white electorate. In the past, whenever they were forced to pull their heads out of the sand as a result of some, normally shocking, event, government propaganda was the antidote to the painful reality that came into focus around them. They accepted the false words of rationalisation with relief, an opiate, so they could get on with their comfortable lives, quietly enjoying the oft-used, envious comment from outsiders, overseas visitors, *you South Africans really know how to live*. Well, the white ones did.

Roger, who in years sat somewhere between Tom's age and the age of his oldest, and estranged, son was not sure where his own beliefs lay. He thought he knew where they

12

should be, but when it came to a political view, he spent a lot of time looking over his shoulder feeling guilty and looking forward feeling apprehensive, not sure where to hang his hat. He generally found himself sitting on the fence for fear of spoiling the conversation, but knowing he would feel self-convicted for the rest of his life for doing nothing.

Recently, looking for a mislaid document, Roger had come across the ID book that had many years ago been his mother's. Her ID photograph had reminded him of his childhood time with her, how caring and kind she was. How easy life was. There was an insert, though, that brought him back down to earth. A required, at the time, government certificate confirming race, neatly folded between the plastic cover and the first page carrying her photograph. It was stamped 'Classified White'. It forced him to remember the darker background to his childhood time in South Africa. His political heritage and its imposed contradictions. Even now, notwithstanding the positive reform that was taking place, the country had seen increasing violence. Aggression seeped through everyday life.

Roger cringed. He remembered as a belligerent, spoilt eight-year-old hitting out in temper with a bread knife at their fifteen-year-old servant, Sifo. Known as a 'house boy', his responsibilities included keeping Roger out of trouble. The memory flooded back to Roger. The young lad had removed the loaf of bread Roger was ineptly trying to cut a slice from, grinning and saying, "Hhhawu, Roger, that's a big mess. Let me cut that for you." Roger

13

looked from the mangled loaf held in Sifo's hand to his toothy grin.

"No. Leave me!" he yelled. Trying to use the flat side of the blade Roger struck at the arm reaching for the bread knife. To his horror the knife had slipped and turned in his sweaty palm, cutting into Sifo's arm. Roger had been severely reprimanded by his parents, but not as harshly as his bandaged keeper for letting him play with the bread knife. For his part the young Roger had felt less chastised and more surprised to see blood the same colour as his own come from black skin. He was transfixed as he watched the cloth his mother held to Sifo's wound turn crimson, blood running down the arm. *So, inside the black skin is just another person like me,* he thought. *Otherwise why would the blood be like mine and not black?*

As he grew to adulthood there would be many times when Roger replayed his epiphany. As have many white South Africans replayed their own, similar epiphanies, and just as many times put them out of their minds.

***

Descending through these scene-setting foothills was one of the farm's herdsman. His name was Bonniface, a name he had been given as a young lad due to the grin that had become part of his features, white teeth splashed across his

14

black face. No doubt a descendant of the rightful owners of the very land he was tasked with herding cattle on, he whistled directions to his bovine charges. Invisible to Bonniface, a pair of dark eyes, nestling in fur the same colour as the veld grass she lay in, watched with deep concentration. Black, tufted caracal ears twitching.

The herdsman was distracted, agonising over a dilemma his wife and he faced. His son, who could speak English, had recently been given a job up at the main house, working with the farm owner, the 'baas'. His wife was very proud of this 'going up step' as she liked to call it. An opportunity to reap the rewards of being accepted by the 'white people'. Bonniface was not convinced. He agonised over the lack of interest his son showed in the traditional values of his people. This desire to have what the white people have. The young had become greedy he thought. His son, Jon, said it was just the desire to have what they had been unfairly denied for so long. Now with democracy they could have anything. With many years of life experience behind him, Bonniface was yet to be convinced about that.

The wild cat, sensing the lack of focus in the herdsman, took a few quick, silent steps forward before lowering herself, turning to stone. The herdsman sighed, thinking how it was that his wife thought only of their son and so little of him and the work he did to keep them. "Jon will learn from Dirk, he is a good man, a smart white man. He shows respect for Jon," she said. Bonniface's father had taught him, as he had been taught by his father, to be thankful for a secure job on the farm. Not to be 'cheeky',

15

as the various white farmers who had owned the farm over the years referred to any work query or indication of ambition from a black farm worker, no matter how justified.

Bonniface worried that Jon was getting beyond himself, he should be humble, accept his meagre wages, be grateful he had a job. There were many others in the surrounding area that did not have jobs, a place to stay on a farm, a farmable allotment, no matter how small. Why could he not just grow vegetables on the land the farmer allocated to the workers and feed a family. And that was another thing, Jon had no family. The young people seemed to not care about getting married anymore. Just wanting to be like the whites, have lots of money, a car, electricity. Distracted by his worried thoughts, Bonniface had no idea he had company. When he turned, whistling, and waved his stick at a wayward cow the cat sank into the grass, disappearing as quickly as if a magician's hand had passed over her.

The ridgeback was huge. He was set apart from both actors in the unfolding drama on this grassy stage. Unseen, but totally aware of every movement. As he often was, he had been with the herdsman all morning, a companion, tracking him, curious about his passage through the hillside. Occasionally running up to Bonniface, exchanging a bark with a few words of Sotho from the herdsman before running off back into the veld. Now he tracked the progress of both from a distance, downwind from the cat, and lying in the tall grass, invisible to Bonniface.

16

The caracal's long, tufted ears swivelled as she pointed them this way and that like a second pair of eyes, but moving independently, replacing light with sound. The slightest rustle was all she needed to triangulate the position it was coming from to within a few inches. Pinpointing any other hunting opportunities or lurking danger in the surrounding grass.

The cat would not normally be so interested in the herdsman but there were no vulnerable calves to target in the herd he tended. She had kittens to feed and, with very little available for her to eat at this time of year, their milk was at risk. As big as she was for a caracal it was debatable whether she could take down the herdsman, but he was old and slight, worth consideration, it was worth testing his strength.

She raised herself slightly off the ground and slipped forward, almost slithered, and froze, and moved forward and froze. The dog tensed his solid frame. A 'concrete block wrapped in fur' is how he had been described by a neighbour farmer who sometimes coveted and often feared the ridgeback for his interest in his lambs. The dog watched the cat closely, readying for her inevitable launch. Bonniface was oblivious, staring into the distance, randomly kicking stones as he watched his animals.

The rattle of these stones blended into the crash of grass as the caracal broke cover, her eyes wide dark pools fixed on the herdsman. A darkness that held thousands of years of predator instinct. The sleek body rose as she accelerated, but Sebete, unobserved and anticipating the cat's move, was already at the point of interception between cat and prey.

As she veered off, the huge muscular canine exploding into pursuit, any bystander observing this unfolding turn of events could not be blamed for expecting the worst for the young feline mother.

***

Nearing retirement, Tom Lenbruikte had moved to Fynberg, the small farming town not far from Caracal Ridge without even knowing the farm existed. He had had a successful and lucrative career as an investment banker and was on the board of several companies he had invested in.   His raised profile had brought him wealth, a wife that was about the same age as his oldest son, Clive, and a successful vasectomy reversal. In addition, he had a young daughter, the result of the reversal, who could have called out to him "Grandad, Grandad!" in public without attracting the curious stares that "Daddy, Daddy," always did.

Tom had decided it was time to be away from big city life. He would travel to conferences and his various consulting assignments. It was a good reason to bring to reality the private pilot's licence he still viewed as a strong possibility, even at seventy.

He enjoyed being a big fish in a small pond, having made sure everyone with influence in Fynberg knew all about his past career history. He also bought the town's only restaurant, hoping to install his son Dirk as manager, given his training was never going to be applied to a legal career. Tom was convinced that training would bring the disciplines and processes needed to run a restaurant as a profitable enterprise. It was worth a telephone call to his son, he decided.

This was the reason Dirk was stumbling around his apartment in Durban, side-stepping empty glasses, scrabbling through piles of discarded clothes trying to locate the ringing telephone that his various girlfriends used with abandon. Naked statues, suddenly mobile, speaking animatedly to their friends, never returning the phone to its allocated home, under the bed. Finally, he and Tom both had receivers in their hands, and his dad proceeded to outline to Dirk a scenario that would ultimately chart a totally new course in life for him.

Having slept on the previous evenings' telephone conversation, and given he had no other ideas for his future, Dirk decided it was worth a look. He threw a duffle bag into the back of his car and headed north to the mountainous farmland where Tom had made his new home. About six hours later he duly made his entrance as the first 'hippy' ever to grace the dusty roads of this very conservative farming community and its *redneck*, Afrikaner-dominated town. On his way to his father's house, he stopped off at the local shop for cigarettes. The aroma of marijuana clinging to Dirk from the joint he had smoked in his car did not go unnoticed. Townsfolk were used to smelling it as it was commonly grown and used by black people. That was OK though, it was just an indigenous thing, but a young white boy? Just too much. And when it became clear he was the visiting son of their newly acquired celebrity businessman from Durban, it was worth some airtime on the local gossip circuit.

It wasn't too much for two young girls who spied Dirk sauntering by. They had learnt, over the last few years, how to survive the perils of their male-dominated environment. It grew in intensity at the end of each school term with the arrival of testosterone-filled high school boys from distant boarding schools for end of term holidays.

They loved that this stranger totally ignored them, not noticing their giggles as they elbowed each other, making comments about his slim fit jeans. Unlike their pimply, overzealous local suiters. To the girls, the boys of the Fynberg, being farmer's sons, seemed single-mindedly determined to prove to their farmer fathers that they were ready to give up school and start work on the farms they were sure to inherit. To do this they needed a serious girlfriend to take home, a potential bride to introduce to Ma and Pa. The two girls made up the town's pool of 'potential brides'.

Had their observations been made from a point less distant than circumstances dictated, they may have found an up-close, Dirk less appealing. Smoking and partying over the last ten years had taken their toll. Nonetheless rose-tinted glasses were a given as they ogled the long reddish mane falling over his face when he eased himself back into his car. Not bothering to look back over his shoulder for other cars in Fynberg's non-existent main street traffic, Dirk pulled away from the kerb and headed in the direction of his father's rather upmarket house. The car's number plates confirming this 'cool' stranger came from a big beach city down south was enough to make the girls blush at the possibilities. Imagine, running off with him to 'Durbs by the sea', lazing around on the beach. As Dirk's battered VW disappeared from view, the girls resolved to find a way to meet their cool new stranger, if indeed he was going to be a local, or at least find out who he was.

Dirk got on well with his dad. He was the only one of the siblings who was not affected by their father leaving their mother for a much younger woman. The girls, angry for a long time, finally accepted it as 'part of life'. Dirk's older brother Clive was the worst affected. Seemingly already estranged from his father, after the divorce Clive had moved to England, and the only person he had maintained contact with was his mother. Rita became the conduit for news from him to his brother and sisters.

**

Clive had left it until his graduation day to tell his father he was not joining 'the firm'. He had studied economics because that was what Tom had convinced him he *should* study. All through school his dad was his career role model, so he was easily persuaded. He hadn't enjoyed it much, slipping business and marketing courses into his university curriculum without Tom knowing, to relieve the tedium of statistics.

"Why would you do that? Lecture a bunch of disinterested students trying to complete their studies as quickly as possible so they can get out and do yet another start up," Tom said with a smirk. "I have you set up for a graduate role at the bank already - it will launch your career. I will make sure of that, I'm a partner."

"Dad, it's what I want to do. I enjoy academic life. Just not economics. But my degree allows me to lecture in business studies. The Dean has already indicated they have a position for me."

"You won't make much money," Tom said shaking his head. "Not the sort you need to afford to send kids to private schools, which will be essential the way this country is going."

"No," Clive retorted. "But if I can help my students make a success of those start-ups, the jobs they create will mean work for people. That is what this country is desperate for. I can make a contribution. Oh, and by the way I don't intend having kids anyway."

Clive had the feeling, watching his father's back leaving his room, there would be no more pats on the shoulder along with 'chip off the old block, aren't you?' comments.

***

Clive found that it was more or less impossible to forget you were South African when you lived in England. It was Madiba's name. There was a 'Nelson Mandela' everything. Square, road, street, close, park, centre, lane, roundabout, pool, you name it. There were at least two 'Nelson Mandela' roads in every town – or at least it felt like it.

And then the people. You knew you had to be from somewhere else when you discovered you alone did *not* think talking about anything but the weather put you at risk of embarrassing yourself or the person you were talking to. And the stoicism, the reserve, unless a rant about the NHS or the transport system was called for.

Clive loved the place though. He loved that he found few people judgmental. Away from his conservative father and the country's Calvinist Afrikaner aversion to anything or anyone who contravened their interpretation of 'God's law'. Especially 'blerry moffies' or 'queers', at the time a still often-used phrase. His siblings, he knew, believed he had left because his father had run off with another woman. Yes, he had been angry. Feet of clay stuff. But it had really just been the trigger to a thought process that allowed him to contemplate 'life after Dad', that his father's one-eyed beliefs were not necessarily the ones he had to follow, that he could go anywhere, be whatever he wanted.

Perhaps *that* day it was the imminent arrival of his father in England causing him stress, or perhaps it was just the fact that he had stomached his daily fellow commuter's sullen, possessive attitude about a stupid seat on a train for long enough. It didn't matter really what prompted it. He had just got to the station early one morning, climbed on the train and sat down in the old fart's seat. In this situation a South African would probably have said, "Hey, you know that's my seat, fuck off." But not the old fart. Stiff upper lip. Stoic. He sat in another seat, turned to look at Clive just once like he was mentally deranged. Then he just glowered, face forward.

As the train picked up speed Clive sighed, got up, walked a few rows down the now rocking coach and said loudly, "Sir, sorry, my mistake, I trust you will find your seat warmed to your satisfaction." He could sense the other regulars grinning to themselves as he sat down in *his* normal seat.

 In some way Clive felt that day that he had lanced the boil of resentment he carried, with his petulant action, believing he came to accept the ways of the English perhaps, made friends with the culture finally. He knew,

24

though, it was unlikely they would accept him, other than superficially anyway, not for a long time.

***

Dirk had not judged his father, nor Clive, for abandoning the family. He typically resisted being judgmental in general, not just when it came to his family, so his relationship with Tom and his new wife and child was comfortable. Nonetheless when he decided he would stay for a while and try the job offered, he was adamant he would find his own place to live.

A few weeks later, a conversation in the restaurant he was now managing yielded the information that the owner of a nearby farm was looking for a tenant to live in the property's farmhouse and, if they so desired, to work the farm as well. The thought of living on a farm appealed to Dirk. Whilst running the restaurant fitted with his desire to learn new, practical, hands-on skills it was not something that related to his dream. A farm however was an unknown. It allowed the imagination to run free in terms of potential ways of learning new skills, earning a living through being self-sufficient.

The transaction was done quickly, and Dirk was soon living in the rambling, slightly run-down old farmhouse with its sandstone walls and rusty corrugated iron roof, driving into the restaurant each morning. He was able to offset his lack of experience as a restaurateur by applying processes and financial acumen he had picked up reading for his law degree. He enjoyed the challenge, and the conservative local customers were coming to like the young 'hippy Dirk', as they called him, the fact that he took such a keen interest in local activities and aspirations, especially polo and the ponies they revered, was well regarded. They were amazed at how much he knew of the history of the game. Where it had first been played, how long ago, what the highest score had been when Argentina played against South Africa and so on. They shook their heads. Who would have expected a hippy could be so smart?

Dirk's real love though was the farm. The bumpy, dusty, bone-jarring morning and late-night drives to and from the restaurant were spent scheming ways to leverage the farm's resources. He acquired more suitable transport for this trip when he traded his car for an old truck, or 'bakkie', as they were called locally. After a few days had passed in his new home Dirk also acquired a house mate that contributed nothing in the way of rent and demanded lots in the way of feeding and affection. A large, muscular ridgeback.

Jon, a young black worker, whom the landlord employed to keep the garden in check while the house was uninhabited, informed Dirk that the dog had been left behind by a previous tenant on his departure about a year ago. He had survived on his own ever since, waiting faithfully for his owner to return and correct his oversight.

The locals named him Sebete, a shortened version of the translation from Sotho would be 'courageous survivor'.

***

Knowing she could not outrun the ridgeback's long legs the caracal suddenly skidded to a halt, turning to face the dog, lowering herself into a side-on position, arching her back, hissing and growling. Sebete had sprayed gravel from his outstretched paws as he came to an abrupt sideways halt as well. The two animals began the standoff routine they had first gone through over a year ago, when the cat was hardly more than a kitten herself. A time when the dog did not regard her as anything more than a curiosity. Certainly not a threat. It was a routine they went through from time to time when their paths crossed in the hillside area they roamed. The cat because it was her home, her territory, and the dog because it was where he had learnt to find food after he had been abandoned. To find prey he had to cross her territory. Normally scent gave warning of proximity and they avoided each other, both more intent on finding other smaller animals to hunt than confronting each other.

Now, panting still, the ridgeback decided to move stiffly to a nearby tree stump. He made the point that he also considered this his territory with a raised hind leg and a nonchalantly aimed squirt. It was the lull in proceedings the cat needed, and she slunk off silently, but gracefully, glancing over her shoulder as she moved off, just in case. This closing routine was similar to all others ending their encounters. Mutual respect as co-inhabitants of the territory kept them from having to dominate. And this time a third party had benefited as well.

Bonniface finally lowered the heavy stick he carried with him at all times. Normally more for support in steep terrain, looking for wayward calves, than protection. A grin, absent for a while, slipped back across his wrinkled, sun-dried face as he murmured in Sotho, *"Yebo, Sebete, u nchebeletse* (you are watching)."

Chapter 2

First Visit

When Georgie and Roger stopped at the end of the track leading up to the farmyard, Dirk was nowhere to be seen. The person they had seen busy with the paddock gate as they drove up turned towards them. He sauntered over to where they were easing themselves out of the car, stretching, slightly stiff from the long drive. He stopped and turned slowly looking into the distance. "He's at the dam," he said, without seeming to need any other words of introduction or greeting, as though he had been chatting to Georgie and Roger for the last five minutes and they had just asked after Dirk. His name was Jon, Dirk's protégé, as

29

Roger would come to realise. Over Jon's shoulder, at the other end of the barnyard, a muscular ridgeback was tethered. He was barking his own greeting. He was tethered to what looked like a small bundle of dirty sheep's wool.

They followed Jon's gaze down a gently falling hillside of golden veld grass that merged into tall reeds ringing a dam a little less than a kilometre away. A reflected search light of shimmering water the size of a large football field. Cattle dotted the hillside, bowing to their task of feeding the milk-making process they embarked on every day. A range of mountains looking down on the dam from the far side seemed comfortable with the clouds that capped their tops and sought ways to escape through the valleys and gullies that separated the hills. As his view came back to the barnyard scene, and the dog, Roger's eyes were drawn upwards to more mountains, much closer, nestling around the old farmhouse like watchful parents. "Helicopter parents," Roger mused.

Georgie, who had been in a relationship with Dirk years before, a first relationship initiated in the latter days of school and ending in University times, saw that Jon dressed in the 60s, hippy style of his boss rather than the basic farm clothes the other African workers wore. Probably would like to have Dirk's long flowing hair and beard too, Georgie thought. Not going to happen. Maybe dreds? Georgie smiled at the image of Jon and Dirk sharing a joint on the farmhouse patio, Bob Marley playing, their gaze descending with the strains of *No Woman No Cry* down into the valley before climbing up to the mountains beyond. Somewhere nearby would be their manicured patch of marijuana plants.

"So, I'm Georgie and this is Roger," she smiled at Jon.

"Yes, Dirk said you were coming to stay, I am Jon. *Sebete, thula ... thula*," he yelled at the dog, but he seemed to bark even louder, jumping from side to side, straining at the rope tethering him.

Either she did not see the dead lamb Roger could now make out or was ignoring it, because Georgie simply said, "Maybe he's lonely?"

Or he doesn't enjoy the company he's forced to keep, Roger smiled to himself.

Whilst Jon was remonstrating with the dog, Roger murmured to Georgie, "I hope you noticed the poor dog is tied to a dead animal! I have to know what that's about?" "How do I know?" Georgie hissed, irritated, mistakenly thinking he was asking *her* why, wanting to have avoided the subject all together. "Ask Dirk when you meet him." Roger widened his eyes in mock disbelief, "Really?" Georgie hissed, "Ask Jon then, if you must know."

"He's swimming," Jon said, looking back from the dog. Roger and Georgie looked at each other bemused. "Oh, sorry, you mean Dirk... right, at the dam...we'll walk down and surprise him," Georgie said giving Roger a 'This conversation is over' look. Jon turned and strolled away, the back of his arm raised in a farewell gesture, brightly coloured bracelets, ANC colours, sliding down his ebony wrist.

Georgie insisted they leave the car there and walk down the track to find Dirk. "You'll love the stroll down into the valley, all the scents, the sounds." She was forever 'introducing' Roger to things. To new music, new ideas, new ways of making love. He absorbed them all happily like he was in a new awakening.

***

Roger had recently emerged from a failed marriage. One of those resulting from the post school new adult process of his age group, a decade before Georgie's generation. Finish your education, find a job, find a girlfriend, go 'steady', get married, have a family. All before you were through the first few years of your twenties. How come parents never said, "Crap idea son/daughter, go and sow some wild oats first, don't do what your mother/father and I did."

Roger had only just completed his enforced army training when they married and within a few years had a son and a daughter. Roger was captivated. There was no baby duty he shied away from, impressing their circle of friends with his nappy changing prowess. They all loved his pooed nappy methodology. Nappy hurled onto the lawn, any poo smell now out of range and with hose spout turned to maximum velocity the old-fashioned cotton nappy was soon ready for a final Napisan soaking. It could fail occasionally if the next-door Labrador, attracted by the fun of jumping, trying to catch the jet of water, grabbed the nappy and ran off. The neighbours, always considerate and wearing gardening gloves, returned the nappy eventually.

He and his wife had married so young that by the time ten years had passed they hardly recognised each other. Their personalities had developed in completely different directions as they matured. From late teenage years to late twenties. They felt like strangers, their children the only common ground. There was no meeting of mind or heart. They had simply changed.

For years Roger and his wife treaded water, neither of them able to find the courage to have *that* conversation. Then suddenly it was over, Roger moved cities as a result of a work promotion. The loss of his children ate at him. He cast around for distraction, the carefree side of life he had somehow missed. To find something to kill the time until he could next drive to the airport to pick the kids up for their monthly weekend with him. A self-imposed early midlife crisis was narrowly avoided when he met Georgie.

***

As Roger and Georgie started down the track, he felt relieved to have avoided asking Jon about the dog. He knew he did not really want to know the answer. Instead he readied himself for yet another 'introduction', the long-planned Dirk introduction. Given all the anecdotes shared about Dirk he felt he already knew him, maybe even liked him. Georgie and Dirk's sister, Eve, waxed lyrical about Dirk, it was an inevitable topic whenever they met. Roger, easily bored when it came to women going on about other men, surreptitiously or so he thought, until Georgie put him right, eyed Eve's abundant shape as a pleasant distraction.

***

Dirk, as a schoolboy, had more or less missed the 60s hippy era, but he was not going to let that hold him back. The prize for completing high school was freedom from rules and the right to enjoy unencumbered hair growth, to emulate the images he treasured in the posters of pop groups hanging on the walls of his bedroom. This required plenty of weed and alcohol, hard partying was a given.

Notwithstanding the laid-back hippy image, Dirk was smart and high energy, similar traits to those of his father whose professional standing in banking was well known. Less known was Tom's one-eyed view of a woman's place in the world. Which in the main was the important responsibility that they had to have, and nurture, babies.

Create the next generation. "A very important job," he insisted. "Not to be taken lightly."

This trait was one Dirk had not inherited. In fact, he was just the opposite. Open minded, concerned about equality and stubbornly opposed to the establishment. Accompanied by lots of partying and intellectual debate, Dirk had eased himself into an academic journey which saw him earn a law degree and use it to avoid a misguided attempt at convicting him for possession of an illegal drug, all within his graduation week. The drug was one Dirk believed would become a prescription medicine if not a recreational drug, similar to alcohol, in the not too distant future. This belief, which he shared in a longish diatribe with the court, did little to help Dirk win over the judge. He did however commend Dirk for having enough confidence in the skills he had acquired studying law to conduct his own defence. The judge did not like the way Dirk dressed, a stained tie and borrowed suit that was too small for him, but he liked Dirk so he commended him anyway.

Roger learnt from Georgie, and later from Eve when he finally met her, that people often commended Dirk. He was one of those people you commended in the presence of others. In case they thought he *was* commendable and resented you for not feeling the same. He seemed to read everything. Years later Roger would be astounded to find that Dirk had subscriptions to both *Playboy* and *Modern Scientist*. Roger always said, 'It was his laugh that got you.' He could share an observation that was quite shocking, jaw dropping, and follow it with a chuckle that made the image he had created unintimidating, even tenable. If not a laugh, an argument, making his observation or postulation a fact of life.

The judge ruled he had had far too little of the illegal substance on him for it to be construed as anything other than for personal use. This in itself at that time was still illegal, however the judge found that the police had been somewhat over-zealous and ruled their evidence inadmissible. Notwithstanding she was unsuccessful getting a conviction, Dirk did however impress the young prosecutor, Marin Belmorjon, whom he later dated and *definitely* got commended by.

Marin, who had already established quite a name for herself in the legal profession, paid for their expensive dinners. It gave her the opportunity to enjoy more intellectual conversation with a young graduate than she ever had with her much older peers. She was never sure whether Dirk was stoned or not. If he was, it did not seem to ever change his demeanour or his ability to articulate a thought process.

Using the curtain to cover her naked body from the passers-by on the road outside, Marin shut her window against the evening traffic. Her apartment was on an intersection, with a traffic light. The noise of cars screeching off when green came on or squealing to a stop for red was starting to get intense. Standing at the window, murky from the salt carried on the continuous sea breeze, it was still light enough to see the white horses. Stirred up by the southerly wind, they danced on the blue Indian ocean in the distance. Marin loved Durban but there were times when it felt like the wind would never stop.

"Enough to make anyone turn to weed," Dirk observed wryly. For a second Marin thought he had read her thoughts about the wind, then she remembered they had been discussing his unsuccessful defence against her prosecution.

Marin unfurled herself from the curtain, "Well you were probably a bit premature attempting to argue your own legal defence, but I am sure you found it a worthwhile learning experience." Marin smiled, "A decent suit would have helped, especially with that particular judge. Very conservative, always has been. But funnily enough he seemed to like you. You must have learnt something?"

Dirk turned his head sideways on the pillow, to face her, one eye closed against the smoke that trailed lazily from his joint. "What I learnt confirmed once and for all that being accepted at the Bar is the last thing I want. Twenty-five years of my life gone by, including university, and what do I know? Not a lot really. Nothing about being independent. I'm being groomed for conformity, been trained to follow the rules, to stay between the lines. Do what society wants. I can barely knot a tie, mind you that's redundant. Lace my own shoes?"

That's also redundant, Marin thought. Dirk's comments were slightly incongruous as he was at that moment naked, sprawled across her bed. She yawned, "You know before I went to Uni, I was a graphic artist. I walked the streets calling on agencies, bruised my ear holding a phone to it for hours, selling my creativity for a buck. Do you think that was worthwhile? More character-building than being in the legal profession? More non-conforming?"

Dirk drew his gaze away from Marin's breasts, his mind returning to an ever-recurring thought process. *We assemble a tool set based on life experiences that we leverage to craft outcomes. Do we want to keep on producing the same outcomes simply to be able to exist? If we don't, we need to be exposed to experiences that will add new life tools so we can engineer different outcomes, the ones we don't yet know we want.* Dirk at least knew he did not want what his education thus far was going to provide.

"If it taught you how to be persuasive enough to achieve an end, to be tenacious enough to achieve an evasive goal, increased your own self esteem by seeing how people reacted to your art, then yes it was worthwhile. Conforming or not is beside the point, if you were equipping yourself to survive in life as a graphic artist. If that was the outcome you wanted? Clearly it wasn't. You went to Uni to equip yourself with a different set of tools."

Ignoring Marin's frown Dirk concluded, "I need to do something that will equip me to be someone I am not at the moment, I'm not sure what that someone will be but it sure as fuck is not a lawyer!"

Marin did not hear Dirk's 'closing argument' as her mind had gone back to her previous career and the things she wished for then. She had never quite been able to grasp what exactly it was she wanted in life, not then and not now, really.

***

The road down to the dam was two wheel-sized tracks bordered on either side by waist high veld grass and divided by a raised section exposed over many years by the endless grinding of cartwheels on wagons drawn by oxen. In latter years, by truck and tractor tyres eating into the gravel, throwing up stones to collect on the natural median. This rocky mound, separating them, meant there was no hand holding as they walked. It suited Roger, as he felt a bit awkward about strolling up to Dirk hand in hand with his 'ex'.

As they descended towards the dam, sun on their faces, the muted sounds of the farm and smells of cattle hung in the air. Georgie was right, Roger thought, this is relaxing and enjoyable. In the zone as well, she had thankfully not shared any more Dirk anecdotes. So quiet. Yet there was a growing awareness of a sound invading the stillness. *Not tinnitus this time,* he thought. Roger, and then Georgie, realised the growing sound was approaching from behind them. Roger spun around to see the dog he had seen earlier approaching at an alarming speed. All muscle and flaying pink wet tongue.

Constrained by just two tracks between the tall grass the speeding animal had had to choose one. It was Roger's. In the distant background, above the salivating canine jaws descending towards him, Roger caught a glimpse of Jon waving at them and in the split second before the dog rocketed past, thumping against his leg, Roger fancied, even at that distance, he could see a smile on Jon's face. The impact forced Roger into a few backward steps before he stumbled, and arms and legs waving wildly like an overturned dung beetle, took off horizontally into the veld grass.

When Georgie turned back towards the dam she saw only the ridgeback continuing his gallop towards his adored master somewhere in the reeds, nothing of Roger who had carved out a sizable impression in the tall grass and was, notwithstanding his traumatic state, conscious that he was grateful the dog had not been dragging the dead lamb behind him.

As he rose to a sitting position, Roger was alarmed to see Georgie bent over double in obvious pain. The dog must have bounced off him and slammed into her he thought. He was opening his mouth to offer words of comfort when Georgie let out a "strangle burp" sound, a cross between a gasp and a yelp, that he only heard when she was laughing uncontrollably. "Sorry, sorry!" she said coming to a more vertical position. "The look on your face!" She doubled over again, becoming unintelligible. Tears streaming.

It was something Roger had never been able to fathom with Georgie in the year they had been together. He knew she loved him, but if something untoward happened to him; he poked himself in the eye whilst putting on his glasses, or they were out somewhere and she spotted he had put on socks that did not match, or anything else that made him really irritable with himself and awkward, she always found it extremely funny. Right now was a prime example. "Excuse me," he said, "I could have broken something you know." Which brought another paroxysm from her.

Finally, gasping, looking down towards the dam and back up to the farmhouse, Georgie managed, "At least nobody else saw that." Roger looked up towards the house. No Jon. He's there somewhere no doubt, having hysterics, Roger growled to himself. A lone cow observed Roger over the barbed wire fence, chewing. Definitely not sympathetic.

Georgie, now under control, but still sniffing and surreptitiously wiping tears, helped him up and they continued down the track. What sort of dog is tied to a dead sheep one minute and then appears as if fired out of a catapult the next? Roger simmered. One that has not seen his human for days because he's been sitting in the catapult waiting to be sprung, he supposed.

For a few minutes while he was walking on the same track behind Georgie and not withstanding his sour demeanour, laced with a good dose of self-pity, he enjoyed her shapely movement. He felt a bit better. Georgie stopped dead in her tracks and spun around. "I heard that thought," she smiled. "What?" His heart leaping. He did love that about her.

They were off the tracks now and walking through the tall grass alongside the dam, quite close to the water. The rustle of the reeds in the water felt like both a welcome and a warning. "We should have brought our swimming costumes," said Georgie. *Another introduction*, thought Roger. *This time to freezing water.* Then he chastised himself for being, as she often commented, "Always so negative."

"We could always skinny dip," he said forcing himself to be cheerful after his mishap. "Well, you could skinny dip and I could fatty dip," he grinned at her, a picture of good humour, patting his stomach.

Roger was just enjoying the mental image of a naked Georgie entering a shimmering surface when, with a crashing splash like a hippo leaving the water, reeds were pushed aside and Dirk and his dog appeared, as if by magic. Both were sopping wet, slick hair glistening in the sun. And naked.

"Dirk, hi!" cried Georgie happily. "I won't give you a hug, you're all wet." Roger joined Georgie in *not* noticing Dirk's nakedness but felt no less awkward. He tried to force his mind down the path of the normality of sporty guys together in the locker room, but it did not work with Georgie there. Her eyes steadfastly staring into Dirk's eyes and then his, strictly horizontally rotating vision only.

Oh God, and he had been concerned about the awkwardness of Dirk seeing him holding Georgie's hand. Roger tried averting his eyes to the dog, hoping to see a trigger for a casual conversation, maybe even about his recent fall, to ease the awkwardness. The segue was not to be. Sebete held his hind leg in the air like he was testing for wind direction whilst he scrutinised his scrotum for who knows what? Like his human, seemingly unconcerned about exposing his intimate parts.

Just as Roger realised he was about to start babbling, he saw that Dirk had found his towel and was mercifully holding it in front of him as he looked for what was wrapped in it. Finally, he flicked a cigarette from a packet. As would be expected of someone living on a farm Dirk's face was tanned and healthy, if not a bit too lined for someone of his age. His wet hair hung down his back. With a languid smile he turned to Georgie. "I was pleased you called and suggested coming down. It's been a long time Georgie." Georgie, maintaining horizontal vision glanced at Roger, "Well, I've told Roger so much about my wonderful time being part of your family, he's met Eve, so I thought it was time he met you as well."

"Eve and Georgie are big fans of yours, Dirk," Roger said, wishing he could stop babbling. "I feel as if I know you already. Thought you might walk on water, but I see even you have to swim in it." Dirk laughed, turning to spread his towel over a bush to dry, and bent to slip on his jeans. Georgie and Roger exchanged glances.

Buckling his belt, Dirk asked after their drive down and whether his directions were OK. "Roads a bit dodgy but the scenery is great so the slower you go the more you see," he grinned.

Taking his towel from where he had slung it, he turned to the dog. "Come on, Sebete, let's take our guests up to the house for coffee. Jon must have decided your banishment for killing that lamb is over." Roger was remembering the image of Sebete descending down the track towards him, like an angel from hell, and Jon in the distance. He wondered if Jon had offered an early parole for their benefit maybe. Georgie was already on her way through the reeds towards the track.

***

The evening they had decided to make this first trip to Caracal Ridge was the evening of their housewarming. Georgie had decided within the first hour that she would never forgive Roger for inviting Brad, his long-time friend, to join them. He had arrived stoned, and so far had burnt Georgie's housewarming gift from her sister, an antique coffee table cloth, with his cigarette lighter, really a *pipe* lighter with a flame that had to be extinguished manually, knocked over a glass of wine and insisted on urinating in the garden in full view of the guests. Fortunately, only his back was visible and because most homes in South Africa had high security walls the neighbours were also spared the image. They however could not miss Brad's loud rendition of *My Ding-A-Ling* as he rinsed his hands in the swimming pool.

Roger was in the kitchen helping Georgie prepare the next round of snacks, and getting lectured on his lack of responsibility, when Brad burst through the swing door with a big grin on his face. "God she's got a pair on her that Eve…oh, can I help?"

"No!" Georgie barely stifled her anguished cry. "Ah, thanks…you're our guest, go and enjoy yourself."

Eve was going to be their house guest that weekend. She had recently moved up to the highveld from Durban and was staying in a communal house close to downtown Johannesburg. The oldest of the Lenbruikte girls, Eve had been somewhat of a shrinking violet until her father left their mother, Rita, for his new wife. It was at this point she had to step up and provide support for her mother. The shy young girl matured overnight, becoming something of a matriarchal figure within the family. Eve was attractive, confident and forthright. Roger wondered if that was why she apparently could not find the right man. Too dominant maybe? Glancing at Georgie he was glad he had not said that out loud.

Having completed his duties and been dispatched from the kitchen under instruction from Georgie to ensure Eve was not being accosted by Brad, Roger found her and asked if she was enjoying herself. "Oh yes, thanks Rog." He hated been called that. "Your friend Brad is interesting, isn't he? From Southern California, he tells me." Roger saw Brad over Eve's shoulder talking to their neighbours, Noddy and Fluffy as he called them, never being able to remember their names and always enjoying the silliness of what he felt were totally apt names for two silly people.

Brad looked somewhat bemused. The couple spoke in unison, saying more or less the same thing at the same time but not quite synchronised. Like listening to an echo. As irritating as hearing your own voice repeat what you are saying on the phone when you get that echo on the line. Brad's head moved from side to side, one to the other, as he tried to follow what each was saying.

"Is he here tonight on his own, is he attached?" Eve asked.

Oh God, Georgie will kill me, Roger thought, and he said a little too quickly, "Ah, Brad's a bit of a lad, plays the field. You're far too nice for him."

"He's so funny, the way he could not keep his eyes off my breasts when we spoke. Looked a bit stoned." Roger gulped, willing his eyes not to move downward whilst thinking that there was no response that he could give that would not get him into trouble.

"Well…ah, well. How's Dirk and the farm going?" Roger blurted out. "Heard from him? We still haven't had the chance to go down that way. I am keen to meet him."

Eve smiled, ignoring Roger's lack of segue, "Well, there has been some strange stuff going on down that way. Let me tell you some interesting news later, when I can talk to the two of you together. But the gist of it…" There was a sudden blast of music and Roger turned to see Brad busy at their sound system. Clearly his solution to their neighbour's non-stop diatribe. He began to gyrate, a bit like a sprayed cockroach looking for escape. Eve moved closer to Roger. "Rog, he won't ask me to dance with him, will he? Please dance with me!" Roger hated the thought of dancing, especially when he had just been called "Rog" twice in the space of a few minutes. With a, "Ha, ha, you wouldn't enjoy being forced into a waltz, would you?" he retreated to the kitchen, waving his arms in apology. As he slipped through the swing door, he glimpsed Brad doing the 'moon walk' towards the stranded Eve.

***

Eve's 'interesting news' was the reason Roger had been stuck behind the steering wheel of his car for the last three hours. It was the catalyst for a long-planned first visit to Dirk's farm that he and Georgie had somehow not got around to. It was now a visit that clearly for Georgie was just too irresistible to put off any longer, well, at least not more than a week, to allow time for some shopping before they left.

The party had gone well enough. Especially after Brad redeemed himself by announcing the existence of a large apple strudel he had made that afternoon and completely forgotten he had brought. Earlier, Georgie had been mortified to see that her guests were requesting second helpings of her own delicious but already depleted dessert. Brad inspired by her anxious comments remembered what he had in his car and returned moments later with a triumphant grin. "Lead me to an oven, your guests have an experience coming."

And they did. Roger, knowing his friend, was in no doubt that Brad's dessert had the gentlest sprinkling of high quality 'grass' over the crust. What Brad whimsically called "Dried mint to balance the sweetness." Those that had not had a helping were soon finding their most earnest conversations elicited involuntary giggles from those listening to them with an empty dessert plate held in their hand. The room was filled with faces etched in either puzzled frowns or tearful mirth. Brad was in his element, fielding culinary compliments with a total lack of humility. *So what?* Roger thought, feeling for his old friend. *He deserves a bit of attention.*

Now, as the car hummed through unbroken farmland, a carpet of golden corn covering thousands of hectares rolling towards the horizon on all sides of him, Roger reminisced about his friend. Brad had recently been dumped by a girl he was head over heels in love with. They had been together for a few years. She had even followed him to the US during a stillborn return to his roots, hoping to be reunited with his teenage daughters from a previous marriage. Her arrival had saved him the accumulating cost of lovelorn long-distance phone calls to her, but could not help the situation with his daughters. Both into drugs, disinterested in Brad other than to hold him responsible for leaving their mother and her succession of bad relationships ever since. Brad decided his quest to win over his two girls would bear no fruit, so they returned. They were no sooner back in South Africa when Suzie decided the somewhat weathered divorcee was not for her. He was devastated.

Roger first met Suzie when they had stayed overnight with him and his ex-wife. They lived in Durban at that stage. They had hidden a key for Brad as he and Suzie were due to arrive very late on the midnight flight from Jo'burg that night. It was about 2 am when Roger sat bolt upright in bed hearing a strangled scream from the spare room occupied by Brad and his girlfriend. Fearing the worst, as you do in South Africa when there is a loud noise at that time of night, Roger bolted down the passage, not hearing his wife calling sleepily from their bed, "Roger, come back, it's not what you think." Even now Roger felt his face redden as he gripped the steering wheel with revisited embarrassment, recalling the image that confronted him as he opened his guest's bedroom door. A gasped, "Oh, sorry!" was all he could manage as he executed a stumbling reverse.

***

Georgie snored gently once in her seat alongside Roger, and his eyes moved from the distant horizon and the hazy, ever-growing line of mountains to glance at her in amused affection. His thoughts went back to Eve's 'news'. After a generous helping of Brad's strudel, her dessert plate still clutched in her hand, Eve was not light-hearted in her delivery of the news she wanted to share with them. It was later that evening when the rest of the guests had left. Dirk was her favourite brother and she clearly was disappointed in him. Georgie had mentioned before that not long after she broke up with Dirk he had been caught in possession of marijuana. Too much to have it treated as a misdemeanour, which was normally the case given that smoking 'dagga' was traditionally the norm with many of the indigenous people of the country. Eve was adamant that although it was thrown out of court, this near conviction was the catalyst for what she referred to as Dirk's current predicament. Roger thought he might have called it Dirk's current 'relationship'.

"It's one thing that Dirk started having sex with a woman who prosecuted him, tried to get him convicted. Another, all together, that he went and got her pregnant. I've met her and don't trust her," Eve said.

Dirk's near prosecution had been old news to Georgie but when Eve delivered her punch line her mouth dropped open. "Knocked her up," Eve grimaced, waving her empty dessert plate at them with abandon to emphasise her point as she spoke. Roger wondered if he should take it from her hand before she caused herself or them an injury. She went on to tell them the woman, Marin, had moved in with Dirk at the farm and they now had a baby girl, Annah.

"Oh yes, and she's quite the little gardener apparently. Dirk has the makings of an English country garden fronting the farmhouse, I'm told. An English rose garden for Annah was essential," Eve smirked. "Marin Belmorjon fancies herself as 'British' although a grandfather born in England is about as close as she gets."

Roger, noting that Dirk was not being commended this time, laughed, "Eve, you sound a bit like an irritated mum talking about her son and an unexpected new partner she did not have the chance to vet. Who, as she foresaw of course, turned out not to be up to the standard she would have liked."

"He is just so irresponsible sometimes," Eve said. "It will never work, you'll see."

Georgie gave Roger a look that said enough from you on this please. He yawned and picking up his half-drunk whisky made for the stairs. He winked at Georgie saying, in his best Humphry Bogart voice, "Here's looking at you kid." Looking back down the stairs he said, "I'll leave you two to catch up. See you in the morning."

***

Roger slowed the car as the farmlands gave way to a smoky, sprawling mass of tin shanties, tiny abodes made from rusty corrugated iron and sheets of black plastic. This township was home to the black people who worked, or aspired to work, in the small town of Brandfort visible in the distance. *How does the 'new' government get power and water to these communities,* Roger mused, *there aren't even roads to run the infrastructure along. It's going to be a tough campaign promise to fulfil.*

This particular, sprawling, high density shanty town of people were Winnie Mandela's neighbours for several years during her banning by the previous white government. Why she was banished to this isolated area is anyone's guess. Probably to keep her away from the action in the main cities five hours away and because she refused to leave the country as decreed in her banishment order. She was initially under house arrest and alone, as her daughters had left home. One sent away to school and the other to America, having married a Swazi prince. Roger remembered reading a report by white activist Helen Suzman, in which she captured the desperate isolation when she wrote that Winnie sat outside the local telephone booth everyday between 10 am and 4 pm waiting for calls from friends and family. In latter years, she was allowed to visit the town nearby for supplies and general shopping. Notwithstanding the fact that the town was predominantly owned and run by very conservative white people, it is well recorded that the attractive and charming black activist won many of them over as the months went by and made quite a few enduring friends.

As the road descended towards Brandfort, the shanties gave way to veld grass for a few miles. The buffer before a more affluent neighbourhood, reserved until recently for white people. Well, affluent in as much as a rural South African town can be affluent. Adorned with rusty old bakkies, in unkempt front yards with weeds growing between the concrete strips running from overflowing garages to the narrow street that led to the small, grubby town centre. It was the last town before Dirk's farm about an hour away and as Roger slowed, Georgie was instantly awake. "Stop at a petrol station please, I need to go to the toilet, there won't be another chance. Eve warned me. She has been caught out before."

**

The last few miles up to the farm were teeth-jarring stuff. Roger feared for the suspension of his car as it vibrated over the corrugations, resolving to use Georgie's car next time rather than his low-slung BMW. Finally, they crawled through the farm gate, an archway of crumbling sandstone with its keystone missing, Roger observed with some concern.

Past the worst of the potholes and exposed rocks, the final half mile of gravel farm track was relatively smooth, winding through a cherry orchard. A stunning view opened before them. A long sweeping valley ringed by hills rising to mountains beyond. At the end of the driveway a sandstone farmhouse seemed to stand like a guardian over the beautiful countryside.

Just off the track a young man was closing the gate of a paddock that held a dozen or so handsome ponies. As he turned to face them, they saw that he himself was as handsome.

***

Roger and Sebete panted in second place alongside each other as they followed the tracks from the dam back up to the house. Georgie and Dirk led the way, Dirk bringing Georgie up to date on his life since they had last seen each other several years ago. The dog gave Roger pink-tongued, salivating looks from time to time, wagging his tail, unaware of any discomfort he may have caused Roger on his way to the dam earlier.

"When I took on the farm the last thing I expected was that I would embark on the venture with a family included. Marin and I only saw each other once a month, when I went down to the coast for weekends. She called one day to say she would like to come up to the farm for a weekend, see what I was up to." Dirk laughed, "When her car pulled up, just about where we are now, I could see from the load she was carrying she was not planning to go back that Sunday evening."

Roger pondered whether Dirk meant luggage loaded in her car or physical appearance.

Georgie was about to ask Dirk how he handled *that* situation, when a striking young woman, baby in her arms, appeared through a rusty gate in the sandstone wall. She was tall and confident, in control. Roger's immediate reaction was Marin looked more like a model than a lawyer. He tried to picture her in court, before a judge, arguing a legal point but all he got was a beautiful photographic image.

"You must be the famous Georgie," Marin smiled. Georgie was taken aback, immediately trying to compute what was imparted by Marin's tone of voice. She decided it was an innocent compliment although she didn't miss Marin's glance at Dirk. "Well, so long as it's not 'infamous', I'm alright," she laughed. "But Marin, if anybody is well known it's you. What with your reputation in the legal world," Georgie said.

Marin laughed, "A career very much on hold right now."

They hugged gingerly, avoiding crushing the baby in Marin's arms. Georgie noted, Dirk had given scant acknowledgment to his daughter, teasing Sebete with a branch fallen from a nearby gum tree. With a smile Marin turned to Roger offering her hand. "Hi Roger. Jon tells me you had a warm reception from Sebete? Turning to Dirk, "For God's sake Dirk now that he's been untethered from it can you get rid of that stinking lamb corpse?"

"Long since done," Dirk said. "We'll dig up and re-engage if Sebete doesn't behave tomorrow," he said without humour. Roger and Georgie concentrated hard on not exchanging glances.

"And this is Annah," Marin said. "Oh, she's so lovely, Marin," Georgie smiled. "We brought you some things for her, I hope they fit." Ah, thought Roger, so that was what the shopping was about.

Pleasantries completed, well mainly pleasant, they moved through the arched gateway in the sandstone wall towards the farmhouse, Marin guiding them to the patio in front of the house. Looking down from the patio wall, Georgie reflected on the surrounding landscape. Ah, so this is the English country garden Eve was going on about. Actually, it is very professional. Very pretty. Dirk went off to make coffee and tea. While he was away Jon arrived to give Dirk details regarding one of his horses. Marin insisted he join them for a drink and, looking awkward, he took a seat.

Roger supposed this situation was being played out all over South Africa with the demise of an oppressive apartheid regime. After years and years of black people being excluded from the lives of white people, except in the role of underpaid maid and 'garden boy' it was a quantum leap for white people to be socialising with people who had finally been recognised as equals. Some would say it was positive support for the new order, others might say it was positioning for the role of being the 'new minority'. Even more likely, cynics would say it was merely posturing in front of other white people, 'doing the right thing', which is where he suspected Marin's motivation lay.

Roger's thoughts dragged him unwillingly back to his childhood, his memories swirling in protest, resisting the images that were on the way. He could see his mother sitting on the sofa, cigarette in hand. Their long-time maid Doris, also his nanny for a few years, had returned out of the blue to visit them after years of being away, maybe retired, he could not remember. *That was a redundant thought,* he knew. *There was no social security for a domestic worker in those days. No pension contributions from an employer like his mother.*

If a white family needed a maid one simply went down to the local labour centre and chose someone randomly from the people sitting around. Unemployed women travelled hours on buses and on foot to get to these centres, sitting around day after day in the hope of being offered a job. If the family relocated the maid was simply given notice. There were white employers who offered some kind of severance payment but there was no legal obligation. They found themselves sitting around with others, overflowing into the parking lot of the local labour centre again.

She sat opposite him, drinking tea with them. Not sitting on a chair, squatting on the floor, in front of a chair, not even leaning her now slightly stooped back against it. Unlikely a black person would be allowed to, or indeed would even if invited to, for fear of showing disrespect. *You did not sit on the chairs of the 'madam'*, Roger mused. The very chairs she dusted every day, adorned with the pillows she re-adjusted every day. They sipped tea and chatted, Roger's mother in her not bad Zulu, looking over her china cup and the old maid peering back over her galvanised iron 'servants' mug'. *God, where had his mother found that after all these years?* Roger saw himself, fifteen or so years old, poised on the edge of a chair, biscuit in hand. Were those tears in his eyes? Because after all those years the woman on the floor showed no animosity, only affection and respect?

Roger noted Jon's gaze was across the valley, seemingly lost in the magnificent view. More likely lost in a mental dilemma as to how he could possibly join their conversation, thinking about the elephant in white people's rooms, concluded Roger. The people they are now including with enthusiasm, they have watched be excluded from all but very basic education, if any, denied any political say, contained like animals in townships without running water or electricity. This is not the history, the background, the education that is going to provide a pool of anecdotes, equip anyone for light-hearted chat over drinks on the patio. *There will have to be patience and understanding on both sides for a long time,* Roger decided. *Learning how best to see past the awkwardness.*

In years to come, as the children of the denied population gain access to the privileged schools within the previously whites-only education system, a new generation of young black people will emerge. Eloquent, worldly wise with the information their teachers have imparted. When *they* chat in this patio environment, will they sound like white teenagers as a result of this education in a still predominantly white school? Or will these integrated teenagers become one and create a whole new dialect to take the emerging new culture forward with? *Time will tell*, thought Roger.

He said, "So Jon, what has Sebete done to get himself into trouble?" Jon turned away from the view with a smile. "He killed a farmer's lamb." Roger noted that Jon's speech had returned to a less flowing 'cool' confident delivery, unlike when they first met on arrival at the farm. He wondered if it was due to the unfamiliar social situation he found himself in, or the dominant presence of Marin, traditionally this home's 'madam', the farmer's wife. Jon explained that one of the local farmers suggested tying Sebete to the lamb he had killed. Something he had done before with his dogs and it seemed to work, breaking the predator habit small farm animals sometimes seemed to awaken in farm dogs, free to roam the bush as they pleased.

"Maybe the smell stays with them, reminds them it is not good, who knows?" Jon was clearly enjoying being engaged in a conversation he could be comfortable with when Dirk appeared from the door to the house with the drinks. Jon sprang up like a firecracker had gone off under him to take the tray from Dirk. Dirk laughed, "Hey man, chill. You buried Marin's dreaded lamb corpse, I'll serve the coffee."

Marin had been rocking slightly in her chair, enjoying the mountains, stroking Annah's hair. Dirk's comment got her attention and she looked away from the vista before them, a slight smile played across her photogenic lips, but did little to hide her irritation. Dirk handed around mugs of coffee, the tea order seemed to have been lost in the trip to the kitchen. Returning a second time he offered a cup with a broken handle containing sugar and a spoon. "God Dirk, you could have put a bit more effort in for your guests, a little finesse. Don't give up your day job," Marin laughed. The others all chuckled as well, hoping to relieve any tension, unsure if there *was* any or not.

Dirk said, "We have a polo game tomorrow, would you guys like to come and watch?"

"Wow, Dirk, since when do you play polo? A man of many talents nowadays I see. I would love to go," Georgie said, and Roger nodded his agreement, "Are those the ponies we saw in the paddock we drove by when we arrived?"

"Some are mine and some Jon's, inherited from the previous farmer here. He taught Jon the basics of the sport when he was just a young drover. Jon introduced me to it when I arrived here and helped me find and train my first string of ponies. The club in the town was by default white people only until I came along. They were desperate for new members though, and when I showed interest were adamant I join. I said I would only have the confidence to join if my teacher played with us as well and they said OK. I think it had just never struck them that they might consider black players, probably didn't even know any existed. Until recently, Jon would never have put his hand up. Hey Jon? the only black polo player in town?" Jon and Dirk roared with laughter. Must be a private joke in there somewhere Roger thought.

"Jon and a few of the guys are taking the ponies into town this afternoon. We don't have a horse transporter, so we just drive them to town and let them rest overnight. There's a place at the field where the guys camp. They enjoy it, especially the beers I make sure go along on the ride. Jon will tell you that wh…" Dirk was interrupted by Sebete jumping up, barking loudly and scattering chairs in all directions as he bolted for the gate. "Jesus, that fucking dog," Marin exploded as Annah began to cry loudly. She stormed off into the house as *that* dog was busy giving Bonniface a rapturous welcome.

Bonniface waved and they all waved back as Jon strolled over to his father, both already engaged in long distance conversation as was the African custom, even though there was still thirty metres between them. It was loud and in Sotho, interspersed with barking from an animated Sebete bouncing around Bonniface like he was a long-lost friend. He had after all been tethered to a carcass for a week, had not been on his regular veld walks with Bonniface.

"Hullo Sebete motsoalle oa ka (my friend)," Bonniface laughed, patting the jumping ridgeback. On his hind legs, front paws on Bonniface's shoulders, nearly as tall as him.

Having righted the chairs, Dirk was busy explaining to Roger and Georgie that the cows on the farm weren't his, belonging to neighbours who paid grazing rights. "Bonniface and other workers keep an eye on them during the day, between milking times. It works well, pays the bills while I develop my other farm projects."

Pointing to the green fields at the bottom of the hill, near the dam where they had met up earlier, Dirk said, "Asparagus, my green gold I am hoping." He related how he came to move from a tenant situation to part owner of the farm. How he had had 24 hours to put a proposal to the previous owners who were arriving that following morning to sign over the farm to liquidators. The end result was that he and Tom, who put up capital, were now major shareholders, the previous owners continuing as minor part owners in return for offering Dirk very good repayment terms.

"Jon and I have been putting in asparagus plants for months now, setting up an overhead irrigation system. I have an agent contact I went to Uni with who says the market in Holland is wide open for fresh asparagus. He supplies cafés throughout the Netherlands with stuff that is a little bit different. Jon's training a team who will do the harvesting, sorting and packing." Dirk looked towards the gate where Jon and Bonniface were still engaged in animated conversation, arms being waved in all directions.

Roger watched Georgie's face as she listened to Dirk. He recognised her expression. It was her 'jigsaw face'. Roger knew she had the ability to foresee the big picture. If incomplete, she treated it as a kind of jigsaw puzzle. Watching and waiting for the missing pieces to appear, as they always did, she said. Georgie collected words, images, snippets of information like random puzzle pieces, anticipating the picture that would emerge. Under the guise of listening intently to Dirk, Roger could see Georgie had mental jigsaw pieces laid out in front of her, a slight frown creased her brow, looking for the first few that would interlock.

***

Later in the afternoon Dirk took Roger and Georgie on a tour of his newly created asparagus packing 'factory' in one of the old workshops adjoining the farmhouse. The work benches were built from timber collected on the farm and whilst rudimentary, Roger thought they were extremely attractive, exuding an atmosphere of farm and country. The feel of the room sparked a thought process in him as he looked through the large windows to the distant hills. He imagined how it would be to holiday here, to wake up to this view and the sounds of animals every morning.

Dirk was just explaining how Jon had been training workers to operate in a rudimentary conveyer belt system, sorting and packing, when Jon strode across the stoep into the workshop. "Ah, speak of the devil," Dirk laughed.

"Sorry Dirk, I had to go with my father to his house to help settle things between him and my ma."

"Same old, same old?" Dirk asked with a smile.

"*Yebo*…yah. But also, my father has a new worry. He has been up on the other side of the mountain," Jon said, waving in the direction of the hills Roger had been gazing towards. "He says it is really dry and we should expect grass fire one of these days if there is no rain. He is worried that the dam has meant there is no river like in the old days to stop a fire from coming across onto our side, up to all the houses."

Dirk put his arm around Georgie, noting her concerned look. "Don't worry guys, it's not likely until the windy season starts and hopefully we will have some rain by then. Jon, maybe we could add some pipes to the dam wall so we can release water if needed?" Jon nodded. "Maybe. We would need a machine to dig the earth out."

Wanting to lighten the conversation again, Dirk got Jon to tell them how the asparagus packing would work and about the jobs it would create for some of the local people desperately in need of work. Roger was really enjoying being involved in their enthusiasm, but he could see they were losing Georgie. It was the cough that came from nowhere, to hide the yawn. Claiming exhaustion after their long drive, she asked for directions to where she and Roger would be sleeping.

Without being asked Jon rushed off to get their bags from the car saying he would show Georgie, who trailed behind, to the room. Dirk took Roger's arm, "Let me show you something," he said as he led him off the veranda towards a raised, rocky outcrop nearby. Sebete was immediately up and running ahead of them, tail wagging, delighted that a walk seemed imminent. When they reached the top, the view, hidden from the room where they had been talking, revealed a vast expanse of green. Silver jets, gleaming in the sun, danced in circles above this green carpet.

"We can go down tomorrow and I'll show you what we've done, but basically what you see is all asparagus plants. All under irrigation from our dam which can supply us for months even though the river feeding into it is very slow at the moment," Dirk said, reaching for his shirt pocket.

"Hence Bonniface's concern, that's his name isn't it? Jon's dad," Roger murmured, almost to himself. "Hard to believe he is concerned about anything. He has such a happy expression."

"Don't be fooled. He's a deep thinker, bit of a worrier, old Bonniface. He's smart."

Dirk, staring straight ahead down the valley, slowly removed what Roger thought was a rolled cigarette from his pocket and lit it. He drew deeply and as he exhaled said, "Farming is a balancing act, Roger. When to plant, when to use resources, when to hold them back. What to give, what to take. It's like that for everything. For life, for our new democracy. Who gets, who must give…for the greater good." He offered the joint to Roger, who against his better judgment, drew deeply, putting the image of Georgie's frowning face out of mind.

***

Dirk finally had to put Sebete on a strong collar and lead in order to get him under control when they went up to the paddock to see the polo ponies off on their journey to the polo field for the match the following day. He was crazy with excitement as Jon and the other riders rounded up the ponies for the trip into town. The big ridgeback was determined to go with them and yelped and barked as they moved off. He jumped at Dirk and Roger who, both still slightly stoned from earlier, laughed and jumped around with him, bringing a knowing smile from the mounted Jon. "See you tomorrow," Jon called. "Good to see Roger and Sebete are friends now." Roger's mood was too good to be irritated at the nuance and he simply waved.

They moved off down the farm road, ponies and their mounted minders raising enough dust to set Roger off on a hay fever attack. "Must be the dust," he gasped.

Dirk laughed, winking. "Or the grass, it does that," slapping Roger on the back. "You're OK, you know. It's going to be a good weekend," he said as they returned to the farmhouse, hauling the resisting and resentful ridgeback behind them.

***

Roger thought he had slipped quietly into the room in order not to disturb the napping Georgie. A 'you smell like a veld fire' groan told him otherwise. At her request he opened the heavy old farm curtains and window. Marin's refurbishing project had obviously not reached as far as this bedroom yet, he thought, hoping the smile on his face could be considered wry. "God, you look peculiar," Georgie said. "Your lips are all twisted, and your eyebrows have gone white."

"Just dust," he said wiping at his face.

Georgie eyed him thoughtfully. "My guess is that our host has introduced you to the other 'green gold' he grows on the farm…right?" Roger smiled weakly. "It seemed appropriate in the moment…" he mumbled as he grabbed a towel from their bed and went in search of a shower. It turned out to be the most enjoyable shower he could remember ever having. Dirk style, there was no shower curtain, and it took him some time to mop up the old timber floor.

***

The evening was going well. They were enjoying drinks on the patio, or *stoep*, as they say in South Africa, watching the sunset from under an old pepper tree that must have been over a hundred years old according to Dirk. Annah dosed in Marin's arms, occasionally waking for more sustenance, which was available on the spot, a deft lift of Marin's T-shirt. Roger chastised himself for being relieved that Jon was not there. He squirmed mentally at his ingrained racialism.

"Well, that's all on the go," said Dirk, as he emerged from the front door having just checked up on activities in the kitchen. "Our cook is doing his chicken special tonight, a sauce he learnt from the previous farmer," he grinned, lifting his beer to his lips.

"He left a few legacies didn't he," laughed Georgie. "Recipes, ponies...Sebete." Dirk had told them the story of the dog being left behind to survive on his own.

"Who kills the neighbour's sheep," murmured Marin. The dog slapped his tail a few times on the slate floor and they all laughed. "I'm hoping that was a coincidence, Sebete," said Dirk, pulling the ridgeback's ears gently. "Only once, Marin."

Roger asked Dirk how he was managing to look after Tom's restaurant and the farm at the same time, now that things were progressing with the asparagus venture. Dirk explained that most of his time regarding the new venture could be allocated to early morning when he and Jon planned the activities for the day, reviewed how certain projects were going and inspected the work done in the fields the previous day. Jon handled most day-to-day activities, managing the workers, ordering and collecting supplies. Dirk's time was taken up on the landline phone and fax, setting up shipping logistics and future distribution in Europe. Internet and mobile phones were in their infancy, especially on an isolated farm.

"I am at the restaurant by early afternoon to oversee the preparations for the evening. No lunchtime opening. The townsfolk's culinary expectations are pretty limited for lunchtime. Hamburgers and fish and chips," Dirk laughed, "which tends to be consumed in the local bars."

"And the bunch that frequent those bars you would not want to have in your restaurant," Marin said. "Too drunk to stand up by mid-afternoon. This is mainly a farming community and if you are not on your farm all day then you're a farmer gone bust, unemployed or a fafi. That's *Fuckall Ambition, Fuckall Interest*," she laughed, seeing the quizzical look on her guests' faces.

"Like someone else we know," Georgie said, glancing at Roger with a grin. He knew she meant Brad, but he said with an innocent smile, "Oh, I'm not that bad darling." They all laughed.

Marin described how the farmers' wives drag their husbands kicking and screaming into the restaurant. The fact that they have to pay for a meal their wife could make for free did not make sense.

"Tom needs to hire a professional chef who can produce some interesting food. Make it worthwhile for the farmers. Enjoy something different, exotic even, a meal they don't get at home," she said. "That's not Dirk or his chef by any stretch of the imagination! Someone asked for toast the other evening and he carried it back from the kitchen in his hand," she said, breaking into a giggling fit that set Georgie off as well.

Despite himself, Dirk laughed along. "Dad and I have been talking about offering Lerryn and her chef partner a share in the place. Would get me off the hook to concentrate on the farm." "Get the poor customers off the hook as well," Marin added. "Seriously that place has always limped along. It has potential though."

Georgie said, "Lerryn would be fantastic in a restaurant. A natural with people. But would she leave her big city life? Roger, do you remember I told you about the twins Lerryn and Pat, the babies in the family?"

Roger opened his mouth to protest the aspersion cast at his memory when Dirk said, "Lerryn's partner is Italian, in this country illegally, from a work visa point of view. We could slip him under the radar out here though. He desperately needs a job. Lerryn is basically supporting him, so the incentive is there for her."

***

As the evening star joined them in the fading orange of the sunset, the colour accentuated by dusty conditions, Marin and Georgie put the baby to bed. Roger wondered what contribution Georgie would be able to make. Probably more a chance for woman's talk. He had sensed an underlying current since Marin joined them earlier that afternoon and knew Georgie would instinctively be drawn towards it, wanting to understand it. Look for missing pieces to her jigsaw picture.

Roger eased himself back in his chair, sipping his wine, he had switched from beer earlier, fearful of Georgie's reaction to any wind in bed later. He sighed contentedly as he enjoyed the darkening hills in the distance. The crickets were all but drowning out Dirk's distant, muted conversation with his cook in the kitchen. It was times like this when one was reluctant to think about the uncertain future the country faced. They were the times that elicited the whimsical, if not cynical, oft-used phrase from South

African white people, "Oh well, another hard day in Africa." Just keep enjoying the lifestyle, we work for it. Let the new government find a solution to millions of unemployed, uneducated, pitifully poor people.

The cook in the kitchen and his helpers? What were they being paid? Probably very little. Did the right to grow subsistence crops on Dirk's farm make up for that? Was it Dirk's farm rightfully? Bonniface, who was now just a worker, with a small land allocation for crops and a few goats, had grown up here. On a farm that he may well have inherited part of from his forefathers had the white people not arrived, uninvited.

Bonniface's instinctive knowledge of this land, the eco system he lived in, compelled him to warn them of the potential for an impending disaster. Concerned for them, as well as his meagre lot. He knew the land. What was building in the dry conditions. He had learnt from his father, who learnt from his.

How far back would one have to go to see them concerned because it was their land, their way of life, their future. Not like Bonniface, who could only be concerned for his employer's lands, not his. How do you make that right, give that pride back?

Roger wondered about the future. Would a time come when the workers began demanding the return of their land? Or began demanding the ANC take action and redistribute farmland? Or take action themselves? A great deal was going to be down to how current white owners sought a compromise. The relationships they built with the people on their lands.

He sipped his wine and thought *I wonder if there is an opportunity for affirmative action at Caracal Ridge.*

***

Dirk's long hair hung perilously close to the flame as he lit a mosquito coil under the table. They had decided to stay on the patio, having agreed the evening was too beautiful to miss by going inside for dinner. It was dark now and the stars blazed across the sky like sequins haphazardly sown on an elegant midnight blue evening gown. Although it was obvious why, it never ceased to amaze Roger how the stars seemed so much more plentiful and brighter away from a city. Dirk had not started the generator yet, so it was darker than usual on the patio.

Roger could see Marin and Georgie in the candle-lit lounge room through the large viewing window, engaged in conversation over a fruity looking concoction they were putting the final touches to. He took the opportunity to ask Dirk what his view was on trying to raise the living standards of his farm workers.

Dirk was animated in his response. This was a subject clearly close to his heart. He told Roger that, practically,

73

he was not doing much at present as he could barely service the overdraft he had taken to purchase the equipment, fertilisers, permits and so on that they needed for the asparagus project. He had not been able to increase wages, but he had given the workers free access to any part of the farm they needed, to grow crops or keep animals provided they employed good land usage principles.

Where it did get exciting, he said, was the equity scheme he was putting together that would allow all the workers to participate in any profits that new projects on the farm produced, according to what work they were contributing towards the project. Contributing through actual work or not, *everyone* would participate in profits though, in some way. Simply because they were, at the end of the day, part of the farm. Had been for generations. *Maybe it was their farm,* Roger thought.

As Dirk spoke the thoughts Roger had had earlier that afternoon in the new asparagus packing room came back to him. "Dirk, I bet there are not too many farm owners thinking about sharing their land with their workers, I'm impressed. I have an idea building in my mind and, after hearing what you have said, I think it might be appropriate. It would create opportunities for workers to leverage that equity scheme you are building. Can I share it?"

At that moment Georgie and Marin returned carrying exotic-looking drinks in their hands.

"Hey, where's ours?" Roger said. "They look like they could have a kick!"

"No alcohol for us, guys, Marin can't and I'm not mad about it," said Georgie. "So, what's your project Roger?"

Dirk sighed, "Not even a small joint later, Georgie?"

Roger, at the same time, "How did you hear 'project' from inside the house anyway?"

"You have a loud voice babe, and yes, Dirk, maybe a small hit later for old times' sake," she laughed, letting it die as she caught Marin's glance.

Over the cook's great chicken dish, notwithstanding their initial cynicism, the women joined in an enthusiastic think tank relating to Roger's 'project'. He had outlined the idea for a very rustic holiday resort on the farm. He visualised accommodation built by the farm workers from locally gathered materials on the raised slope behind the farmhouse, offering a 270-degree view over the main buildings across to the rolling hills and mountains.

An enthusiastic Dirk added that the individual, self-contained chalets could indeed be built by the farm workers, many of whom already had thatching skills and mudrock wall-building skills as they'd built their own tiny homes in a similar fashion. The chalets would need to be bigger though, to accommodate two adults and two kids as a minimum and as close to a standard expected by resort visitors as possible. Using local materials, they could be built relatively cheaply and on a stage-by-stage basis, as patronage grew and funds became available.

In addition, there was already a swimming pool that could be brought back to life from its current muddy state and parts of the farmhouse outbuildings could be converted into a kitchen and dining area. Roger was right, the project would be another vehicle for Dirk's worker equity participation scheme.

The subject, with side-tracks, took up much of the evening and included some outlandish ideas but, by the end, seeds had been sown in Dirk's mind, Roger could see it. They decided to make a day of it and get to bed early, as they had the polo match to go to the following day. Or as Marin put it, "Three hours of mad, mounted Afrikaners effing and blinding at their poor horses, blaming them for their own gross incompetence and lack of skill."

***

As he eased himself under the duvet, Roger whispered, "Well, what an interesting day!" but Georgie was already well on her way into a deep sleep. He listened to the night sounds of the farm. An owl in one of the gum trees nearby, a jackal howling in the distance, a quick bark from Sebete in response, warning it about the perils of crossing into his territory, polo ponies stamping the ground from time to time in their sleep.

He tried to imagine himself a farmer. Then he remembered the dead lamb and the sounds of the cook chasing a chicken around the yard earlier before catching it and wringing its neck for their dinner. He sighed and decided he should stick to his office job. He blew out the lamp, enjoying the whiff of burnt oil as it extinguished.

Chapter 3

Polo

Sandwiched between the truck door and Georgie sitting in the middle of the cabin next to Dirk, who drove at breakneck speed along the dilapidated dirt road to town, Roger was distinctly aware of his immortality. He felt like he was in the catapult David used against the giant, about to be slung into oblivion. If he survived this, he thought, he might consider going to church next Sunday. Their skeletal frames shook violently in concert with the truck's vibrations as it skidded from side to side, barely under control, across the corrugations in the road. Georgie, in the middle position, was slightly raised due to a small pillow used to suppress the probing interest of a broken seat spring. Fortunately, she was short enough to avoid banging her head on the unpadded ceiling of the truck's roof every time it bounced.

"D-d-damn g-good idea that of y-yours," Dirk yelled, competing with the truck's vibration and the hammering noise of its incessant rattling.

Roger, determined not to unclamp his jaws for fear of his teeth chattering so hard they would chip, nodded his head violently hoping that it would suffice for an "Oh, thanks." Georgie turned her head to him from alongside, looking down at him, an eyebrow raised.

As the rear wheels slid from side to side, behind them Dirk, cigarette in his mouth, lent forward over his hands resting on the top of the steering wheel and clutching an open box of matches. For fear of an imminent accident Roger tried to touch Georgie's arm to get her attention, to indicate by pointing, she should light the match for Dirk, but the truck lunged and it became a prod in her breast which got him a quizzical look from her. His sign language confused her even further, so he gave up. Dirk threw the match box onto the dashboard and exhaled smoke.

They were 10 minutes into the 40-minute drive to Fynberg and its local polo field, and Roger was already wishing he had not even heard of polo let alone making this dangerous journey to watch it. He decided to feign sleep in order to avoid conversation and possible disintegration of his teeth. Closing his eyes and putting his head back in a relaxed position resulted in his head being slammed successively against the door as they entered and exited a pothole. True to form Georgie burst into laughter, accompanied by Dirk who caught the episode in his ever askew rear-view mirror.

Notwithstanding the juddering and shuddering Georgie managed, "Ag Roger, you banging your head on the wall 'cause it's so nice when you stop, hey?" in her best impersonation of a surly Afrikaans prison guard. They all laughed this time.

Five minutes later they were mercifully off the dirt road onto a rudimentary tar road that had avoidable potholes and no corrugations.

"Phew that's a bit better," said Georgie.

"Yeah, now we can get up a bit of speed," replied Dirk.

Wonderful, thought Roger.

***

The polo field lay on the edge of the small town, surrounded by oak trees that must have been planted a hundred years ago at least. As Roger and Georgie climbed, with considerable relief, from the cab of Dirk's truck, he explained that the ground was originally an agricultural show ground where farmers from miles around came to trade cattle, horses, pigs and all manner of produce.

Mountains in the near distance marked the border with Lesotho, the tiny, land locked mountain country enclave that in the past became the haven of choice for white political activists on the run from South African security police. A long walk, sometimes very cold, but relatively easy to find a way past the border control point, especially under cover of darkness. Donald Woods, editor of the banned *Daily Dispatch*, was one who took this escape route. From there a flight could be arranged to political exile or freedom, depending how one viewed it. Some, like Chris Hani, stayed, operating remotely until cross border raids by South African security forces in the 1980s made it too dangerous for him.

The oaks and the actual polo field were a green oasis in the dry golden veld grass that swept up to the mountains beyond. Several horse trailers were parked off to one side and groups of horses grazed contentedly in the shade of the trees. Their minders laughed and joked with each other loudly in Sotho, and Roger noticed that one seemed to be taking bets. On the match result no doubt, he thought, and asked Dirk. "Oh yes," he laughed, "it's a big thing for them, who will score first, whose baas will fall off first, who will win the match, whatever they can find to bet on."

Roger looked over Dirk's shoulder as they chatted, towards the mountains and Lesotho. He wondered if these workers could afford the trip to the capital, Maseru, which had a casino.

Many affluent white South Africans had made the trip to the Maseru Casino over the years. Gambling had been banned in a Calvinistic South Africa and enterprising hotel groups had set up casinos in the government's so called 'independent puppet states' and legitimate neighbouring countries like Lesotho and Swaziland. The newly set up puppet states, being independent were not subject to the regime's laws. The South African government couldn't have it both ways.

"Weird," said Roger. "South African arrivals in Botswana, one day a security force raid, the next, tourists to their Casino." Dirk nodded, "Yes, those were strange days indeed. There's Jon, let's check on the horses." He turned and strode off.

Roger observed Dirk as he walked away from him, newly fitted spurs jangling, long ponytail dangling.

Georgie and Roger hung back on the periphery, Georgie nervous of the stamping, shying horses. She remarked that they seemed somehow to be excited by the prospect competing, galloping around like crazy. Or, thought Roger, just protesting at the stupidity of chasing around after a little rolling object, being pulled this way and that by their riders.

He had seen a collision once in a professional international match that had broken the neck of a pony, killing it instantly. The memory of it being dragged off the playing field under a tarpaulin came back to him and he shuddered. Georgie smiled, prodding him gently in the ribs, "What, shaking with excitement, would you like to have a go?" He was busy manufacturing a smart retort, when she waved over his shoulder at someone behind him. "Hello Tom, it's been ages! How are you?"   She hugged what Roger would have described as a Mr. Magoo look-alike.

Tom Lenbruikte was nothing like Roger expected after all he had heard from Georgie and Eve. He had created an image of a tall, lean, suave, dark-business-suited 'captain of industry'. He was in fact shaking the hand of a smallish, slightly balding man with a four-year-old girl clutching his hand. Roger could not mistake the energy though, the sparkle in Tom's eyes. The look of a successful vasectomy reversal?

After they had exchanged pleasantries and Georgie had inquired about both Tom's ex-wife, Rita, and his new wife Mandy, all three good friends nowadays, Tom finally introduced his daughter. "And this is our cheeky daughter. Kerry, say hello darling, to Uncle and Auntie."

Oh boy, thought Roger. *True Afrikaner tradition. Show respect kids. No first names without a title in front when talking to adults. White ones that is. He can't speak a word of Afrikaans, nor his kids either, but insists on*

Afrikaner protocol. He made a mental note to stay away from any political conversation with Tom.

"Daddy when is the game starting? When will the horses run fast around?" Kerry said, tugging Tom's hand. "Soon darling, soon, and it's run *around fast*, not *fast around.*"

Georgie and Tom were soon deep in a 'call back the past, do you remember old so and so' conversation, so Roger, not knowing a single person they were talking about, invited Kerry to go and see the horses getting saddled up. "Ooh, yes please Uncle," she said taking his hand confidently.

Roger was quite taken. His children from his first marriage were teenagers now and it had been a long time since he felt a little child's hand grasp his hand so tightly, skipping excitedly alongside him. Getting control of the lump in his throat, he guided her around the prancing group of horses to where the first ponies to participate were being saddled.

Three burly farmers were standing around Dirk and Jon giving them rapid fire instructions on the strategy they were planning to employ against the team from the neighbouring district. Then one said, "Jon, keep away from that old bugger with the grey hair who plays defence for them. He will go after you. We will keep an eye on him, don't worry. Koos here will donder him if he gets too clever," he laughed, punching Koos on a big muscular arm.

Walking up to them with a smile, Cor Onderbann, a sergeant in the local police said, "I hope I am not hearing any plans for assaults on the opposition from my teammates. You know I will have to lock you up?" They all pointed at each other saying 'it was him, sir' very seriously. Then Cor said, "And you, Dirk, all you have to do is not fall off like last time." They all roared with laughter, slapping Dirk on the back. Jon allowed himself a grin, an amused splash of white teeth contrasting with his handsome features. As it was, after all, his boss, he refrained from joining in the back slapping in front of Dirk's farmer peers.

Roger had forgotten how dramatic the sound of eight galloping horses could be, and as amateur as these teams might have been, he and Georgie were nonetheless transfixed. The ground thundered as advancing horses, nostrils flaring, leaned into each other, riders jostling for position over the ball rolling in front of them, often towards spectators on the side-line.

They were more than relieved to see the horses veer off at the last second as a rider reached down to swing and connect the ball with a 'thwack' of wooden mallet on hard ball. Roger marvelled at the ability some riders demonstrated, reverse swinging the mallet on the opposite side of their crouching bodies, to make contact with the ball.

Dirk, being new to the sport was a bit hit and miss, but Jon was clearly enjoying himself. He and his horse seemed as though they were one. At the end of the first chukka new ponies were introduced and some of the team interchanged.

Sipping a cold drink during the break, Georgie prodded Roger playfully in the ribs. "So, what's this I see, *Mr. Broody*? A little girl stole your heart? I saw the look on your face. Don't get any ideas, buddy," she laughed.

Roger watched her face carefully. That sounded more like a 'When are we having a baby?' to me, he said to himself.

Jon did not experience any issues with the opposition and, on the contrary, drew some admiring, good natured curses from them for his skilled horsemanship as he slipped between them to reach the ball. A small crowd of locals had gathered to watch. Mainly family of the players, but Roger noticed two young girls on the side-line who seemed to be more appreciative of Dirk's skills than any of the other participants on horseback.

It was over an hour of huffing and puffing, shouting and cursing before the final chukka was over. After dismounting from their sweating ponies, Dirk's team and the opposition gathered under a large oak, leaving their mounts to their workers. Wives and helpers had set up a charcoal braai on which boerewors and steaks were already sizzling. A nearby basin was overflowing with ice and cold beer in bottles. There was much back slapping and teasing. Jon excused himself to check on his team, watering and grooming the ponies before their ride back to the farm.

"He knows what he's doing on a horse, that boy of yours."
Roger cringed at the derogatory term used unthinkingly by
the farmer. The terms 'boy' and 'girl' were long dead,
used historically for black people, whether they were five
years old or fifty. They hated it. The term was obviously
still alive and well in this farming community. Dirk
opened his mouth to respond when one of the other
farmers interceded with an ironic smile, "*Jong*, Koos you
know it's the new South Africa, don't say 'boy' hey."

"Oh jammer, sorry, I didn't mean anything." Roger got the
feeling Koos was genuinely embarrassed and sorry for his
slip up.

Just then there was an indignant bellow from a truck
parked nearby, "*Jong, swart, ek sal jou moer* (Damn it,
black, I'll beat you up)." A burly male of about fifty had
emerged from his truck, marching angrily towards Jon and
the two girls.

Roger had earlier noticed the girls intercept Jon as he
strode towards the horses. They had introduced themselves
and were just exchanging handshakes when the father of
one of the girls noticed. The girls had seen Jon and Dirk
talking constantly both on and off the field. Embarrassed
to approach Dirk directly, they decided to see if they could
get the lowdown on him from Jon. Maybe even get an
introduction to Dirk.

Dirk took off at speed, getting between the irate father and
Jon. "What's the problem, sir?" he said calmly. "Jon is my
foreman...and friend."

"Listen, you hippy shit, I don't care if you are a *swart boetie*, I am not having him touch my girl."

"They were just greeting, shaking hands, like normal people? Do you really think you should be swearing at us for that?"

"Pa, Pa…" his daughter pleaded.

"*Klim die motor in. Ek sal julle albei 'n klap gee.* (Get in the car. I'll give you both a hiding). Do you want a hiding, hey?"

Taking a stride towards Dirk he yelled, "En jy hippy, I will punch your blerry teeth…" He never got the words out because Koos' big fist clamped around his collar, yanked him back and threw him towards his truck. "Go on, bugger off, you don't talk to my boys like that." He grinned at Jon and Dirk, "Ag not boys, teammates hey."

The father sized up the towering Koos, thought better of it and walked towards his truck.

Koos looked at the girls. "Take him home, girls. He's been at the brandy, in the car, I can smell it."

Roger could see the girls were mortified. Dirk, feeling their discomfort said, "Don't worry girls, we all have fathers who embarrass us sometimes. See you around another time," as they walked away to follow the father to his car. The man's daughter, turned back to Dirk and Jon, "Yes, but do your fathers slap you around as well?" Roger wondered if the slight smile that teased the other girl's lips was conspiratory or embarrassment. The image of Tom or Bonniface slapping their respective sons seemed ludicrous.

Behind him, one of those fathers was hanging on to his four-year-old daughter who was tugging at his hand, keen to get closer to the adult action. Tom, resisting his young daughter's urging to join the action, gave Koos a thumbs up.

Roger wondered if it was just him who saw signs of positive change in the events he had just witnessed. Afrikaans farmers minding what terms they used to refer to others? And defending a black guy threatened by a white guy? Drinking beer and chatting with their workers instead of ignoring them, leaving them to wait around after tending to the farmer's horses while they enjoyed themselves. Roger had a sudden image of himself as the manifestation of oppression. How *could* these warm-hearted people have been so openly supportive of apartheid. He chastised himself, *English South Africans had been different. Not really. Not trying to do anything about the country's injustices made you just as culpable. Voting for some white minority opposition party during that time was not a vindication.*

He asked Georgie what she thought, hoping to distract her from her still shocked state, standing like a statue, recovering from narrowly escaping what looked like a potentially violent confrontation. "Positives? We *will* have positives when you men stop being such arseholes," was

89

all she could muster. Walking away she said, "I should talk to that girl. I think she may need help with that monster. He needs a good talking to."

Roger was going to say he was glad the girls had left as it might not have turned out well while the father was still around, but thought better of it. Anyway, to his relief Georgie was already introducing herself to one of the wives who had brought her a cold drink. *No confrontations today.*

He could hear the likely gossip in the town. "This damn hippy is going to cause a revolution. They say his workers call him by his first name?"

***

Roger had drunk enough to feel oblivious to the perils of Dirk's driving. His offer to drive was greeted by a dismissive shake of the head from Georgie and an invitation to enjoy the middle seat of the cab.

"Given the number of beers you have had, I am sure you will not notice the discomfort I had to put up with coming here. Dirk are you OK to drive? You and Roger had about the same number of beers, didn't you?"

Dirk smiled and shrugged his shoulders, "Farm roads, it will be OK. Unless you want to drive?" "Sure," Georgie said, but Dirk only grinned and got into the driver's seat before anyone could comment further.

They had carried on until sunset before departing with much back slapping and promises of meeting again soon. Even Georgie got a few unexpected bear hugs from sweaty farmers who had taken to her directness and inquisitive conversation about farm life, the responsibilities taken by farmers' wives for ensuring there was a supportive community where life could be tough.

Roger sat next to Dirk as they thundered along the decrepit road back to the farm. Their shouted conversation covered many subjects, but mainly around developing the resort. When he saw the horses ahead (Jon had left much earlier with them) Dirk slowed down to a snail's pace edging along on the far side of the road ensuring the ponies were not frightened. Stopping momentarily, he exchanged a few words with Jon that had them both laughing before waving and speeding up. Roger didn't catch what was said but wondered again about inside jokes.

***

As Dirk's truck rattled off into the distance leaving a cloud of dust behind it, Jon reflected on Dirk's parting joke about both narrowly escaping being bitten by a 'rock spider', as white English-speaking people referred to Afrikaners when feeling irritated or annoyed. He smiled again to himself about Dirk's comment. *From someone with an Afrikaans name who only speaks English?*

The confrontation at the polo field had not really rattled him, he had experienced aggression from white people from time to time in his life on the farm and when visiting the town. He had been surprised, though, at his newfound resentment to the way he was spoken to that afternoon by the girl's father. Clearly, he had got accustomed to the environment Dirk had been developing at the farm. Dirk spoke to everyone as an equal. Respect and appreciation had replaced tolerance and irritation. There were only requests, no demands. They were fast becoming a community. He had banned terms like 'master' and 'baas' and insisted on being called Dirk only.

Jon had spent his whole life on the farm. It was all he knew. As kids he and his sisters had walked to the local school a few miles away, barefoot along the dirt road armed with a piece of chalk and a small blackboard to write on. They were taught the very basics of spelling and arithmetic. There was little in the way of books.

In the afternoon, Jon joined Bonniface in the fields where he learnt how to herd the farmer's cattle and tend to the animals' various needs. His sisters helped their mother on their small ploughed allotment where they grew mielies and other vegetables.

It was a daily routine that varied little, but they were happy. They had space and something of their own. Well, nearly. Unlike some people they knew, cousins, who lived in the shanty township of Brandfort. Crammed together, insufferably hot in the midday sun. Under dilapidated, bits and pieces of corrugated iron for roofs and plastic sheeting for walls. Freezing through the winter nights, hence the countless open fires for warmth, creating a canopy of dark pollution over them day and night.

Children of the farm workers gathered occasionally at the dam to paddle and giggle about the boys who tried to catch their attention with their antics in the shallow water. Which of these would be their husband in years to come?

As he got to his teen years Jon had participated less in activities with the other kids preferring to read any books he could get his hands on. He had used the rudimentary teaching he had had as a foundation for self-learning and had over the years become a competent English reader and writer. He had little interest in girls which worried Bonniface as he was looking forward to his son marrying and the increase in land allotment the family would receive. Jon for his part was intent on developing his skills and therefore his potential as a worker for a local farmer, or even in one of Fynberg's shops. He would have to find a way to get to the town each day though.

He had already been sought out by farmers wives as a gardener and houseboy. They had heard of his ability to speak and write English, and although they were generally Afrikaans speaking, they spoke English as well and Jon offered the attraction of easy communication. It was through these part-time jobs that Jon had access to discarded newspapers, and he read everything he could. As he busied himself with some chore or the other in the kitchen he listened to conversations between his employer and visiting farmers and the news on the radio in the kitchen. By the time he was in his late teens he had a good understanding of the political situation in South Africa.

In the last few years since Nelson Mandela had been released, he had become increasingly excited about the possibilities liberation might hold, even for him. Dirk's arrival at the farm, the new responsibilities he was allocated and the potential Dirk's plans for the farm could offer had him lying awake at night with excitement and anticipation.

His father, Bonniface, was the only damper on his spirits. He continually warned Jon of becoming distracted and of the need to focus on having his own family. And, in particular, querying why it was necessary to spend so much money on clothes and grow his hair. "You want to look like your Baas? You are black, how can you?"

In each of these conversations Jon knew what the next question would be even before his Father made the gesture, the forefinger of his right hand moving backwards and forwards through the circle he made with the thumb and finger of his other hand. "What about this?" Bonniface pleaded, "Have you done this with a girl yet?"

Jon did not have the heart to tell his father that up to this point the only emotion he had been able to muster for the female species was for his sisters and mother, and that was ongoing irritation for the former and undying love for the latter.

***

As they drove, Dirk shouted to Roger over the rattling that Tom had confirmed that Lerryn and her chef boyfriend, Luigi were moving to Fynberg and were going to work in the restaurant. "I just got fired," Dirk laughed. "Thank God."

"Yeah, but how will you make up the pay while you are getting the projects going, getting cash in from them?" Georgie asked.

"I thought you were asleep! Always the practical thinker," shouted Dirk. Roger smiled to himself and hiccupped.

"Dad wants me to keep a watching brief over the operation for which he will continue to pay me half my salary, so I will get by. The only question mark is over Pat. She is devastated that Lerryn is moving and has asked Dad to try and organise something up here for her and Gus, her husband. They are very close those two, Lerryn and Pat," he explained for Roger's benefit.

The return trip seemed to Roger to have gone a lot faster. They were already on the last stretch of bone-jarring farm road. They shouted words at each other through chattering teeth. Roger was much taller than Georgie, so when he bounced on the wayward spring in the bench seat, he did not escape the low roof as she had. Despite being taller she had insisted it was his turn to have the uncomfortable middle position. His head narrowly missed the truck roof's metal ceiling above him every time the truck leapt over a hump in the road. Forcing him to lean his head forward, out of the way, risking impalement on the gear lever which had long since lost its plastic knob. Its bare, threaded tip polished by Dirk's constant gear changes seemed to point menacingly at him.

Georgie pulled him back, pointing up, meaning he should sit up, away from the gear lever. He thought she meant he should look up at something on the truck ceiling which he tried to do with disastrous results. Looking up coincided with the next bump in the road and the next bounce, his raised forehead connecting the unpadded truck roof with a resounding thud. "You OK?" Georgie shouted. Roger knew she was desperately trying not to laugh. Dirk was cackling like an old crow, like he did when he shared one of his controversial observations.

As they pulled up to the house, its windows already dark in the dying light, they saw Marin in the nearby barn entrance, struggling with the generator. Pushing strands of hair back over her head, she cried, "Yay, you're back just in time. This thing is a mystery to me. Mandy just called, they're all coming over for dinner. To talk about the new chef, I guess your dad told you. Need to start being a cook myself now, bye."

As Marin trotted across to the main house and disappeared through the kitchen door, Roger couldn't help admiring her good looks. That image and the fact that their vehicle had become blissfully silent, stationery, caused his spirits to rise considerably.

* * *

Watching Dirk fuss over the temperamental generator, Roger reflected on the environment Dirk was creating for himself. Not long ago, Dirk had probably never even seen a generator let alone tease one into action. He was learning new skills fast in his attempt to leverage the farm's potential, being creative with its resources without losing sight of involving and rewarding the farm's community. Not a bad start on a journey towards feeling fulfilled by what you did to earn a living.

As instructed by Dirk, he held a lever that did god knows what on the generator. He wondered about Dirk's own personal 'community' though. He and Marin and their baby did not seem to be in the idyllic relationship an outsider might expect of a young couple with a new baby and a farming adventure ahead of them. He wondered if Dirk felt Marin had used the baby, and its dependence on those that brought it into their world, to thrust herself into the new life he had only just started to build. Roger got the impression Dirk felt responsibility for his family but not necessarily love.

"Shit, Roger remind me to call my mate Basie," Dirk exclaimed. "Jon and the guys need to rest over at his farm tonight, those ponies are bushed…forgot to call him…just remembered…come on mother fucker," he grunted, pulling the start chord again. At that moment the generator finally sprung into life and Dirk trotted towards the house, and phone. He yelled, "Pull that lever you're holding up to 'off' after two minutes…I'll call Basie," over his shoulder and the thumping generator.

As he counted off "one Mississippi, two Mississippi…" Roger's thoughts went back to his hosts. Dirk was here because he did not want a legal career, Marin was here because she had a baby, desire for a legal career or not. Roger could see there was potential for resentment on both sides. He was at "one hundred and six Mississippi" and reckoned two minutes must be up.

After pulling up the lever, as instructed, Roger turned back towards the house, all lights blazing now. Through the large window he could see there was lots of action in the kitchen-cum-family room. Everybody, including Georgie, fresh from her shower, helped prepare the evening meal which had been started in candlelight, much to her delight. For the second time in the last half an hour or so Roger was admiring a woman, this time through a window, unobserved. Even in the candlelight Georgie's fine features were noticeable, her blue eyes flashing as she spoke and laughed with Marin. He had always enjoyed her, fresh from a shower. It seemed to refresh her, raise her spirits. She was pushing back long blond hair from her face as she leant over the stove. Boy, you're becoming quite the voyeur, Roger thought to himself as he left his position at the window.

He walked in through the rear door that opened from the kitchen onto the large dark back lawn. The coal stove Georgie had been working at also heated the water in the house. Its heat had taken the chill off the evening air, so the atmosphere was warm and inviting. Dirk appeared from his call to Basie with a bottle of red wine in each hand and a grin that said all was good with Jon and the horses encamped at his friend's farm.

There was a large wooden table running most of the kitchen length that Roger thought could probably seat a small army. Dirk and he took up residence at the far end out of the women's way. Roger had hardly taken a sip of his wine when car headlights splashed across the dark farmyard outside and through the kitchen, now only lit by candles. Georgie had insisted the newly acquired light from the generator spoilt the atmosphere.

Kerry, led by a barking, over-excited, Sebete, burst through the back door, "Dark in here, switch on the lights, hello uncle Roger!"

"Hello, hello…easy with that torch," Roger said, shielding his eyes, feeling somewhat pleased that he was the only one singled out for salutation, although Sebete's paws placed on his chest also had to go down as a greeting, although somewhat daunting.

"All the better for ghost stories later," Marin said tactfully as she picked Kerry up and hugged her, heading off Dirk's likely response which was probably not what Kerry wanted to hear. Tom and Mandy arrived from the front entrance of the house, clumping down the passage, the old farmhouse timber floors creaking. They had avoided the dark route across the farmyard that Kerry had taken with Sebete. She had their only flashlight anyway.

"Evening all," Tom called, jovially. "Mandy, this is Roger and Georgie…and this is Mandy."

Roger observed, as opening pleasantries were exchanged, wine poured and glasses clinked, that Mandy's role was more one of doting older daughter and carer, for both child and husband, than wife. The age difference between Tom and his wife was considerable, over thirty years, Roger guessed. When Mandy wasn't fussing over Kerry she was fussing over Tom. Was he OK on that stool, shouldn't he have a chair with back support?

It did not take Roger long to realise the reason Tom was visiting so soon after seeing them at the polo was less about the new chef and more about repositioning his image, away from that of an aging parent he was forced to project earlier, as a result of Mandy's absence from the match, needing to manage some issues at their restaurant.

To reset the perception lest it become ingrained that he wasn't an influential professional.

The meal was relaxed, and compliments flew. Marin and Georgie deferred to each other and finally, laughing, linked arms and took an exaggerated bow. As the evening progressed, and after Kerry had been put to bed, twice, Tom shared some interesting anecdotes, some funny some scary. Not the least of which was the time he and Dirk were caught in a dust storm in the light aircraft Tom, as a fairly novice pilot, was flying. Roger wondered how he would have felt in that situation given Tom's age and limited flying hours. Dirk seemed to have been unconcerned.

No matter what the subject, Tom seemed to have had some experience that made him more knowledgeable about the subject than the others. This was an attribute that was naturally essential for him in order to fulfil the role of Lenbruikte family head. Roger could see from the looks on the faces of those around the table they all accepted, or were resigned to, how important Tom was to his family. *And to business, to the community and to the world in general,* Roger thought sarcastically.

Eventually there was some discussion regarding Lerryn and her boyfriend Luigi, the new chef. He had some ideas about Italian dishes he would introduce to make the restaurant a little different. More desirable to the farming community. So, they were not 'paying through the nose' for the same food their wives could cook at home, as Marin had claimed the day before.

"Of course, we will have to pay him more than the woman who has been doing the job, but that's just how it is."

Marin said, "More? Why, is he more qualified?"

"Not really."

"Then why?" Marin smiled.

"Because he's a man," Georgie said. "Exactly," Marin said.

Roger held his breath, casting around for the bottle of wine that had apparently disappeared. He seemed to remember last seeing it just before Mandy said, "Tom don't have another glass of wine darling, you won't feel good in the morning sweetie."

Dirk having second guessed Roger, had already collected a fresh bottle from where he had put it near the stove to take the chill off. He positioned himself over Roger's shoulder, pouring some into his glass. "Here we go," he murmured near Roger's ear. Roger was not sure whether he was referring to the wine or the debate that was about to ensue. "Dad's favourite."

Tom had already launched into a diatribe about how overstated male female equality was, so once again Roger wasn't sure whether Dirk was referring to the wine or possibly the fact that this was Tom's favourite subject.

When Tom began lecturing on the important role women played as mothers, nurturing the next generation, Roger could feel Georgie and Marin shifting uncomfortably, rolling their eyes. So far, they had resisted folding their arms. Mandy, having heard this lecture many times before, left to check on Kerry who was supposed to be sleeping, having already had a bedtime story from both Marin and Mandy. "Check on Annah while you are there please," Marin called, as Mandy tiptoed down the passage. Roger noticed how smoothly unobtrusive Mandy was in removing Tom's half-full wine glass and taking it with her, without him noticing.

"If women were paid equally and therefore incentivised to follow careers, who would be at home to bring up the children? In this so-called new South Africa, having a maid to look after kids is going to become very expensive. It won't be possible. Yet another consequence of equality and equal opportunity that no one has thought of," Tom smirked. "Hey, where's my wine?"

Georgie said, "Tom, I can't believe you just said what you did. It is just wrong on so many levels."

"Just male bullshit," Marin said.

Mandy, returning, burst into laughter as she picked up Marin's comment. "Maybe Tom has bitten off more than he should have."

"Maybe Tom should be lecturing males on putting a bit of effort into participating in their children's lives," Marin went on, with a glance at Dirk.

Roger had noticed that Tom's voice was getting louder and his index finger higher. Mandy had joined in now, so Tom was taking on an intimidating trio of intelligent women, Roger felt. He will swing even further towards politics Roger thought, it's his best way out.

Tom was loudly denouncing Georgie's postulation enthusiastically supported by Marin and Mandy, of a world where men and women were able to share in a child's upbringing as a result of positive support from employers, corporate and government, for equality in the workplace. Dirk was trying to break in with a legal technicality when Mandy let out a scream.

Standing in the doorway was Kerry, the front of her nightie wet and red. There were gasps and chairs scraping before Roger spotted the empty wine glass dangling in her hand behind her back and laughed.

"I had the cough medicine you left by my bed Mummy. It's not very nice and I spilt."

Giggling with relief the women fussing around Kerry as Tom knelt down before her. Taking the wine glass from her hand he started, in fatherly fashion, to lecture her on the perils of helping herself to something without an adult to supervise her. Kerry was nodding seriously when her little shoulders shook once and she threw up over her serious-faced, now temporarily blinded, father.

***

Roger had a flashback to a particularly traumatic evening when he and his ex-wife had been exposed to a home movie at a friend of a friend's home featuring *The Exorcist*. The 'home movie' evenings were popular then, with the old projectors and their big wheels filled with celluloid.

They were 'at home' events because it was popular to hire a banned film (even *Playboy* was banned by the Calvinistic Afrikaner government) under the counter and invite friends over for a barbecue and illicit movie. Chairs were set up in the double garage with a screen, or at worst a white sheet pegged up, and a whirring, fan- blowing projector.

In that particular evening's movie when the young protagonist projectile vomited, teeth bared and eyes agape, as the priest hovered over her, Roger felt ice-cold perspiration appear on his face like he had been sprayed with a hose, his stomach clenched into a tight ball. He stumbled from his chair through the gloom and nausea to the exit door like a stricken zombie.

Groping his way down the passage he collapsed, panting, into a large chair in the host's lounge room. Transfixed on the movie no one had even noticed his hurried departure, or so he thought.

"Oh, Roger you look awful. I don't blame you, awful movie, I don't know what Bob was thinking, choosing that movie! I'll get a damp face cloth." It was Margery, their host.

She was back in a trice, bending over Roger gently wiping his face. She was close enough that he had nowhere to look but down her front as her blouse sagged forward. His nausea was rapidly being replaced by another involuntary reaction, growing in the flimsy board shorts he had worn because the evening had started with swimming and a pool barbecue. "There you are, you're a bit less pale now," she cooed, close enough for Roger to feel her breath. Roger tried to surreptitiously lay his arm across his board shorts.

At that moment his wife came through the door. "Roger why did you leave, why are you and Margery sitting on that one chair together? Come on Roger up you get, give Margery some space, she can't sit on the arm of the chair like that. Come and sit here with me," his wife said, as she sat down on a sofa patting the fabric beside her.

Roger was stricken. He presently could not even move his arm for fear of exposing circumstantial evidence relating to his previous wanton thought process, let alone stand up in his shorts.

Both women were looking at him expectedly. Knowing time was what he needed Roger suddenly bent over double, sliding to the floor, groaning, "Oh my God, the cramps are back," as he slid to the floor in a foetal position, buying a least a few minutes for the incriminating evidence to disappear.

***

Coming back to the present, two different women were staring at him now. "Roger, where are you?" Georgie exclaimed. "Marin asked if you wanted coffee or a whisky."

"Definitely a whisky," he managed.

"Me too," said Dirk, back from seeing Tom and Mandy off, an already sleeping Kerry in the back of their car. "What an evening!"

Chapter 4

Between visits

On the trip back, Georgie was ominously quiet, and Roger wondered if she was miffed at him about anything. The grass smoking? Hell, she did her share in the past. Maybe he had been over-sensitive about her Brad aside. *She's bound to say I turned a joke into something mean,* he thought. Then it struck him. Nope, she was probably back in mental jigsaw puzzle mode. God knows she must have discovered lots of interesting pieces during the last few days. He decided to remain quiet and concentrate on his driving.

They hummed through the countryside into the setting sun, storm clouds on the horizon, full of empty promises, teasing the farmers on their dry lands. Roger let his mind wander. He began reflecting, with some enjoyment, on some of the weekend's events and conversations. At breakfast they had all chuckled over last night's drama with Kerry. Tom's face was a picture! Regurgitated red wine dripping from it, as he attempted to downplay the demise of the smart new designer jacket Mandy had insisted he purchase recently.

Later, having cleaned up, looking totally out of character in a pair of Dirk's jeans and T-shirt, Tom had cast around for his wine. This was how he discovered that the wine had got into Kerry's hands as a result of Mandy sneaking off with his wine glass. He now blamed her for the whole saga. Georgie and Marin tried to defuse the situation by shouldering some of the blame. It had after all become a heated debate, stoked up by them, they suggested, looking contrite.

Tom was having nothing of it. He growled in Mandy's direction, "You always interfere. Taking my wine like that. I'm not an 'alchie' you know."

"OK darling, I'm sorry," Mandy purred. "But let's go now, it's been a long day." She winked at Marin and Georgie.

After Tom and Marin had left, the four of them moved back to the patio for a nightcap. The sky was a sparkling canopy spread over them from mountain top across the valley in front to cliff top behind them. A huge dome of far flung galaxies. Gazing upwards, they could almost feel themselves travelling through them at that very moment.

In the silence, as they sipped their drinks and soaked up the wonder of the view. Roger found, with the help of the whisky, he was feeling philosophical. He murmured, to himself he thought, *what really insignificant travellers they all were in the journey of the universe. Where their journey was taking them, and why, they had no idea.* "We sure don't," Dirk responded, catching the last part of Roger's observation.

Roger listened as the others engaged in a hushed conversation about a greater universal force orchestrating things. Not necessarily God, but an energy of some kind. *Their voices low out of respect for the tranquillity of the night or nervous about offending God?* he wondered.

***

"Do you have no idea why Jon gives you that impression?" Georgie's voice came through the hum of the car, startling him from his reverie. He was fascinated to note, as he always was when he did the 'daydream' driving thing, he did not seem to remember anything of the last few miles of the road.

"Uh…sorry, not with you."

"Well, you've been going on about Jon getting at you, haven't you?" Georgie said.

"Yeah, as I was saying earlier it seemed he resented my being around, at times. Maybe just my imagination. Paranoia, hey?"

Georgie had already made the point that Jon setting Sebete free to gallop down their track could have just as easily ended up with her flat on her back. Further, Jon laughing at him sneezing was not exactly sinister either.

"It was just that… I don't know. Every time Dirk and I were engaged, and Jon was around, there seemed to be an atmosphere. An awkwardness maybe?"

"Well, you were a male in his territory."

"What do you mean? His territory? What about Dirk and Tom?"

"Exactly. What *about* Dirk and Tom? Tom is Dirk's *father,* so no threat, get it?"

"And Dirk?"

"Well, I'll leave you to think about that a bit more Roger. I would love to hear your conclusions," Georgie laughed, shaking her head. "You *men!*"

Much of the rest of the trip was taken up by Georgie asking for his thoughts on various incidents and interactions between people during the weekend. Roger was happy with the distraction. He was not keen to go back to the Jon conversation, as he had a feeling he knew where it was heading and would need considerable processing.

In any event, as they drew closer to home their minds turned from the farm to their own occupations. To the deals that were being worked on. To their meetings planned for the week, with customers, with bosses and in Roger's case, errant salespeople in his team.

***

Brad was one of those errant sales guys in Roger's team. He had been made redundant over a year ago and finding a new sales management role at forty plus years of age had not been easy. Affirmative action meant a strong focus on increasing the number of black people in the work force. The pool of candidates for any white-collar role had grown exponentially overnight.

Georgie claimed that instead of waiting for recruiters to call him, it would have been a lot easier for Brad had he put some effort into leveraging his network of contacts in the industry, which backfired on her when Roger, feeling sorry for his old friend, offered him a sales role in his team. Brad was delighted. It may have been a demotion, but it was a job, a good one, and with his considerable experience in the technology world he was bound to make up the reduction in base salary through commission on sales.

After a few months however, Roger was starting to regret his subjective decision. Brad was not delivering results. He was away from the office a lot. That was good if he was making sales calls. Roger was not convinced he was. A few days after returning from the farm, Roger was still debating how to approach Brad on his lack of performance when Brad himself stuck his head through Roger's office door and said, "Fancy a beer after work. Need to pick your brain on something?"

"Sure. The Rose?" Roger smiled. "Say 5.30?"

An opportunity to end the procrastination maybe, thought Roger.

"Done," Brad called, waving through Roger's glass partition window as he continued down the passage away from Roger's office. "I'll get the first round."

***

Roger, thinking he had got to their local bar before Brad, slid into a bench seat away from the main bar counter. Looking around the room he noticed his two other sales guys, Peter and Rolf, ensconced on bar stools holding forth over their beers to a standing Brad who was just being served their drinks. Seeing him they all waved a greeting.

Edging his way back from the bar through the jostling revellers, Brad put their drinks down on the table, sliding along the bench seat until opposite Roger. He noticed Brad's nails needed considerable attention, as did his unruly hair which had fallen over his face as he leant down to deposit their glasses. Brad combed his fingers through his fringe, pushing it off his face, mumbling, "Need a haircut."

"You sure do, looking every part the tatty bachelor Brad my boy," Roger teased. "When are you going to find a woman to get you on track?"

"How did you know that's what I wanted to pick your brain about?" Brad smiled, face in mock surprise. "How was the farm by the way?"

Roger gave Brad a rundown on the weekend, trying to make the details of a very eventful two days as succinct as possible. Brad's eyes widened at the mention of the grass smoking incident saying he could not imagine Roger smoking a joint. "Dark horse, hey Roger," he laughed.

"Anyway, oh ignorant one, what question about women do you need to ask the *guru*?" Roger asked as innocently as he could, having already being tipped off by Georgie.

***

Struggling through the front door with two suitcases Roger nearly knocked Georgie over. She was standing in their small hallway, overnight bag in one hand, phone in the other. It had rung as she put the key in their front door. He heard the conversation as he struggled up the stairs.

"Oh my God," gasped Georgie. "I mean, Eve really? Are you sure you want to get involved with *Brad*, he's quite a womaniser you know? The proverbial bachelor and schoolboy-mannered."

"It's the Californian way," called Roger over his shoulder from the top of the stairs. "I wonder if he used the same opening line *we* heard in the kitchen, to her directly." He bit his tongue as he realised how loudly he had spoken, Georgie, phone to her ear, waving her finger in front of her lips indicating he should shut up.

Eve sighed down the line, "Well, I was surprised actually. There's a lot more to him than meets the eye when you get to know him a bit."

Arriving back on the landing, Roger could not resist, "So your friend's gone for a 'fafi' has she?" He dodged the pillow that flew in his direction as he came down the stairs. Georgie said Brad had called Eve after their party to ask her out. Against her better judgment and more out of curiosity than anything she had accepted. They had gone out to dinner, Brad on his best behaviour and very charming. Eve apparently was smitten. During Roger and Georgie's farm weekend, Brad had invited her over for a home cooked meal and she had ended up staying over.

***

Now, in the increasingly noisy bar Brad sipped his drink. "Well, I know I am guilty of making lewd comments about Eve and I regret that a lot. We have been seeing each other since the party and I am sorry I was so disrespectful to such a lovely person. I want to continue with the relationship. Should I confess to her about my comment to you and Georgie. You know, fess up and apologise in case it comes out."

"Probably. Or pray that Georgie never mentions it to her," Roger laughed. "Maybe Eve would laugh it off anyway. Nah, that's asking a bit much."

Roger, putting his hand over his heart, trying to keep a serious face said, "I suggest you hold thumbs and let sleeping …br…ah…*dogs* lie."

Brad snorted, "Very funny." He raised his shoulders and let them fall with a deep sigh, raising his glass to his lips.

Notwithstanding the fact that he would have preferred not to be doing it in a noisy bar, Roger decided he should raise the work issue with Brad.

Pointing out that although he could be assured he would be given ample time to get his sales pipeline looking good, he nonetheless in return needed to show more commitment to his sales activities. Was he sure all the time away from the office was in pursuit of new business?

Brad assured Roger that it mainly was, but in the last month he had had major issues with renewing his residency visa. They were making him jump through the hoops. All kinds of paperwork needed to be renewed. Even a medical.

"It's because I forgot to re-apply in the allowed time and they came after me. Threatened to arrest me and deport me. Don't worry it's under control now. I will make sure there are no more distractions, OK? I'm on a restricted visa for a year though. On probation. I need to let them know where I am going if I travel inter-state. No big deal."

"Well, OK. Let me know if you need any help. Any letters confirming your employment contract or whatever." Roger was relieved to get a plausible explanation and hoped that would be the end of Brad's lack of focus.

What Brad failed to mention was that he had also been caught in possession of marijuana. He was pulled over at an RBT check point. Although he was under the alcohol limit the police spotted a joint he had carelessly left in the car's ashtray. After checking his passport in the absence of a local driver's licence, he ended up being arrested for both being an illegal immigrant and possessing an illegal substance.

After an uncomfortable night in a holding cell, Brad met with both Immigration and drug squad officials the following morning. They told him if he was charged with the drug offence any chance of renewing his visa would be gone for at least a year and he would be deported. In this case, given the minimal quantity they would not charge him, however he was going to be on their database and further drug-related incidents would have dire consequences.

***

It had been a challenging but enjoyable few months for Lerryn, now ensconced in Tom's restaurant. Her role as *Maître D'* was a far cry from her previous job as a lawyer, and she loved it. She used her good looks and personality to charm patrons of the restaurant and with help from Luigi and Dirk she quickly became familiar with the operational side of running the restaurant.

She had even dug out her guitar and performed a few folk songs on some evenings. Mixed reviews from the farming community and increasing requests for old Afrikaans '*liedjies*' had been a damper though. When, as the final chord of a Bob Dylan song faded, she overheard a farmer at a table laugh, "*Jong*, don't clap too hard she might sing again," she returned her guitar to its case knowing it needed to stay there.

Patronage was up, food reviews were great and the new décor, designed and project managed by Marin, a hit. The challenging side of the last few months had nothing to do with getting to grips with the logistics of running a restaurant. It was more about the discomfort of watching a metamorphosis in Luigi.

Once a loving partner, he was now a temperamental chef, winning the hearts of customers who ate his food and driving the people who helped him make it crazy. His kitchen staff spent a lot of time nonplussed, mouths wide open. As was Lerryn, when he regularly stormed into the dining area to rant and rave in Italian about some ingredient that had gone missing. The diners assumed it was part of the new European atmosphere. Some even

119

mimicked his gesticulations and accent which simply added oil to the flame.

The black workers were historically used to being shouted at by their white bosses but seeing someone yell and throw whole pots of boiling vegetables or sauce out the window because they were not to his liking was very new. Their favourite was the sobbing when recipes went wrong. Once, a worker was kissed on both cheeks for his initiative.

Then there was Pat. She had been on the phone several times to Lerryn bemoaning the fact that she had been deserted by her twin sister. Abandoned to a life with a toothless husband and his kids. Pat said it was all the grass he smoked. Rotted his teeth. She said he had lost his dentures some time ago when he got stoned, took them out and left them on the seat at a bus stop.

Lerryn knew that she and her sister were destined always to live in close proximity. It was just the way it needed to be. They had always looked out for each other, 'Those redhead kids', and nothing had really changed when they became 'those girls with the red hair' at school.

***

"Is jy ook rooi daar onder?...is your hair also red down below?...is jy ook rooi daar onder?" was a bilingual chant the Lenbruikte twins had to learn to ignore on the school bus.

It came from obnoxious, Afrikaans twelve-year-old boys whom the girls from the private girls-only high school were forced to share the bus with in the afternoons. It referred to their startling red hair, the one and only physical attribute the fraternal twins shared. The one in the form of a long shining mane, the other short and close cropped.

Lerryn was a startlingly beautiful young girl, elegant and graceful. Her sister Pat was plain and ungainly, thin and boyish. Both had minds as sharp as a razor and were, despite the difference in looks and relationships with others, devoted.

When Tom Lenbruikte agreed to his wife, Rita's, suggestion that they start a family, he insisted the process should be executed with haste. He was after all a busy professional, but he understood the need for procreation. He needed to get it over with as quickly as possible though. Which he did, adding a vasectomy as the full stop in the phase.

His poor wife had in accordance delivered five babies in quick succession. A whirlwind of childbirth remembered as a collage of endless sleepless nights, fighting siblings, tantrums and rampant colds and flu. It included a final set of twins and by the time these siblings were in their teens, to those who knew no better, they were in such close chronological order they all seemed the same age.

A positive consequence of this closeness in age was in their latter teens they were able to enjoy a more or less common level of intellect. The family was thus close knit, spending hours involved in conversation, debates or board games, the older siblings supporting the younger ones where necessary.

All was not always rosy though for the youngest, the twins. They had to learn to defend themselves, and each other, from time to time in sibling wars. This only increased their devotion to each other. They still giggled about the time all those years ago when Pat had just had enough of the boys on the bus. She had got up, marched down the centre aisle to the back of the bus and slapped the ringleader so hard the rest of them were open mouthed. There was giggling and pointing at the spreading wet patch he tried to hide with his cap for the rest of the trip.

After that, the best they could offer in girl baiting on the bus trips were a few smirks, carefully hidden behind school caps.

***

They still spent a great deal of time together even when they had each had partners of their own. It had however become more about Lerryn supporting Pat as they reached their late twenties, and relationships with others were prevalent in their lives. It was easy for Lerryn with her beauty. She could walk into a room and know that heads were turning for her. Everyone, male and female, wanted to be her friend. Pat did not mind this one-sided situation. Indeed, she was Lerryn's greatest admirer, more focused on *her* wellbeing than her own.

When they were in a crowded, rowdy club or bar Lerryn knew Pat was keeping a wary eye on her male admirers lest their attempts to get her attention became ungentlemanly. As the years went by it became increasingly awkward. Pat did not have many admirers and Lerryn found that her dates often ended up as third wheel. However, when she did get into any kind of serious relationship, she was not often forced to ask Pat to give her more space. They were so close Pat instinctively knew when her sister needed to be alone.

Lerryn thought Pat would eventually find her soul mate. It was only a matter of time. How stupid could men be not to look past looks and see the person inside; the wonderful human being her twin was.

As the years went by Lerryn began to feel uneasy with the situation. She agonised over what to do if one day Pat would become desperate and knee jerk into a relationship that she viewed through rose-tinted glasses, born out of

frustration and loneliness. That's exactly what had
happened.

***

Back in her and Lerryn's hometown Durban, well, ex-
hometown for her sister, darn her, Pat felt frozen in time,
freshly washed plate in her motionless hand, staring
listlessly out the window of their tiny kitchen into the
almost as tiny courtyard. Through the vague, misty from
the hot dish water, image of herself in the glass, Gus
played some kind of game outside with his two boys. The
indistinct outline of her face formed their playground.

It was like she was out of body, looking into the world she
had created for herself through the image in the window.
Is this it? A degree. No job. Mother to both the father and
his two boys. Raising an adult as well as two children. The
reflection in the glass was unsympathetic. She saw, as she
always did, a dowdy, freckled face with overly sharp
features. She smirked at the reflection. No wonder she had
had to settle for a man her father referred to as a 'rescue'.

***

Pat had indeed met Gus at a shelter where she and Lerryn volunteered. Serving soup to sad homeless souls in need of a meal. He had teeth in those days, and dreadlocks. Pat thought he was handsome in a sad sort of way. Lost. Needy. She liked that he was not immediately staring at Lerryn, as most men did, ignoring her.

Lerryn was immediately on her guard. She spent most of her teenage years and young adult life picking up the pieces after her twin's bad choice in boys and then men. Some might say desperate choices. Not seeing when a relationship she entered was doomed. Mostly not caring. It was almost as if she did it on purpose. To punish her sister for being so stunningly good looking. For leaving her with the crumbs in the relationship stakes.

As she got to know him, Gus reminded Lerryn of that shifty, rabbit cartoon character. Only without the teeth. Not just the front ones, all of them. He slinks from lamp post to lamp post, then suddenly is completely lost from sight behind the pole. Always on the lookout for easy pickings. It seemed to her he was one of those men who made a career out of being needy.

Gus had been in a relationship with a young black girl who had produced two boys who looked like their mother, not Gus. They never lived together because, until reform started in South Africa, only white people qualified for social security. Gus figured that being associated with a black woman might disqualify him from the unemployment benefits and he would have to face the distasteful idea of finding a job.

From time to time he had sneaked into the township where his boys and their mother lived with her parents. There was plenty of time during the day to be alone with them. Her parents had to get up at four in the morning to get an overcrowded bus to travel hours to their jobs in the white-people-only suburbs. They returned, exhausted, in the evening. They both needed to work in order to provide for themselves as well as their daughter and her boys.

After meeting at the shelter, it seemed a very short time before Pat and Gus were living together and not much longer before his ex-partner dumped their two boys, three and four, at the door of Pat's tiny studio.

Lerryn and Pat's social time together went from going to exhibitions, shows or clubbing to walking in playgrounds, separating two fighting kids, uptight from the stressful lives they had already had to endure. It happened literally overnight, it felt like.

***

Back in her tiny kitchen, Pat opened the door of the cupboard below the sink and started to pack the newly washed dishes away. Time to start thinking about what to cook for dinner, she thought. Time to do a shop, then. She picked up her duffel bag she had left lying in the hall and slung it over her shoulder. It had some of her possessions in it. Overnight stuff. She wasn't sure when she had put them into the bag. Still, plenty of room for groceries. Pat closed the door to the tiny studio. She waved to Gus and the boys as she walked down the communal driveway. "Off to do the shopping." When she reached the pavement, she turned left towards the shops. Then stopped, turned around and walked the other way.

**

It was a beautiful, sunny morning and Tom and Lerryn were enjoying a coffee together. Tom had called in to review how things were going with the restaurant. He could tell from what his accountant told him that things were on the mend.

Given the positive situation, Lerryn seized the opportunity to broach the subject of finding a way to get Pat closer to her. Maybe Pat could help in the kitchen. Be a calming influence on Luigi. They had always got on well together.

"I can understand Pat could be a help to you in the restaurant Lerryn, but what's Gums going to do?" Tom responded.

"Don't call Gus that, Dad. You've got Dirk doing it as well and it's not funny."

"Well, he needs to get a job and buy some new dentures. He looks ridiculous," Tom snorted.

"Who would have thought one of the consequences of smoking grass was you lose your teeth? Your brother better be careful as well!" Tom grinned at his daughter. She punched him gently on the arm.

They were sitting on the veranda of the restaurant which was located in an old sandstone house, not unlike Dirk's farmhouse. It was in the quieter end of the town, so the appearance of a local taxi, as usual a dilapidated white van, was not expected. It was overcrowded, of course, with slightly fearful black faces peering forward, partly because they wondered if the driver had taken a wrong turning and partly because in these battered, overcrowded taxis one had cause to be slightly fearful generally.

As she spoke, Lerryn absent-mindedly observed the taxi drawing nearer. She was in mid-sentence when she noticed the white face and shock of red hair amongst the twenty or so black faces. Her mouth dropped open as she recognised her twin sister waving wildly.

Lerryn nearly fell as she raced down the veranda's old wooden steps. Tom sat opened mouthed, coffee cup on its side after Lerryn's hasty departure. The driver was still getting out of his taxi to open the sliding passenger door for his passenger when Lerryn yanked it open. With much laughter from all the passengers, Pat crawled over the passengers sitting next to the door into her sister's arms.

They bounced around together yelling out greetings. "Speak of the devil!" Lerryn laughed.

Everyone on the bus clapped their hands, enjoying the reunion. No one understood the preciousness of family love and reunion like indigenous South Africans. Over the years many of them had felt pain at the loss or injury to a dear one because of apartheid. An elderly woman said in Sotho, "Now we see the unhappy white girl has a heart full of love although she looks like she is full of sadness. Now her face smiles as bright as her red hair."

"*Mokotla oa hau,*" someone laughed at the back of the taxi, and Pat's bag came flying out of the doorway into her outstretched arms.

"No, I won't forget it. It's all I have, thank you my travel companions."

She waved as they pulled away. "*Sala hantle!*" she called after it. Pat had heard the greeting as people got on and off the taxi during the trip.

***

Pat told Lerryn she did not feel guilty about walking out on Gus. The boys she had mixed feelings about. She worried about how Gus would cope with them. It was her or them.

"I felt like I was about to slip into a bottomless pit of despair. I didn't feel sorry for myself, just afraid it was the end of my life I was experiencing."

You can think it, Pat, but don't say it. That it was me moving away that was the final straw, Lerryn thought to herself. She said, "Well some things are meant. Let's just take one day at a time and all that."

Over the next few days and after considerable family deliberation, it was agreed that Pat should move to the farm rather than be in another third wheel with Lerryn and Luigi. At Caracal Ridge she could contribute by helping Marin with Annah and working with Jon in the new asparagus venture. Everyone was happy with this arrangement, including Sebete who could never find enough people to go on farm walks with.

***

Roger had just unpacked the dishes Georgie had placed in the dishwasher earlier and was busy re packing it to his liking when she walked into the kitchen.

"Hey, I just got off the phone from Marin. Interesting news and an invitation," she said.

"OK, give me a minute and I will join you in the lounge. Want a drink?"

When he had made himself comfortable with his drink, Georgie gave him an update on things at the farm. She said she had had a call from Eve earlier as well.

Not knowing them, Roger could not draw any conclusions about either Lerryn or Pat playing a role at the farm or restaurant. He did find the fact that Pat's estranged partner had two black children intriguing. That would create a bit of conversation if she ever took them to watch a polo game, knowing some of those guys he had met last time.

"So, Marin has a maid now; and a white one at that. Very proper," Roger said putting on his best wry smile. "I wonder if that will make her a bit happier?"

"The only thing that will make her happy is some attention from Dirk," Georgie said. "Some interest in Annah as well. I never saw him pick her up the whole weekend we were there."

Georgie had concluded from their weekend at Caracal Ridge that Dirk and Marin were not heading in the right direction with their relationship. She was convinced it was mainly Dirk's fault. He clearly was not committed to any long-term family situation. Roger asked why she was so sure that was the case, and immediately regretted it.

"Dirk is committed to one person. Dirk. Believe me I have been there. He is a very self-centred person."

"Hang on," Roger said. "What about all his plans to involve the people on the farm in his ventures? To make sure they share in the profits? He is very focused on the wellbeing of others from what I can see."

"That's true. But the jury is still out on that as far as I am concerned. I hope it doesn't turn out to be self-serving. As it always does with Dirk. Look, don't get me wrong, he's a fantastic man. But boy does he look out for himself." Georgie switched on the TV. "Like father, like son."

As she flicked through what was showing, Roger thought, "There endeth the lesson."

She switched the TV back off. "Oh, and we have been invited down to the Cherry Festival weekend at the end of the month. Interested?"

"Sounds great. What happens at a Cherry festival?"

Georgie explained with considerable enthusiasm that apparently amongst other events there was a major open-air art exhibition by famous South African artists. Roger was immediately interested. He loved the work he had seen done by the few black artists that seemed to have been able to pursue their calling despite working under arduous conditions in the townships. He marvelled at what they achieved in their shanties with limited access to materials, by candlelight at night, or in the heat or cold depending on the time of year, in a room or two shared with several family members.

All kinds of other arts and crafts were on show and a big rock n' roll party in the local hall on the Saturday night.

Georgie was keen to get dressed up for the rock n' roll party. The very thought made Roger cringe with embarrassment. One of Dirk's joints might come in handy for that.

"This will make you happy. If we go, Eve wants to go down with us and, *drum roll*," Georgie waved her hands up and down in a not very good impersonation of a drummer, "she has invited your big buddy Brad, *yay*."

Despite himself Roger had to laugh at Georgie's theatrics. He gave her a hug from behind the sofa and with a giggle she squealed, "Get off me, Romeo."

Chapter 5

Second Farm Trip: Remembering

Roger said, to nobody in particular, that it would have been better to use Georgie's car given the state of the last section of road approaching the farm.

"You've said that three times since we left, Roger, and we've all agreed each time it would have been very uncomfortable in my small car even if it does have a higher clearance," said Georgie. "Can we all agree if he says it again, we leave him on the side of the road?"

"Yes," from Eve.

"Yes," murmured Brad, responding to the poke from Eve's elbow, engrossed in the operating instructions for the new camera he had bought that morning.

Roger looked into the rear-view mirror to wink at Eve, and noticed her head was on Brad's shoulder. Their romance was certainly in full bloom.

***

Georgie and Eve first met when Eve arrived at the high school Georgie attended in a small town deep in the midlands, about four hours north of Durban, the city the Lenbruiktes lived in. Onderstroom was predominantly Afrikaans-speaking, but boasted good high schools and junior schools of both English and Afrikaans persuasion.

Tom, whose brother and wife lived in the town, decided that it would be a good environment for Eve's last school year, in order to improve her very poor Afrikaans skills. Although he rarely spoke it himself Tom thought it fitting that all his children have a good grounding in both 'official' languages of the country.

When the ANC took power there were eleven official languages established, but English has always been promoted by the ANC as the official language for government, even though it only accounts for less than 10% of first language speakers. About 14% of South Africans speak Afrikaans as a first language.

Neither Eve nor the twins had any desire to be proficient in the Afrikaans language, despite the heritage their name might imply. This had been the subject of heated debate more than once at family mealtimes. In fact, the young Lenbruiktes all felt the further they could get from any association with Afrikaans the better, given the apartheid connotation. Oldest brother Clive, always subjective in these arguments, suggested it was a credit to Eve that her Afrikaans was poor. The dominant white government of the time was almost exclusively Afrikaans.

Notwithstanding the fact that well over half of the country's Afrikaans speakers were not white people, it was a language hated by many of the black people. Not only because of its association with oppression but because it was the language the apartheid regime used in the very separate black education system. A big impact on black education over the apartheid years, gaining momentum after the dark times of 1976, had been the burning down by young people of their schools in protest against the enforced use of Afrikaans in the system. The government of the time of course promoted this protest activity as an example of why black people were not fit to be included.

Lerryn and Pat were devastated at the loss of their older sister for a whole year, and insisted they go as well. Tom's brother and wife were more than happy to have the extra money offered for being foster parents to three girls for a year, so Tom agreed to the demands of the twins to join their sister.

So, it was then, to Georgie's delight, that she acquired a friend who came from a big city and not the little town she lived in and so despised. Someone she could talk to about more than just what movie was on at the one and only local bug house. Someone whose brother Dirk was already at university reading law and whose other brother Clive, was a lecturer in Business Studies. Not like the young men of Onderstroom, driving around in noisy cars yelling out invitations and lewd remarks to any girl they drove past.

By the end of the first few months Eve was a bit of a celebrity amongst the girls, coming from a big city environment with her worldly-wise demeanour. The boys of course were more captivated by her looks. To Georgie she was, first and foremost, a living conduit to a world outside the small, narrow-minded town she had grown up in. Light at, less than a year away, the end of the tunnel. By association, she already felt free.

The twins, on the other hand, had become more infamous than celebrity. The way Pat dealt with the boys on the bus in their first few weeks in Onderstroom was already a legend. The beautiful Lerryn and her 'minder', who took no prisoners when provoked, were held in awe. Each for very different reasons.

Three months in, it looked like the Lenbruikte girls had made a good, if not controversial, start to their new school environment. Popular already and appreciated for their non-judgmental attitude towards others it looked like they were set for a good year.

Until the sleepover at Eve's.

***

Georgie awoke in the darkness of Eve's room to see her down on her knees looking out of the window into the neighbour's back yard. It must have been around midnight. Hearing Georgie getting out of bed, Eve lowered the curtain carefully, "Oh my God he's putting a ladder under the maid's window."

"What? Who is? whispered Georgie.

"I think it's Mr. Witkop, our neighbour. Maybe not?"

Georgie had joined Eve on her knees at the window. The dark figure below was carefully manoeuvring the ladder to ensure it was stable. He tested it by gripping a rung, rocking it to see how firm it was on the surface of the wall. The room, part of the garage structure but on this side of the Witkop's garage where the ground level dropped away steeply, required a ladder to reach the window. The slope of the ground meant the ladder was standing in a precarious position almost parallel to the wall, but the climber was determined.

Satisfied, the figure began to climb the ladder, one uncertain, shaky step at a time, careful not to allow his body weight to pull the top of the ladder away from the wall. Just then the window lit up dimly and a woman's outline appeared, a silhouette against the curtains. The climbing figure stopped, looking up expectantly.

"What is he doing? whispered Georgie. "What's he want?"

"To bonk the maid of course, you dummy," said Pat.

Georgie and Eve jumped at the unexpected voice behind them, letting the curtain fall. They broke into giggles.

"Shut up you two. You'll wake Uncle," Pat hissed as she joined them at the window, gently raising the curtain again.

The curtain of the room outside was also moving, pulled slowly back, a black face appeared in the window. With the curtain open, light fell on the climber's face.

"Hey, that's not Mr. Witkop!" said Eve.

"No," said Georgie, with a sudden intake of breath. "It's the dominee, the priest in the Witkop's church."

They both stared at Pat as she fist-pumped the air saying, "Yes."

"What? what?" Georgie and Eve asked, getting no answer.

The figure in the window was gesticulating, with some conviction, for whoever was on the ladder to go away. He for his part was just as committed to continuing his upward journey. Two arms were lit by the light from the now open window as they reached down and took hold of the top rung of the almost vertical ladder. The climber made the mistake of taking his hands off the ladder, clasping them together as he held them upward.

Pat, giggling, whispered, "Is he begging for a bonk or for her to not push the ladder?"

All three were now giggling uncontrollably as they watched the ladder beginning to move slowly away from the wall. The dominee's arms began to wave as he struggled for balance, rotating like a drunk aircraft marshal in a silent movie trying to guide two planes to their parking positions at the same time. Seconds before, the girls' bedroom door had swung open to reveal Eve's aunt, looking more than irritated at being woken up by giggling girls.

"What's going on?" she demanded as she strode across to the window, reached above the three girls' heads and pulled the curtains open. "Oh my God…oh my God," she gasped, as the ladder crashed to earth.

Down below, the climber was now hanging in a tree upside down, held by his jacket hooked on a branch. The ladder he had been on had toppled backwards after being firmly pushed, sending him flying into the canopy of a tree at the bottom of the steep incline. The ladder itself finally crashing down onto a metal fence with a clang and screech of metal that sounded like a major motor car accident.

Lit up by the security lights Mr. Witkop had switched on, the dominee, white faced and upside down, looked like an acrobat in a midnight circus performance. His audience made up of six faces in the 'upper circle', which included Lerryn, who had now joined her aunt and the three giggling girls at Eve's window and, next door, the maid, who stood at her window looked down as well, transfixed by the spectacle. The 'lower stalls' consisted of the two upturned faces of Eve's uncle and Mr. Witkop below the tree, looking into the distraught upside-down face of the dominee. Long strands of hair, normally a comb-over for his bald head, hanging downwards from his head like the tentacles of a jelly fish.

Several grinning neighbours watched the spectacle, arms folded on top of their respective boundary fences, dogs barking wildly alongside them. In their striped pyjamas they could quite easily have been part of the night's performance. Grinning clowns at the edge of the circus arena waiting for their act to begin after the acrobat finished.

***

Georgie and Roger often laughed over anecdotes about her times with various Lenbruikte siblings. When she shared the story of the dominee incident with Roger, it had immediately brought back memories of his childhood and some of his mother's mischievous Afrikaner profiling. It was at the height of the apartheid era and the enforcement of the Immorality Act. Subsequently renamed the *Sexual Offences Act, 1957*, it prohibited sexual intercourse or 'immoral or indecent acts' between white people and anyone not white. This version also increased the penalty to up to seven years imprisonment for both partners.

Like any law considered 'academic' in the environment of the day, there were transgressors, but unless it was blatant, and public, convictions and jail terms were not that common. In day-to-day family life, the fact that there was a law did somehow make rumours about transgressors just that much more spicy, though. Notwithstanding the law, white people were incredulous, at worst, but more likely amused, to hear of 'sex across the colour line' incidents.

In addition, in those days there was limited social interaction between black and white individuals generally. Cinemas, bars, beaches, public events, etc. were 'whites only'. Such gathering places often did not need a sign at the entry point indicating this exclusion, like those always found on a park bench or public toilet. It was a given for both groups, they had grown up with it.

So, in this light, it was not unusual to find transgressions often took place in a domestic environment. Sneaking into the maid's room, conveniently detached, at the bottom of the garden. Or a business owner cavorting with the office cleaning lady in his car in the park after dark.

This created the opportunity for many 'love across the line' anecdotes for white folk. A dinner time smirk and raised eyebrows. "Guess what my hairdresser told me today about her boss and the cleaning girl..." or "You won't believe what I heard happened in the changing room..." or "The people next door have sacked the maid they hired only last month. Apparently, the husband..."

Roger smiled to himself, remembering that due to the seldom admitted to acrimony between English and Afrikaner, each language group had an assumed likely perpetrator profile for love across the line. For the English, including his mother, he could still see her winking, it was always a dominee, head of the church the Afrikaners attended, the Dutch Reformed Church, who was likely to be caught with his hand in the cookie jar at the end of the garden.

***

The Onderstroom Dutch Reform Church dominee told the church elders at the inquiry that the Devil himself was responsible for what had transpired during the week. He had only been in the area a few times before. Recently, when invited by the Witkop family for dinner and coincidentally the following evening to visit briefly the guardian of the Lenbruikte girls who lived next door.

The parents of a young boy had notified the school that one of the Lenbruikte sisters had, without provocation, slapped him and poured a bottle of water over his pants. The school had asked him, as an independent party, to raise the matter with the Lenbruikte girl's uncle, her guardian.

***

Standing before her seated uncle and the dominee, Pat had been accused of being a bully and disrespectful to the school. The dominee railed that her behaviour was typical of a person who did not attend church regularly. A person who did not ask for God's guidance in their daily life, like he did, could not be a good, clean-living Christian like he was.

During his lecture, all Pat could think of was Mr. Witkop's daughter telling her and Lerryn, at school lunch break that day, how the dominee behaved when he went to dinner there the evening before. She said when the maid cleared the table after they had eaten, all the dominee could do was ogle the poor girl. It was so obvious that Mr. and Mrs. Witkop were clearly embarrassed, as was the maid, eventually sending their daughter upstairs to do homework.

After his lengthy tirade that included Pat not ever being welcome in his church and bringing shame on her foster family, the dominee asked if she had anything to say for herself. Pat responded to his charge calmly and in a quiet voice.

"Yes, I did slap him, for being rude and uncouth. No, I did not pour water over him. The little shit pissed himself with fright."

"Pat! You are talking to the *dominee*!"

"Well, was the dominee told that the boy was referring to whether our pubic hair was red like the hair on our heads, in his stupid daily chant on the bus?"

Both men turned crimson. "OK, Pat you can go to your room," her uncle said quietly.

Pat's uncle conferred with the dominee for some time suggesting that it sounded like there was blame on both sides. As the dominee got up to leave, Pat appeared in the doorway with his coat, looking contrite. "I brought your coat, sir. Sorry if I caused trouble. Goodnight." She turned quickly to avoid the smirk she knew would be on his face.

When she got back to her room, Lerryn looked up, raised her eyebrows at her sister. Pat smiled at her twin as she closed the University Southern Coast note pad Dirk had given her and returned it to her drawer.

***

It was the week following the dinner, the dominee continued to the Elders, he had found a note in his coat. At the bottom of the page was written the name of the young maid who worked for Mr. and Mrs. Witkop. It said she had seen him looking at her when she served at the dinner and wanted him to visit her. She said there was always a ladder left lying by the garage so he could come in through the window without Mr. Witkop seeing. The dominee pleaded that we all know how persuasive the Devil could be when feeding on man's weakness. "*That* weakness we *all* have, good elders," he said nodding slowly with a deadpan expression. He went on, just like Adam, also God's servant, he had been tempted and he deeply regretted his actions.

The dominee concluded he knew it must have been the Devil's note and not the maid's when he saw, hardly noticeable, that it was embossed with the crest of the University Southern Coast. A known liberal academic institution in Durban that was considered a breeding ground for the Devil's disciples.

Where would the maid get writing paper like that? She probably could not write anyway? The elders agreed to accept his explanation given that it would be impossible to find another dominee willing to live in Onderstroom and the last thing they needed was to fire him and start a witch hunt that might wake up all kinds of sleeping dogs.

***

All was quiet in the car for the moment, Eve and Brad dozing in the back seat and Georgie and Roger wondering how things would look at the farm. Three months had passed since they were at Caracal Ridge and they were looking forward to renewing the friendships they had initiated. Having Eve and Brad along as well made it even more interesting.

Staring out across the endless flat fields of mielies they were speeding through, Georgie wondered how much Pat being part of the household might have changed the dynamic in the house. With help available maybe there had been a lift in Marin's mood. And Eve joining them for the weekend? She was clearly excited about seeing her brother again but had not said a word about Marin. *Oh yes, it was going to be another interesting weekend.*

Roger for his part was more preoccupied with thoughts about reengaging with the resort idea again. Over the last few months he had thought often about their discussion that night on the patio. He wondered how Dirk might differentiate Caracal Ridge as a place to visit for a break. He liked Dirk's ideas about it being super rustic. They had all laughed when Roger said, "You mean after check in you get handed a roll of toilet paper and a shovel?"

Turning to the back seat, Georgie said with a laugh, "Oh my God Eve, that reminds me. At the risk of getting Roger back onto road clearance again, have you ever done the trip into town with Dirk? In his bakkie, or truck, or whatever he calls that wreck?"

Eve, coming out of her nap, listened with a smile as Georgie gave a graphic description of their trip to polo the last time they were there. Eve chuckled from time to time but, noticing she had gone quiet, Georgie turned in her seat to ask her if she had ever seen Dirk play polo. She had drifted off to sleep again, head on Brad's shoulder. One-handed, he had the camera to his eye, pointed at Georgie. She turned her head back to the front quickly. "You'll be the one left on the road if you're not careful, mister" Georgie said, trying not to sound irritable, forcing a smile. "You, and Roger!"

"Hey? What?" Roger said, coming out of his 'farm resort reverie'. In the far distance was an elongated cloud of smoky pollution. It hung in the cooling afternoon air, over the township Winnie Mandela had been banished to. It signalled they had arrived on the outskirts of Brandfort, the last town before the farm. About an hour to go.

"Are we making that last stop at Dodge City, gals?" Roger said in a hopeless impersonation of a John Wayne drawl.

"Yes," said Georgie and Eve together. Eve instantly awake as her radar picked up the mandatory toilet opportunity she had previously told Georgie about.

***

It was still light when they arrived at the farm, and the first people they saw as they drove up the track through the cherry orchard were Marin and Annah. Marin stood in between a row of trees scarlet with fruit, a basket on her arm and Annah tied on her back with a small blanket, Sotho mother style. As they pulled to a stop, she waved at them, beckoning them to come over.

"What a lovely mother and baby picture," Georgie exclaimed. "In a cherry orchard full of fruit."

Eve said with a wry smile, "At least she had something to eat while she waited hours for us to arrive to 'by chance' catch her in that pose."

"Oh, Eve," Georgie laughed, "give the girl a break already."

Roger and Brad, knowing better than to get involved, climbed out of the car and headed through the cherry trees. Spotting them, Sebete came from nowhere at a gallop, barking a greeting. After a few sniffs he seemed to remember Roger, or at least accept him, wagging his tail. Brad he was wary of, sniffing his outstretched hand once and trotting off towards Marin.

Eve and Georgie had caught up, and they all followed Sebete through the orchard to Marin and Annah.

"Hey guys! So nice to see you again. It's been, what, about three months? And Eve much longer? When I was still on the coast," Marin said hugging each of them, getting an introduction to Brad from Eve as she was shaking his hand.

Raising the basket of cherries slightly, Marin said, "I thought I would make a cherry pie tonight. Seems appropriate given the weekend, yeah?"

"Fantastic," said Brad with a smile, "My favourite, being American it would have to be."

Roger said, "And if he offers to help with the baking, watch him, he's prone to lacing his desserts with you know what."

"Why not?" laughed Marin. "Would not be the first time in this house. Talking of which, let's head that way and we'll get you something to drink. Sure you need one after your trip."

Roger drove the car the last few hundred yards whilst the others strolled along with Marin and Annah. Sebete covering the distance about three times over as he raced laterally to and fro after rabbits, racing through the grass before disappearing down their holes.

**

At the same time, up in the hills without his erstwhile protector, Sebete, Bonniface scanned the skyline demarcated by rugged mountains and the bright blue beyond. His dark brown eyes were framed with wrinkles as he squinted against the glare. He glanced down briefly as one of his charges stumbled as she clambered across a rocky outcrop in search of further grazing. Bonniface sniffed the air as he squinted. After a few minutes he was satisfied. No fire around.

It did little to assuage his concern that a grass fire was imminent. There had been little rain for ages and the lands were tinder dry. The winter that was so good for the cherries meant there was little chance of rain for months.

Further up the hill, another set of eyes scanned for danger. A black nose also sniffed. In addition, the cat listened for sounds to guide her towards any unexpected arrivals. Her black tufted ears rotated as she watched her two kittens in the distance. They were getting big now and roamed off

151

on their own a lot but only for a short time, preferring to be near to her, or at least near enough to pick up her scent. They would soon leave for good to find their own way in life, but for the present the caracal mother had to keep an eye out for predators.

Satisfied for the moment, she moved back into the cool darkness of the cave she and her ancestors had used as a lair for generations. Something made her stop and return to the cave entrance. She stared through the haze. Had she heard her mate? He had been gone since her kittens began to grow inside her. Was that movement in the grass him? Was he looking for her? She didn't trust him near the kittens. Not if he was looking for her.

Her ears rotated, nose raised, but all she could identify were her kittens. Both play hunting with more bravado than was good for them. Once more she turned to her lair to wait for them to return to her warmth. She needed to rest a while before the night's hunt, leaving her kittens safe in the lair to await her return with a kill for them to practice their predatory skills on.

Chapter 6

Cherry Festival

They had just settled on the patio, Brad raving about the view, when Dirk and Jon arrived from the asparagus fields down below in the valley. Dirk carried a sack of fresh asparagus spears they had just harvested before returning to the house.

After introductions, Dirk passed a few spears around for them to admire. "You arrived in time to enjoy some of the first crop to appear out of the ground," he said. "We'll grill some with herb butter for tonight."

153

Brad bit a piece off his, "Delicious. Vegetables like asparagus are best eaten raw," he munched at them. Roger caught the slight roll of Georgie's eyes skyward. Sitting alongside Jon, Brad became engrossed in a conversation about asparagus growing.

Roger was interested to observe how natural the conversation sounded. He found, nowadays, white South Africans were likely to appear to be trying too hard at being natural with black people. Treating them almost like they needed an overdose of reassurance, the way one treated a friend who arrived late at the party, through no fault of their own. Going over the top to make them feel at ease. Well, thought Roger, after years of apartheid they *had* arrived late at the party, had they not.

Brad interacted with Jon as an equal. Naturally. Interrupting and asking him to repeat anything he did not pick up as a result of the Sotho accent, without feeling self-conscious. At times unconsciously cutting Jon off in mid-sentence to respond enthusiastically to something he had said. Interruption in a conversation is always tolerated if it is spawned from enthusiasm.

"I can take you down in the morning and show you around the asparagus section if you like," Jon said to Brad.

"Good idea," Dirk said, "Let's all go."

"Well," Marin said, "How about this, we could take some sausages and salads and we'll go for a bit of a walk around the farm. Stop somewhere in the fields for a lunch time barbecue?"

They all thought the idea was a good one, including Sebete, who had cocked one ear although he looked like he was dosing until his tail thumped once.

Marin suggested Dirk take Annah in their backpack kiddie chair. He was humming-and-hawing about whether they should, given it was a long way and she would get tired, when Pat appeared through the patio door.

"Oh, for God's sake big brother just do it! If she gets tired she'll dose off on your back. She wants to have fun too. Anyway, I have to help with the restaurant tomorrow so I can't look after Annah."

"I love your work, Pat," Marin said as Pat leant down to kiss Annah on the forehead.

After putting her arms around Georgie from behind her chair and kissing her cheek with a, "Hello favourite non-sibling!" Pat introduced herself to Brad and Roger. She turned to Eve and after a long sisterly hug she led her off towards the garden to update her on the situation with Gus. "Sorry guys, sister stuff. Be right back," Pat called over her shoulder. Sebete followed them on the off chance a walk was imminent.

Going back to the picnic debate, Georgie said, "Yes, and the last time I looked we had two other husky men to help carry the load. Three if you come, Jon, are you coming?

Of course, you are, you're the asparagus 'tour guide'." She felt slightly awkward about maybe being seen to have initially excluded Jon.

"Sure," Jon said, glancing at Dirk who smiled as he walked from the patio into the house saying over his shoulder, "Those husky men will be needed if we take all the stuff Marin's going to want to take, Georgie." Marin gave Dirk's departing back the finger as he disappeared through the door and Georgie laughed.

Good for Pat, Roger thought. He liked her confidence. She took control. She had an energy about her that kind of drew one along with her. You just knew she was a natural champion of the underdog. *Georgie's right. Dirk and Marin don't look like they are very close.* He noted how Dirk kind of took it for granted Marin could or should stay at home with Annah.

***

The following morning, they all sauntered down the track Roger and Georgie had used on their first visit. Only this time Sebete was way ahead, trotting along, ears peaked, head swivelling left and right. Like he was the one-man advance party of an invading army, Brad observed. Better than thundering down behind them like some out of control cavalry charge, Roger commented and then regretted it as Georgie launched into a description of his demise at the hands of Sebete the morning of their first visit to the farm. Everyone laughed, Annah as well, not knowing why she was but keen to laugh along.

Jon said, grinning, "Yes, I was trying to change his collar and he slipped out and was off to find Dirk." Roger slowed his pace, looking over his shoulder at Jon as he spoke. Seeing if there was any indication that would confirm his suspicions that the accident was pre-meditated.

Eve, the only Lenbruikte girl on their walk, poked him in the back, "Come on slow coach, before it's me that tail-ends you this time." Pat hadn't joined them for the walk. She took Dirk's bakkie and, as she had said on the patio the previous day, drove into town to help out at the restaurant where they were preparing for the big Cherry Festival night.

The long carpet of asparagus fields started near the dam where Georgie and Roger had met up with Dirk last time. Roger murmured to Georgie, "Last time we saw Dirk down here he was naked, remember?" Georgie nodded and grinned.

They worked their way through what looked like acres of bright green rain forest ferns, the 'chuk chuk chuk' of the overhead irrigation sprinklers adding sound to the sunlit backdrop of asparagus fronds from which sparkling drops of water fell. Annah waved her hands in delight as spasmodic arches of water, hurled upwards by the rotating

157

sprinklers, passed over her. Each time leaving one or two diamonds of water on her face which she tried unsuccessfully to wipe away.

Seeing her excited expression, Roger could not resist the impulse. He slipped her from Dirk's backpack kiddie carrier thing, exclaiming, "Let's race the water squirts, Annah."

She was a little apprehensive at first as he carefully lifted her onto his shoulders. Holding her firmly under her arms so she would not feel insecure he hopped over each asparagus ridge and furrow trying to keep up with the falling drops. Annah squealed with a mixture of excited apprehension and delight.

As he leapt from furrow to furrow, Marin joined them holding Annah's outstretched hand. The others laughed at their antics, Brad standing with his camera in hand seemed oblivious to any photo opportunity.

It wasn't long before Roger was gasping for air. Sliding Annah expertly from his shoulders to his chest he collapsed ungracefully into a furrow, back leant against a ridge, asparagus spears poking up from the soil all around him. He laughed up into the little girl's face as she giggled and smacked her hands on his chest.

Roger look up and behind him to find the others and looked directly into a face with an expression that caught him by surprise. Marin was looking at him with undisguised affection. As he looked back to Annah, enjoying the cool drops of irrigation water in the warm morning sun, he knew instinctively just how much Marin needed Dirk to love her daughter the way she did. Roger realised, with sudden clarity, that it was not a loss of career that played on Marin's mind. It was in fact the lack of a loving father for her daughter.

Roger looked towards that very father. Standing with an empty child carrier slung on his back staring out across his asparagus treasure. He smiled up at Marin, "You know I seem to spend half my time at your farm lying on my back in the dirt."

As they continued their walk, Jon and Dirk gave them an overview on the creation of the asparagus fields. They were fascinated to learn that asparagus roots could go down to a depth of ten feet or so. Notwithstanding these aggressive root systems, the plants still had to be irrigated and the fields had thus been located near the dam so abundant water was nearby. Roger understood what Bonniface had been saying though about losing a natural fire barrier. The river that once flowed through the valley had been reduced to a stream by various farmers' dams in the area.

It was around midday when Dirk pointed out the spot a little way up a hill that he used for a picnic from time to time. Thorn trees surrounded a small *boma* fire pit dug into the ground. In the distance they could see that Sebete, after detouring to the nearby stream for a drink, was already there, lying in the shade of a thorn tree, no doubt looking forward to any scraps from the braai.

***

 When Pat thumped off the end of the gravel road she had been on and started up the town's main street in Dirk's bakkie, two pairs of eyes had long since spotted the truck. Ever since that day at the polo game when the girls had seen it for the first time, they kept an eye open for it.

As it got closer, they were disappointed to see that the red hair behind the steering wheel meant the driver could not be their idol. Disappointment turned to anguish when they saw it was a young woman driving.

"Oh no!" one of the girls groaned. "Do you think it's a girlfriend, or even his wife?"

"Well, the girl who runs the restaurant now also has red hair, and her name is Lenbruikte so she must be Dirk's sister." She had heard her parents talking about yet another Lenbruikte in town. "Maybe this is just another sister."

They were nonplussed when Pat suddenly stopped the bakkie right opposite them and waved them over to the open passenger window. "Hi girls, you wouldn't by any chance be interested in some part-time work? Helping out at the restaurant tonight? Normal hourly rate for around here. Whatever that is?"

The girls exchanged looks. Their imaginations concocting romantic restaurant situations, all of which featured Dirk of course.

"What are your names? I'm Pat, Lerryn's sister. She's the manager there."

"I'm Marta and this is Marie."

"Oh great, Marta and Marie, we could have 'M&Ms' in our restaurant," Pat laughed. The girls giggled. Not without some relief mixed in, discovering they were talking to Dirk's sister, not his wife or girlfriend!

Marta, daughter of the guy who accosted Jon and Dirk at the game, said, "We would have to check with our parents."

"Mine won't mind. They're always saying I should find part-time work during the school holidays," said Marie with a grin.

"OK, if you're on, come up to the restaurant after lunch and we'll see what we can organise. See you later." Pat pulled back into the main street, leaving the girls in a small cloud of diesel smoke from Dirk's not very well tuned engine.

They looked at each other, jumping up and down with excitement. They made tracks to Marta's house and her dad. This was going to be the challenge.

Pat parked the bakkie in the street rather than the restaurant parking place, as she knew Tom would growl if he did not have a parking place for his flash car. She found a place about 50 yards up the street so her arrival at the restaurant was not announced.

Deciding to enter the restaurant from the rear where the kitchen was located, Pat walked silently up the grassed side garden. This gave her a chance to pick a few flowers off the large camelia shrub in front of Lerryn's office window. Lerryn always admired its blooms, but never got around to picking any for her office vase. Pat thought she would surprise her twin with some.

She began breaking off some of the newer blossoms when, looking through the shrub, the inside of Lerryn's office came into focus through the window. There, knelt down in front of the safe, was Luigi. He appeared to be stuffing something into his pocket. The wad was thick, and he stood up slightly so access to his pocket would be easier. Pat saw then that the wad was actually money.

She froze as something made Luigi look towards the window. His face was anxious, and guilty. Pat could tell from his expression he could not see her through the dense shrub. So long as she did not move. Standing in the dark shade of the huge camelia she merged into its dense foliage. He knelt down once more and closed the safe slowly, turned the combination lock wheel a few turns and stood up. Pat was shocked to see him take the kitchen cloth that was draped over his shoulder and carefully wipe the lock and the entire top and front of the safe.

Luigi had left the office, closing the door behind him. Pat heard the door close through the open window rather than saw it, as it was out of her line of sight. She collapsed slowly to her knees, heart thumping.

What had she just seen? Luigi was a lovely guy. She got on really well with him. Lerryn and he appeared to be so in love with each other. *Oh my God,* Pat whispered to herself. *Now what. Lerryn could not possibly be party to what she had just seen, surely. Oh my God!*

***

Having Luigi as a client had been something of a challenge for Lerryn in her first year out of law school. She worked in the immigration division of a law firm handling clients who were struggling to get permanent residence visas. The problem Luigi had was that, as good a chef as he was, he was inclined to 'skim off the top' wherever he worked. It had been fairly petty, the odd bottle of wine, the odd sick day when he watched Italian soccer in the early hours. The complaints had followed him from part-time job to part-time job, and along with an actual formal dismissal his application for a visa was not looking good, which is where Lerryn's firm had come into the picture.

The challenge for Lerryn was trying to get Luigi to realise that his misdemeanours could not be passed off as 'naughty little boy' stuff, to be dismissed with a shrug of his nubile shoulders and charming smile. At least not with the government's Immigration Department.

Long before she had managed to convince him that he needed to stick to the rules and hope that his bad marks faded with time, they had become a couple.

***

On the way back after their barbecue they had taken a circular route and were now approaching the farmhouse from behind, climbing up a shallow ravine below the sheer rock face that rose to the high ground overlooking the farmhouse buildings. The ground rose gently towards the hidden buildings and as they got closer Dirk said, "I have a little surprise for you and Georgie, Roger. You will see what I mean once we are over that ridge ahead."

As they climbed up the gentle slope, a thatched roof appeared in their line of sight. Nearer the summit the sandstone walls upon which it sat came into view. The wooden windows completed what Roger decided was a perfect holiday cottage overlooking the farmhouse, the distant valley and mountains.

"I'm assuming this is the first of your 'farm stay' holiday homes, Dirk," Roger said.

"Call it a prototype if you like. Lots of guess work and trial and error, but we think it will work. Come and see what you guys think."

Bed frames and tables were built out of timber sourced locally and left largely in their natural state. The rough finish gave the room a rustic feel and in a juxtaposition with the modern bed linen and bathroom fittings. Dirk's conviction that Caracal Ridge Resort would have a very rural theme was endorsed by Georgie's double take.

"No door to the bathroom," she exclaimed. "How does that work?"

"Creates an open plan feel, roomier and cheaper to construct," after all the rooms won't be shared by couples who are strangers."

"Yes, but what about…you know…embarrassing stuff," Eve said.

"Exactly," Georgie laughed. "I think the toilets down in your proposed dining area will be popular, with their lockable doors!"

Marin joined in, "You should never have made the joke about handing out a spade and toilet paper on arrival at reception. It gave him ideas."

Roger stood in the infinity shower area looking through the window. The shower was large with no glass screens and a floor of sandstone. "I love that you can shower and enjoy the view across to the valley and hills," he said. "Will they all have views?"

"Yes, if topography allows," Dirk replied.

Notwithstanding their reservations about open plan toilet facilities, everyone congratulated Dirk on making the first step towards a resort happen.

"Thanks, but I have had lots of help. Jon has managed to find the skills we needed from amongst our own farm workers and Pat and Marin have been great at sourcing the fittings."

Dirk went on to explain that the plan was to complete this first room and invite a few couples to the farm for a few weekends and get some independent reviews before proceeding with any further rooms.

They were just moving off when Brad said, "Hey, what's that over there, that green patch all by itself?"

Dirk and Jon had built their vegetable patch as far from the farmhouse as their irrigation pipe would allow them. This obviated any problems with the smell of the cow manure they used for fertilizer and also kept Dirk's marijuana plants out of view. A fence covered in a creeper kept small animals out. It was hidden in a hollow about 500 metres from the farmhouse.

Roger wondered why Brad was so determined they go across to what Dirk had already explained was just the farmhouse's vegetable garden. The women were all tired, but Brad was determined. "You girls carry on," he said. "We'll go across, hey guys," he said striding off down the slope, camera clutched in his hand.

Roger saw Jon was watching Dirk for direction. He was clearly apprehensive about the way things were unfolding, looking to his boss for reassurance. Roger guessed that the vegetable patch no doubt also housed their source of marijuana.

Where Dirk would be dismissive of any such discovery, Jon, coming from a background of oppression, would find it difficult not to expect the worst outcome given this white guy's zealous desire to visit their vegetable garden.

Brad suddenly seemed to lose interest in the garden after walking around a bit and strode off up the slope. "You guys stay there. I want a picture taking in everything. A landscape, garden, farmhouse, asparagus, hills, the whole lot," he panted as he climbed to a high point above them.

After being asked to face in Brad's direction and do some play acting, Dirk having to point out towards the hills, they moved off towards the farmhouse leaving Brad to catch up. Sebete glanced over his shoulder every now and again as if to keep an eye on this new visitor to his domain.

Roger noted that Brad seemed to have had his fill of photography for the day. Packing the camera back in its holder he slung it over his shoulder. In fact, Roger never saw it leave the holder again that weekend.

***

The three lookalike Elvis Presleys from Caracal Ridge and their respective 'chicks' in pleated skirts and bobby socks had finally made it to town in a mini-van Jon had hired from a friend who used it as a taxi.

Jon drove them as he did not drink and was not going to the dance anyway. Elvis Presley and the 'rock and roll' era were literally unknowns to him, and the thought of meeting up with Marta's father again did not fill him with desire.

Dirk had insisted he at least join them for the dinner at the restaurant, and after some persuasion he had agreed. Jon was cautious when it came to socialising. It could be stressful at times. As good as his English was, he missed some of the nuances which meant he spent a lot of time smiling for no reason, better than a blank face at the wrong time. Back at the farm Jon's sister, Bongi, was babysitting Annah, with Sebete keeping an eye on both from his place in front of the fireplace.

Tom and Mandy were already seated at the rapidly filling restaurant, Tom in deep conversation with Lerryn. When the group of slightly dusty, and a little drunk, 'rockers' burst through the door their mouths dropped open. Pat and Lerryn were in hysterics.

Georgie, Marin and Eve had done the best they could with the boys. They had smeared black gel into the hair of Roger and Brad and combed their heads into a passible Elvis slick back and quiff. Dirk was more of a problem, refusing anything more than a fringe quiff, the rest of his hair was off limits.

The clothes were easier. Unbeknownst to the men Georgie and Eve had paid a visit to a dress up place and hired an assortment of Elvis paraphernalia, giggling uncontrollably throughout.

"Dirk, my *boet*, Elvis with a greased up, black fringe and ginger ponytail? Really?" Pat called across the room. "And Roger, a very tall Elvis? Did Elvis also have his ankles on show?"

"I know, I know," Georgie laughed. "Those were the longest trousers they had."

Roger, relaxed after sharing a joint with Dirk before leaving the farm, tried to waggle his hips but only succeeded in knocking his knees together painfully and a wine glass off a table, bringing a wry smile to Georgie's over-made-up face with blue eye shadow and pink lipstick.

"Brad, you look the best of the bunch," said Lerryn, as she was introduced to Brad and Roger.

Brad, inspired by the compliment, tried a moon walk with his tuneless, "It's 'cause I ain't nothing but a hound doggggg, crying all…" but tripped on a chair leg. He was saved by a vigilant Jon, who had been half expecting an accident ever since he had seen Brad sneak a whole joint to himself before they left the farm.

"Ah, different era, I think Brad darling, the dance I mean," Eve laughed. Tom and Mandy laughed along, but unlike the others noted the 'darling' in the observation from Eve.

Mandy said, "Well actually, I think you girls have stolen the show with your cherry head bands!"

"I *know*," said Marin. "I asked Bongi, you know, Jon's sister, to make us something for our hair and she weaved them using thatching grass during the week and added the cherries this afternoon. They're amazing!"

"Are you as clever as your sister?" Mandy smiled at Jon.

"Nah, he just grows the grass," laughed Dirk with a wink at Roger as he put his arm around Jon, who was sitting next to him. Making sure not to look at Georgie, who he knew would be computing, Roger wondered if he had just seen a fatherly hug or more?

Pat had a large table set up at the restaurant to cater for the Lenbruikte family and friends. Lerryn was too busy to join them but for fleeting visits to the table. However, Pat had done some intense training of the girls, Marta and Marie, that afternoon. She decided she could supervise the 'M&Ms' from the table so she could enjoy the evening with the others.

Marta had approached her father about the waitering job at the restaurant and, to her relief, he was in such a hurry to get to the pub for his lunchtime session he deferred to Marta's mother. She was also distracted, focused on getting ready for the fancy-dress cherry festival dance that evening she simply nodded and waved the girls away.

Now that she was not fully occupied with the girls, other than the occasional surreptitious directive using her eyes, Pat's mind went back to her experience that afternoon. She agonised over raising what she had observed in the office with her sister. Would she be offended, think Pat was not minding her own business? Dismiss it as a misunderstanding?

**

The following morning, notwithstanding hangovers, everyone was up early to share anecdotes from the previous evening over breakfast. Brad, everyone agreed, had attracted most attention at the dance with his spontaneous rendition of *Jailhouse Rock* whilst the DJ was fixing a technical problem with his turntables. His uninvited, badly out-of-tune entertainment was enthusiastically received by all, Koos alongside him doing an impersonation of the 'warden playing on his saxophone', lips pursed, huge sausage fingers pressing imaginary keys.

Roger was unsurprised to see there was not a single black face amongst the revellers. *At a predominantly Afrikaans gathering in a conservative farming community? Early days yet in Fynberg for that kind of integration.* Roger decided Jon had probably been astute in his decision not to go to the dance, although a few polo players he met as he mingled asked if Jon was coming. There were hearty greetings and back slapping from them, especially from the big Koos. He thumped Roger so hard on his back the fake glasses he was wearing flew off and were stomped on by a large farmer doing a frenzied gyration across the dance floor.

Roger saw through the dancers, as he retrieved bits of his glasses, that Georgie had been in demand. Bear hugs for a long-lost friend, from farmers she had met only once at the polo last time. Also, as a dance partner, spun around like a ballerina to a thumping Bill Haley. It was Eve, though, who got most of the attention. In a tight-fitting red jumper worn in reverse, buttons at the back, as was the fashion of the rock 'n roll era.

He also noticed Dirk was engrossed in a conversation with Marta's dad at one stage. They were smiling, so he assumed there wasn't going to be an incident.

"What was that about?" he shouted at Dirk over the music, later.

"An apology of sorts, I think? Then a lecture on the dangers of allowing black people too much freedom. He said he understands that I am only trying to do the right thing, but did I realise the dangers of allowing what he called, 'these damned blacks' to get too uppity?"

Moving back from shouting in Roger's ear, Dirk, with a grimace, clenched his fists and shook them in mock frustration.

"Yup, there are always going to be a few who will never change," Roger shouted.

"I'll say. And by all accounts he's *still* assaulting his teenage daughter, Marta. Slapping her and yelling at her, that is. You met her at the restaurant," yelled Dirk, and then gave up any further attempts at conversation in the booming, festive environment. He grabbed Mandy by the hand as she walked past with Tom and dragged her protesting on to the dance floor.

Luigi had gone home directly from the restaurant, so Pat and Lerryn had spent most of the time together. Either in deep conversation, yelling into each other's ears or dancing together. Both seemed to be having fun, enjoying a twin's version of 'me' time.

***

The next day they got back to the farm from the art exhibition around lunch time. Bouncing up the driveway to the farmhouse, still all together in the borrowed taxi driven now by Dirk, with Jon as navigator. The exhibition had been set up at the far end of the valley in a location that took some time to get to from the farm but not if you knew all the short cuts as Jon did.

The setting for the exhibition had almost been an artwork itself. Paintings, grouped by artist, were set up at the base of a towering sandstone cliff face which leaned forward creating a cool protected area. The shaded location seemed to have its own eco system. Not quite a rainforest environment, but protected from the harsh afternoon sun, was more moist than the surrounding veld and accordingly had a greater variety of trees, evergreen plants growing beneath them.

Roger and Georgie wandered from painting to painting, sharing their views on the works, observing the artists in conversation with those interested in their work. Suddenly, she had lost him to a painting, he had stopped, transfixed.

It was a painting inspired by a David Goldblatt photograph that Roger had seen in an exhibition recently. On the sidewalk of downtown Jo'burg, a slightly portly, smartly dressed black gentleman was looking over his shoulder,

174

down at a young white boy of five or six pointing his toy gun at the back of the man's leg. A stick up.

It was the expression the artist had captured on the man's face that had Roger captivated. A kindly, smiling face but at the same time simulating surprise and fear at the boy pointing the gun at him. The young boy caught up in the action, real in his mind, maybe even irritated that the man was not taking him seriously. Well, not seriously *enough* anyway.

Roger searched for the word that would not come to mind, describing the scene. Irony? Juxtaposition? Parody?

Roger was lost in the scene, struggling with the reality of the time it represented. A time when the little boy would have been privileged, living in a comfortable white suburb. The man probably in dusty, dangerous Soweto.

***

Nursing several bruises, feeling he would like to die, he had been hanging around at the foot of Draken *koppie*. A tiny hill that was the highest point in a flat sprawling terrain of wind-blown shopping bags and densely packed shacks with rusty corrugated iron roofs and black plastic walls that was Soweto. The crest of the *koppie* was the favourite meeting place of the Dragon Boys gang. The gang was named after the *koppie*. The English translation of the name, of course. He liked to watch them from a distance. It gave him some hope that there was another life. He loved the way they seemed to belong together, how they seemed to *enjoy* being together. He watched them now as they laughed and jostled each other, some playfully threatening one of the gang with mock blows to an already scarred scalp, rocks gripped in their already damaged teenage hands.

He yearned to be part of the gang, to belong, to laugh. Last night his father had beaten his mother because there was no money left for drink. His father had shouted that she had stolen money from his pocket for food. It did not matter if she had or not, he would have beaten her anyway. Later his father had beaten him as well, because he said he wanted to live at his granny's place with his mother.

One of the gang noticed him staring up at them. Beckoning him, rock still clenched in his hand, he called out, "*Umfaan*, come up here." He spoke English, the gang's signature. They liked to emulate the American gangs they saw in the occasional movie they watched at the community centre. Talk like them. "Do you want a life of crime, buddy?" The others all laughed, pointing at his short pants, making him feel self-conscious and silly. "I need a small boy for a job. Do you want to make some money?"

They returned to Soweto with a bag loaded with valuables
including watches, jewellery, an electric shaver, hairdryer
and even some cash. After a visit to the shop they knew
purchased stolen goods, the twelve-year-old found himself
clutching his share of the spoils. It was over a hundred
rand. He felt like he was reborn. His accomplice even said
he did well. "You OK, *umfaan*. You are our 'small jobs
boy' now. One day you may be in our gang," he laughed.
He had immediately gone to a shop and bought himself a
pair of trousers. No more shorts for him. He had to
persuade his mother to tell his father she had stolen the
trousers from a shop, or he would have been suspicious
about where the money came from.

***

Roger became aware of Jon standing alongside him taking
in a painting by the same artist, of a young boy staring
towards the top of a *koppie* where a group of boys who
looked older than him were gathered, a shanty town spread
out behind them as far as the eye could see. It was
desolate. One of the boys at the top seemed to be pointing
down to the young boy. The artist had captured the
arrogance in his expression and the sadness etched on the
young boy's face. Roger was about to say something,
when he noticed the tears running down Jon's face and

177

turned away so as not to invade his space. It brought him face to face with the artist. Somehow Roger had assumed the artist would be white, but the person standing before him was a diminutive young black woman who was barely out of her teens.

She smiled slightly, "These scenes are inspired by photographs I have seen by David Goldblatt. He captures the pain of apartheid with such accuracy."

"I have seen a book, a collection of his photographs and read the background to each. You have shown the story behind these pictures just as well without using a single word," Jon said, wiping his cheeks with his sleeve.

Later, as they headed back to the van, Georgie said, "I see you made some purchases big spender, what are they? I can guess what one of them is, I reckon. How much?"

Roger said, "Later."

***

As they rattled to a stop alongside the sandstone wall that separated the house from the parking area and stables, Pat, who was with them this time, said, "Hey, Lerryn's car is here. She never said anything about her and Luigi coming over today?"

"Let's hope he brought leftovers from last night. That food was great. I'm famished!" said Brad.

They tumbled out of the van, and Marin was just saying, "OK, what do you all want to eat. I've got…" when they heard Pat, who had already strode through the gate to find what brought Lerryn over so soon, say "Oh my God, where did you two come from. Come here you little rascals."

"Patty, Patty, Dad says we're here for a holiday!"

The rest of them crowded through the gate to find Pat down on her knees being hugged by two young boys. Gus's boys, no doubt, thought Roger.

"Where's your dad?"

"We're going to milk a cow and ride a horse," Gaza yelled.

"Hang on a minute, Gaza. Where's your dad?" Pat said, again still on her knees.

"Driving himself and Luigi to greener fields I guess," said Lerryn, walking through the open double doors onto the patio, her face puffy, still showing signs of distress. Eyes red with crying. "They must be home by now. Luigi is probably on the beach. Oh, and by the look of the amount of stuff Gus dumped with the boys they are not here for a holiday. Something a bit more permanent is my guess."

"What an arsehole," Pat said through clenched teeth, as she stood.

"Can we see a cow, can we, can we?" this time it was the younger, Vula.

"Why is Luigi with him? What's he up to?" Pat asked Lerryn.

The others took over the boys as Pat led the now crying Lerryn into the house.

***

Luigi and Gus had been in cahoots for some time. It started when Luigi had called Gus to ask him, with as innocent a tone as he could muster, when he might be visiting the farm.

"Why would I pal?"

"Oh, I thought you might be coming to see Pat" Luigi said trying to sound as unaware as possible of any domestic issues between him and Pat.

"Ah, that's where she is, the bitch. Dumped me with the boys and buggered off." Gus growled.

"I thought they *were* your kids?" Luigi said before he could stop himself.

"Doesn't matter, it was Pat's fault my wife dumped them with us in the first place. She was pissed off with Pat and I getting together. Now Pat just buggers off and leaves them with me. She's not doing her share."

Luigi was way ahead of Gus. He had been planning his escape from this one-horse town for a while now.

"OK, so why don't you bring them up here. Leave them with her for a while. She should have a turn, you can have a break from the kids. By the way, I need to get back home and if I got a lift back with you I would pay you what the train fare would have cost me. You could make a few bucks at the same time." Catching a train was the last thing Luigi wanted to do. Not from what he had seen of rural train services in South Africa.

Luigi knew Gus would be thinking he could make it a permanent 'break'. Dump the kids and be off. He could hear the boys yelling in the background as he waited for a response from Gus.

"I think I like the idea," Gus said. "Give me your number and I'll call you back."

"No, I will call you tomorrow. I don't want Lerryn to suspect anything," Luigi said, hastily cutting the call as he heard Lerryn's car in the driveway. Luigi pursed his lips as he listened to Lerryn's high heels clomping up the old wooden veranda steps and then the key rattling their door lock.

He was not looking forward to telling Lerryn he was leaving. That he wanted to call off their relationship. He doubted she suspected anything. He would delay telling her until the last minute. He did not want to risk her losing it and changing the safe combination. He needed a few more opportunities to skim some more off all the 'cream' going into that safe. After all, the increased takings were as a result of his fine cooking, and Tom refused to pay him any bonus. Tom insisted it should come out of year-end profits. That was bonus time, he said.

Luigi's handsome features lit up as he smiled at the thought of being back down south with money in his pocket. There weren't any good-looking women to appreciate him in this dump. He hadn't been able to flirt with any admiring women in months. Just farmers' wives and a few silly young girls. That had made Lerryn happy but not him. At least she had stopped accusing him of having wandering eyes.

He was tired of her. Tired of the whole Lenbruikte family and their devotion to their 'know it all' father. Be patient he told himself. A little from the safe each day. Accumulate. No one will notice.

Without a work visa he needed to accumulate some cash to survive whilst he looked for other informal work. He needed to get a visa. He wondered if Lerryn's previous company would still act for him if they knew he had run out on her. Not likely, he sighed.

***

It was a full six months since Georgie and Roger, feeling somewhat sombre after the events of their final afternoon, had driven down the bumpy farm track away from Caracal Ridge. As they drove home, Eve and Brad dozing in the back seat, they had contemplated how things would turn out at the farm with the addition of two small boys and two damaged relationships to the rather fragile environment that already existed.

They had not heard from Dirk at all other than through Eve. She said he had told her there was a lot keeping him occupied and he would contact her soon. She had subsequently not heard anything from him. Roger and Georgie were not really that close to Dirk, so when they arrived home late after Friday evening work drinks to find a battered truck parked in their driveway, the last thing they expected was to see Dirk climb out of the cab with his wry smile.

Chapter 7

Big Smoke Visitors

Taking their details, Dirk was not sure what he saw in the eyes of his first guests. It was not excitement, for sure. But then he was not sure what he should expect.

The first six chalets were complete and, notwithstanding the open-plan bathrooms everybody had resisted, looked very stylish and cosy. Maybe it was just the very rustic bar and dining area with numerous cats darting between the chairs, and Sebete's repeated overzealous greeting every time he returned from seeing off one of the cats that had them distracted?

Dirk had decided to go ahead and build six chalets, all similar to the one already built, rather than use the first one as a prototype on a few guests. He had tentatively placed an ad in a travel magazine and this couple was his first response. It was a bit early, but he was keen to get feedback before investing too much more. To be honest he also wanted to see how comfortable he would be entertaining complete strangers as 'mine host', as well.

He and Jon had moved the asparagus packing operation up to a big room next to the stables and converted the vacated area into a dining/bar area. The farm workers had built the bar, tables and chairs from wood hewn from a local forest, leaving the wood partially unfinished, showing the natural look of the timber. People at the travel magazine had been very complimentary when they saw the photos he submitted to them.

"But then they would," Marin had said. "You're paying them."

"And they loved your gardens," Dirk countered. She just shrugged.

Dirk sat at the bar tapping a keyboard. He did not know what their relationship was, but the guests had taken separate chalets. The young woman was friendly, short black hair framed the startlingly blue eyes in her round face. She seemed to be studying her surroundings with care whilst her companion responded with their registration details. He was also in his late twenties, maybe a bit older than Dirk. Certainly, a lot less laid back. A frown wrinkled his forehead and he picked at a pimple as he gave his address. They were both from Johannesburg, on their way to Cape Town.

They had arrived just before dinner so, after formalities, ordered drinks which Dirk served from the new bar. He had told them they were his *first* guests, so he was looking forward to their reviews. Reaching for a bottle of wine from the fridge, he laughed over his shoulder that they should not hold back, he needed to know where he could improve.

He caught Jackie, that was the girl's name, observing him intently as he turned back to the bar. Like she was trying to read him. *Sad eyes*, he thought. Her companion Dave turned chatty halfway through his first drink, asking about the farm and what they grew on it. Where were they allowed to explore? Was anything off limits? The more chatty he got, the broader his Afrikaans accent became and the more glances he got from Jackie. After a while she relaxed too, and they had a few laughs together, Dirk sharing anecdotes about how he came to acquire the farm and some of Sebete's escapades.

As the evening wore on Jon joined them from the kitchen next door where he had been watching over the meal preparation, much to the displeasure of the cook. Thomas was Jon's older cousin and irritated by this young *mosemane*'s silly questions. But Dirk had explained to

Thomas that Jon was responsible for the running of the dining operation and had to be sure all Dirk's requests were followed, even in the kitchen. Thomas grumbled but consoled himself with the fact that he, not Jon, would get the tips left by the guests if the food and service was good.

Jon's arrival gave Dirk the chance to slip away and join Marin and Annah for their dinner up at the house. He excused himself, telling his guests Jon would see to their needs. They waved their acknowledgement, happily enjoying the view of the mountains backlit by the moon light. Dirk gave a surreptitious smile and a thumbs up to Jon as he walked out, which Jon knew was 'good luck with your first time as a 'mine host''.

***

When Dirk arrived back at the bar later, his guests had finished eating and were relaxing with a second bottle of wine. The two of them were deep in conversation when Jackie spotted Dirk walk past the window. She leaned back quickly to terminate the conversation with Dave, switching focus and expression as he entered, "Dirk, that was wonderful. Our compliments to your cook, so tasty. And Jon has been a great host."

"Thank you, Jackie, I will make sure Thomas knows you enjoyed it," Dirk said as he entered the bar, noting Jackie's English accent had faded since he was last there.

"It's great to get your feedback on our first resort dinner. The resort is a dream come true for *all* of us on the farm. Everyone shares in the success of whatever we do," Dirk was saying as he poured himself a drink and joined them at their table.

"You mean by creating jobs?" Dave asked.

"Yes, of course, but everyone who lives on the farm will participate in the profits to a lesser or greater degree, depending on their contribution. There will be a minimum reward though, no matter what they contribute, for anyone who was an occupant of this land the day I bought it."

"Wow!" Jackie said, "That's quite something, Dirk!"

Jackie seemed fascinated by his plans for Caracal Ridge. She insisted he "start at the beginning," how he even came to be here, considering he had a law degree?

Jon must have told her that whilst he was away, Dirk thought. He loved to stretch the truth and tell people that his farmer boss was *actually* a lawyer.

Dirk explained how Tom had persuaded him to come up this way originally, and how it evolved from there, including Jon's involvement as well. He had joined them having finished in the kitchen. Dave yawned his way through the Dirk's story until the part about their first polo match, which had everyone laughing.

"Here's to the new South Africa," Jackie said raising her glass. "May we find our way successfully through the maze."

Dirk, feeling a level of irritation that surprised him, noticed Dave looking at Jon with a smirk to see if he understood the word 'maze'.

"Sometimes when I am walking between the asparagus ferns, I feel like I am in one, but I always find my way eventually," Jon said, exchanging a smile with Dirk.

Dave and Jon had long since gone to their beds when Jackie and Dirk moved onto the patio to finish their drinks. Jackie was saying how much she respected what Dirk was doing in the spirit of 're-distribution of wealth'. How it was people like him who were going to make a difference over the next few years, as the country tried to make up lost ground. She had just put her hand on his arm and was saying how much she would like to find a way to contribute as well, when Marin strode onto the patio.

"Is there any chance you might be coming to bed tonight?" she said between clenched teeth.

Dirk stood up slowly and started to introduce Jackie. "Marin this is our…" but Marin had turned on her heel and strode off.

Jackie looked mortified.

"Well, that's a wrinkle in the resort operation we will have to look at," Dirk smiled.

"Don't worry. I have forgotten it already. My problem for making the staff stay up and talk," Jackie smiled back.

"It was lovely though. I am off to bed," she said as she strode into the darkness towards her chalet. "I've got my torch," she said, waving a shaft of light backward and forwards into the darkness above her and then onto the rough, newly laid path.

***

Despite all the inquiries about the places on the farm they could explore, Jackie and Dave did not move far from their chalets or the main buildings the following day. Wandering around the gardens Marin had created, they met up with Pat and Gus's two boys. There were the normal quizzical looks given the boy's dark skins and Pat's red hair and pale, freckled face. Pat was long since comfortable with the reaction, as she was with the awkwardness strangers felt when they realised they had not been able to disguise their curiosity.

As Dave joined in the boy's game of kicking a plastic ball, Jackie introduced herself to Pat. "And that's Dave. Sorry if I was gawking. You know. Oh shit!" she said getting flustered.

"Hey don't worry, no problem. You should have seen people in the supermarket when I and my ex, who is also white, walked in. Now that's gawking...they were, are, his kids actually, Gaza and Vula, the younger one."

Pat wasn't sure whether it was the woman's open contrition, or the fact that she had not spoken to a woman she wasn't related to in some way for months. For some reason, she felt compelled to tell Jackie how she came to be on the farm with the boys, on her own.

"So, he just dumped them. There must be a legal aspect to that. Can't Dirk help you with that, from a legal point of view?"

Sounds like Dirk has also been parting with background information, Pat thought. *Hope he hasn't got the hots for her, just what you don't need with your first paying customer.*

"Well, it's not too bad. There's lots of company for them with all the worker's kids around. I decided they should be stimulated so I started home schooling them in the morning before I go into the town to help out my sister in our dad's restaurant. She runs it for him."

The boys were way in the distance with Dave, possibly having lost interest in the ball and gone for a walk maybe? Pat was saying how Gaza and Vula liked to invite their farm friends to join them with their home-schooling activities and, before she knew it, she had parent after parent approaching her and Dirk, begging to be allowed into the '*sekolo*'. Dirk had decided it was right in line with what he wanted to achieve on the farm, so he had moved the generator outside into a lean-to and allocated the shed to Pat for a classroom. Pat had used some of her savings to equip the classroom and they now had about twenty kids each morning, learning the basics. They called Pat 'Teacher, Malakabe', meaning 'flame' in Sotho, due to her now long red hair hanging down her back.

"My God, you and your brother are quite something," Jackie said. "What motivates you to do all this?"

Pat laughed, "Just going with what you can do to make a life. Maybe share some of the rewards with others along the way. I know Dirk is driven by being able to learn skills that allow him to leverage the resources he discovers. He loves to learn how to do new things. Sometimes it looks self-serving, but he likes to include others if he can."

***

Dirk had decided Saturday nights would be barbecue, or braai, nights at Caracal Ridge and he and some of the workers had built a *boma* just off the patio facing the valley below and the hills beyond it, rising steeply into the mountains. His vision was for guests to stand around the fire, warming themselves in winter, drinking in the view, or what was in their glass, or both, whilst their meat, grilling over the *boma* fire, gave off tantalising aromas.

Tonight Marin, Pat and Jon had all joined in, Marin apologizing for her abruptness the previous evening. After Dirk had made the point to her that evening when he got to the house that they were paying guests, their first, Marin had admitted she was out of line and promised to apologise when she had the chance.

The hand she put on Dirk's arm as she spoke to Jackie was clearly a *keep your hands off, lady,* signal.

Pat said, "OK, now that we've got that out of the way can we get pissed and have a laugh?"

The evening had gone extremely well, so Dirk was slightly surprised that Jackie and Dave unexpectedly said they were going to turn in early. Dirk hoped that nothing else might have offended either of them. Pat said he was being paranoid. Maybe they just wanted to be fresh for their following morning's travels.

***

In the morning when Dirk got to the dining room to get the breakfast started in the kitchen Jackie and Dave were already there.

"Morning," Dirk said. "Ready for the next part of your journey?"

"Is there somewhere we could speak privately?" Dave said coldly.

Dirk looked from one to the other, mind racing. What could have happened?

"Here's fine," Dirk said. "I will just close these doors. The feedback can't be good then?" he grinned as they sat down at one of the tables.

His inaugural guests both opened their Police Identification cards in front of him.

Dave said, "You are Dirk Lenbruikte of Caracal Ridge, is that correct?"

"Yes," Dirk said, heart pumping.

"In accordance with the 'Illegal Substance Act' we are hereby arresting you for the growing of an illegal substance for purposes of dealing," Dave intoned.

Open-mouthed, Dirk looked from him to Jackie. She looked away, but not before he saw what looked like tears welling up in her eyes.

"What the fuck!" gasped Roger, throwing himself forward in his lounge chair.

"Oh no," said Georgie quietly.

They had settled down in the lounge with Dirk and demanded he update them with all the news from the farm over a bottle of wine.

"What sort of people do they have in the police force. Arrest you for a mickey mouse patch of weed you grow on your own property for your own personal use. That's bullshit!"

"They were actually from the drug squad and that's their thing, they take it seriously. Under cover, act like a guest, find the evidence. Even got pissed with us. I should have picked it. Jackie, if that was her name, letting it slip she knew I had a law degree. I thought it was just Jon mentioning it while chatting to them. Nope, they must have seen my file," Dirk shrugged. "There must be a file, because of my previous near conviction. It was all pre-planned. They had been tipped off. They knew the grass was growing amongst vegetables, just not where the vegetable patch was. Some bullshit about Gus's kids wanting to take him to the vegetable garden. He would have asked them, more likely, to take him to where the vegetable garden was. He knew somehow our grass supply was growing in a veggie patch. It was the only time either of them left the buildings."

Dirk laughed, "You should have seen Pat, I thought they were going to arrest her too when she went off at them. She actually shoved the woman cop, called her a devious bitch. Instead of getting angry, though, she just looked sad, waved off her colleague who tried to intervene. I almost felt sorry for her. Then Pat said, "And you can pay your fucking bill before you go anywhere with my brother.""

Roger and Georgie both burst out laughing. "I have always thought Pat is not the one you want to piss off," Roger grinned.

***

The workers, trying to be inconspicuous, going about their jobs, watched in horror, eyes flicking to and from the scene, as Dirk was led in hand cuffs to the cops' car and helped in. It was not uncommon for them to see black people taken away like this from time to time, for some transgression of a random apartheid law, *but their white baas?* They were stunned. Jon had already climbed into Dirk's bakkie, intent on being at the police station to see what happened next. Pat was trying to console a panicking Marin. "I'll call my dad. He can meet them at the police station. He will be able to do something," Pat said, going into the office to dial Tom and Mandy's number.

When they walked into the charge office the Sergeant on duty, Cor Onderbann, looked up, almost grateful that there was some action in his boring day. With the end of apartheid and the scrapping of the 'dompas', the hated ID document all black people were forced to carry, the number of arrests that arrived in this charge office had gone from dozens to about one a day. Then his mouth dropped open. Appearing from behind the two individuals he had never seen before was Dirk. Here *in handcuffs* was his polo teammate. He jumped up so quickly his chair fell over with a clatter.

The two undercover drug squad police identified themselves and explained why they had to formally charge Dirk. The Sergeant looked from Dirk to the two officers and back to Dirk. Cor and Dirk had become friends over the last year or so since meeting up at polo. From time to time, on his rounds, he called in at the farm and had coffee with Dirk and Jon. He knew that they grew a small amount of cannabis for their own use on the farm and turned a blind eye to it. Dirk, in turn, never took advantage by smoking a joint in front of Cor or anywhere in public for that matter.

The Sergeant also knew that recently the Constitutional Court had been asked to rule on a controversial dagga law which automatically turns dope smokers into dope dealers if they're found with more than a handful of the weed, because it states that persons caught with more than 115g of dagga in their possession will be suspected of dealing in the drug, an offence that carries far more serious penalties than mere possession. The Court believed the 'suspicion' clause was unconstitutional. Growing it, though, was a whole new ball game.

He smiled briefly at Dirk and turned to the officers and said, "*Jammer ek moet met die Kommandant praat.*" He turned and walked off to his station commander's office to explain the situation. Five minutes later a tall man with a handlebar moustache and piercing blue eyes appeared through the door, Cor in his wake.

"Good morning Mr Lenbruikte," he said to Dirk. "Good morning officers, Sergeant Onderbann has explained to me the process you would like to initiate, but perhaps you could enlighten me yourselves?"

"Of course, sir," Dave said, "We..." He was cut off by the Kommandant raising his hand slowly. With a smile that held no humour, Kommandant Berghof said, in a calm tone that did little to disguise the menace in his voice, "In particular, I would like to understand what you are doing operating in my jurisdiction without my knowledge and why I have no documents from your superiors requesting our cooperation? Why you have not presented any documents to Sergeant Onderbann confirming the authority vested in yourselves to process a legal arrest in my jurisdiction? I would also like to know why you did not present yourselves to this police station to inform us of your arrival in the area in an official police capacity? I would also like a copy of the warrant you presented to Mr. Lenbruikte before searching his property."

Dirk's recent guests exchanged looks of total disbelief and then dismay as they realised the station commander had just made them look totally incompetent. Dave, if that was his name, said, "Kommandant, you are right. We apologise. We have not crossed all the 'T's in this case. May we phone our office to rectify this?"

"No, you may not. On your return there, you may ask your *office* to send me a formal request asking me to investigate any matter that has come to your attention in my jurisdiction, and I will take the necessary action. I will inform you of the outcome before handing over to you, if necessary. There are however a few 'T's you can uncross though," he said, turning in Dirk's direction. "For example, the handcuffs on Mr Lenbruikte. Please release him. Mr Lenbruikte you are free to go. I apologise for the inconvenience."

The Kommandant then asked his desk sergeant to take the two drug squad Officers' details and write up a report. "Good morning, Mr Lenbruikte. Good morning, officers. Have a safe trip back," he said, as he left the room.

Tom arrived back from church to be told by Mandy that Pat had called to tell them Dirk had been arrested. White-faced, he jumped back into his car and raced off to the police station where he narrowly avoided crashing into a car carrying a young man and woman. The driver did not look back as he U-turned in front of Tom's car, and with a squeal of tyres on tarmac drove off up the road. Tom pulled up at the police station just as Dirk finished telling Jon, who had been waiting in Dirk's bakkie, the outcome. He climbed from his car to see Jon hugging Dirk like a long, lost brother.

Dirk and Jon were well on their way back to the farm by the time Tom and Kommandant Berghof had finished having coffee together, sharing anecdotes about the impulsiveness they saw in young people nowadays. Sergeant Onderbann was also well on *his* way, through his typed report of the last hour's events, thinking how much he was looking forward to his next visit to Caracal Ridge and the laugh they would have about today. He reminded himself to phone Dirk and tell him to get rid of that dammed patch of marijuana in case his commander sent him out there to follow up on what he had just been told by the two undercover officers. Dirk was lucky this time. Especially with a 'previous' hanging over him.

***

"Well, thank heavens there was a good outcome" Georgie was saying as she refilled all their glasses.

"You know it still intrigues me just how they knew about the patch," Dirk said. "Certainly could not have been anyone from the town. Cor is the only one who kind of knew, and he would never have bypassed his commander to inform the drug squad."

"Someone in town who knows someone up here in Jo'burg?" suggested Roger. "Maybe one of your workers let slip to some other farmer's worker? A farmer that had it in for you?"

"Nah, my only potential enemy is that young girl Marta's father. But he is very unpopular in town. Especially with the black people, apparently, who have seen him assault his workers. They would never tell him anything even if he asked. Even if they knew."

As she looked around the spare room to make sure she had not missed anything that Dirk might need, Georgie wondered why he had not yet said a word about Marin and Annah. When they had got out of Roger's car, exchanged hugs and ushered him inside out of the highveld cold he had simply said, "You will never guess how the first guest weekend at the resort turned out," and launched into his recount before they had even sat down. After detouring to the kitchen to check on the oven and collect another bottle of wine she folded herself into her lounge chair, as Roger said, "Ah, you're a star darling, thanks, another wine Dirk?"

Georgie said, "Dirk, how are Marin and Annah, you should have brought them up with you."

"They *are* here. Have been for a month. Marin has left the farm. Says she's had enough. Wants the big city again."

"Oh no, that's not good," Georgie said. "Wow, your news items are major!"

Roger shook his head slowly. "Sorry pal, but I had a feeling she was not very settled."

Dirk explained they had come to an agreement that Marin and Annah would stay with her mother for a few months and they would see how things turned out. Marin was going to do part-time work with a legal firm in the city. Her mother was only too happy to babysit Annah. Dirk would visit them every few weeks and this was the reason he was here. He had decided it was best not to stay with them though, hence his request for a bed that night.

Slightly irritated that he had not called beforehand, Georgie was about to suggest she would have liked to be more prepared when Roger grinned. "Anytime Dirk. Just rock up when you need a place!"

"Of course," she said.

Over dinner Dirk updated them on the other developments on the farm. The asparagus venture was doing OK. Notwithstanding having to overcome the challenges of working with incompetent export and freighting agents, they were getting repeat orders from Europe. Volume was still low but at least there was a contribution to outgoings. Jon's little packing operation hummed along and there were over 20 workers involved who previously had no jobs.

"On the community side of things, Malakabe's school is thriving, in fact looking more like a community centre now." Seeing their blank expressions, Dirk said, "Oh, of course it's been a while and we've just fallen into it. That's Pat. The mothers and their kids gave her that name when their kids started going to the school she originally created just for Gus's two boys."

Giving the impression he was rather proud of his little sister, Dirk went on, "It actually means 'flames' in Sotho, for her red hair, which they all admire. Even Jon, he's started calling her Malakabe as well!"

With Luigi absconding, Tom had decided the restaurant was just too much trouble and had decided to sell it after some debate with Lerryn over its viability and her motivation after being let down so badly by Luigi. He had never contacted her, and the last she heard from an ex-colleague he was still working illegally.

Lerryn had decided to use her share of the profits from the sale to set up a firm in the town offering low cost legal services to disadvantaged and marginalised people and communities, products of the apartheid regime of the past. Tom was helping with some funding and he was using his connections in government to try and get her firm some additional, more permanent funding. She was once again thriving in an environment where she felt she could make a contribution in her new country.

By definition, Lerryn had expected that her clients would be predominantly black people but she had been surprised to find how fast the number of her white clients was growing. Equal opportunity practices and affirmative action were starting to bite into white privilege. Certainly, more and more white people were finding the previous abundance of employment opportunities under job reservation for white people was diminishing day by day. They were struggling to earn enough to keep themselves out of debt.

***

Dirk surprised both Roger and Georgie when he informed them that he had nearly completed twelve villas. The final few would be available in about a month.

"It's amazing what you have achieved in such a short time Dirk," Roger said.

"Well thanks Roger but remember it was your idea and that is the main reason I am here. I need your help again," Dirk said.

Georgie thought that it was only a matter of time before Dirk's self-serving motivations rose to the surface in the conversation and asked, somewhat apprehensively, how they could help.

"Well, the villas are nearly complete and now I need your help with an idea for the launch of the resort. To get Caracal Ridge Resort's name out there. Or at least initiate the process. At the moment we are getting one or two stays a week through information bureaux, but we need to kick start some momentum. We need an event."

"Funny, I've been thinking about that actually."

"I knew you would say that Roger. Knew you wouldn't disappoint," laughed Dirk. "My main marketing man!"

Roger took a sip of wine, "OK, I have read, a few times recently, about events organisers running what they call 'Agatha Christie Mystery' weekends. They invite a whole bunch of people to an hotel, stage an event at the start of the weekend, a simulated murder, say, followed by a series of other events that create incriminating clues along the way as to who the perpetrators are. One of the guest couples are the offenders, only they don't know it until the end when each other couple presents their conclusions and evidence as to 'who dunnit'. Each couple is told that if they perceive circumstantial evidence is mounting up against them, they need to start thinking about creating their own alibis, alliances." Georgie could see Dirk's eyes lighting up. *Seen that a few times in the past.* She pushed that thought away fast.

"You could do a Caracal Ridge version and invite twelve or so travel journalists or 'weekend away'- type magazine editors," Roger finished.

"It's different from the normal freebie weekend they get offered as tacit request for a decent write up, I reckon. Journos will see it as a chance to write a fun column. I like it, Roger!" said Dirk.

"Yeah it's a good idea," agreed Georgie. "But I think you need a few couples you know to be there and complicit in your contrived plot. They could leave clues in real time without being noticed like you or Pat would."

"Good, that confirms you and Roger will be there and helping out, right?" Dirk laughed.

Chapter 8

Murder on the Caracal Express

It took three months to get ten appropriate journalists confirmed as weekend guests and the plot ironed out.
Of course, once Eve and Brad heard of the weekend, they had insisted they would be there as well. Roger decided to keep the planning of the weekend mystery plot to Dirk, Georgie and himself, though.

"Less who know the better when you commit a murder," Roger smiled at Georgie's quizzical expression.
"Seriously, I know Brad, he will want to take control. He

is super competitive, let him focus on solving the mystery rather."

Georgie laughed. "We're a bit possessive of our idea, are we?"

There would be mock-up shooting under cover of darkness during the first evening's dinner. People would be milling about at the buffet or at their tables for four. They would not remember who was in the room or who wasn't after the lights came back on. Except who they were talking to at the time.

As soon as Dirk flicked the main switch and plunged the whole place into darkness, in a spare room down the passage their mate, Kris, from the polo club, would fire off a blank, slide the club's starter pistol under a cupboard, crush the capsule of fake blood Roger had bought in a hobby shop and lie down concentrating on not smiling. Dirk and Roger had warned him that if he did smile when the guests came running in, they would reload the gun with a live round and re-shoot him.

When the lights came back on, things would unfold spontaneously from there, Roger hoped. Everyone had been informed that no matter how realistic events might seem they were in no danger, all was fake and they should do what they wanted to keep abreast of the intrigue and, therefore, the game. They would also be told, after the shooting, that although they had not noticed him early in the evening, the murder victim was the ex-Minister for Communications in the government. He had been a rampant anti-press advocate therefore most people in the room might have a motive.

**

A storm had threatened in the early afternoon before the arrival of the guests. Pendulous clouds hung over the distant mountains above and beyond the farm dam. Refusing to deliver any rain as had been the case for months now. From time to time sharp crackles of lightening left the base of the clouds taking a super charge of electricity to mother earth. Trails of jagged light followed by rolling thunder echoed in the amphitheatre that the valley and surrounding hills formed.

Much to the consternation of all on the farm, one of these fiery spears had started grass fire high up on one of the hillsides. Fortunately, before it had covered much more than one side of the hill the wind had turned back in the direction of the fire and, starved of fuel, it had burnt itself out. Dirk was relieved that, with the stiff breeze blown towards the fire, there would be no smell of burnt grass hanging over his guests when they gathered for his late afternoon welcoming drinks on the patio.

Sebete had been up in the hills with Bonniface when the fire started so they had seen it unfold from close range. After he had driven the cattle he was watching over off the hillside into a safe area, Bonniface remembered Sebete. He scanned the hillside for him, but he was nowhere to be seen. During their walks it was normal for Sebete to go off in different directions, following up on new scents in the grass, Bonniface knew, so he was not too concerned as he watched the fire's progress down the hill. It was slowing as the wind turned towards it.

He turned and looked back in the opposite direction, eyes looking from left to right across the slope as the veld rose towards the farmhouse in the distance. No Sebete on his way home. Seeing the farmhouse and the small dots of people on the front lawn looking towards him and the fire Bonniface said to himself, "Yes people, see the warning of what can come. Let some of your dam water back into the stream. Let it become a river again, for your own sake. For all our sakes."

***

The last of the guests had checked in, settled in their chalets and joined the others on a patio bathed in late afternoon sun. Everyone agreed that Caracal Ridge's location added a whole new meaning to Friday afternoon, 'end of work week' drinks. Partners had been invited as well so the atmosphere was relaxed and happy as they all got to know each other. Some quite excited about involving themselves in the mystery aspect of the weekend, others just delighted to enjoy a relaxing free weekend. All agreed the beauty and stillness of Caracal Ridge made it special.

In his jeans and long ponytail, Dirk was also impressing them with his unorthodox, for a resort manager anyway, hippy image. Normally on these complimentary weekends they were exposed to rather stuffy owner-managers angling for good reviews. He quickly won them over with his obvious intelligence and empathy for the farm and the people who lived on it.

As part of his welcome address he gave them a brief run down on what was grown on the farm, excluding the personal use marijuana patch which had now been moved so it was camouflaged in the centre of the asparagus field. He also outlined the overall objective of Caracal Ridge which was to create an environment where all those that lived here could benefit from participating in various projects. The resort they were here to review was one such project.

Dirk also mentioned Pat's little school, giving some background to how quickly it had grown from just her own two boy's home schooling to over twenty of the workers children. "They call it 'Malakabe's School', meaning Pat's school."

"Of course, they would," a young woman sitting on the patio's surrounding wall laughed. "I know some Sotho, 'Malakabe' means something to do with flames, that would be Pat's long beautiful hair, right Pat?"

Pat raised her thumbs with a smile, and they all laughed.

Dirk was just thinking how well it was going when someone said, "Dirk I think your dog has also been busy with a project of his own and is bringing you some of the fruits, a rabbit."

They all turned to look in the direction of the track that wound up from the dam. Nearing the farmhouse Sebete was striding purposefully, forelegs slightly apart to accommodate the dangling body of a small animal held in his jaws.

"Oh, shame," one of the women said. "So sad."

"Has to find his supper," said another.

Everyone seemed transfixed as Sebete drew ever closer. Pat, who had seen Sebete arriving with dead rabbits many times before, had not bothered to get up from her seated position at one of the patio tables with Roger and Brad. Georgie and Eve had been circulating amongst the guests doing some informal PR.

"Hang on," the guy who had first spotted Sebete said, "Dirk, unless your rabbits have long tails, that is not a rabbit, more like a cat."

Pat was out of her chair in an instant, pushing through the gathered observers and on her way across the lawn towards Sebete.

As they neared each other Sebete stopped and lowered his prize, which he had carried for over three kilometres, to the ground.

Pat slowed, not wanting to intimidate Sebete. Make him pick up the animal and run off for fear of losing his prize or get into trouble as he had with his lamb experience.

"Good boy, Sebete!" she cooed. "Good boy, well done. What have you got there? Is that for me?"

***

The lightning bolt had startled the caracal as she lay in the cave with her kittens. They snuggled closer to her, frightened by the thunder. After a few minutes, a strange sound drove her to the mouth of her lair to check on her surroundings for any threats. She found one. The fire Dirk had seen from the farmhouse had started quickly in the dry veld grass. She could hear the snapping and cracking as small twigs in the grass burst, splitting into fiery sparks. Instinct told her the cave was not the safest place to wait out the fire. Not with the wind blowing this way. She needed to move her young quickly. She had a small window. She ran back in and scruffed one of the kittens and returned to the entrance. One look told her which direction to move in to get out of the fire's path.

Reaching a rocky outcrop, the caracal, even carrying a kitten, leaped easily over the boulders upwards out of reach of the fire. The kitten was motionless and calm as they always are when scruffed by their mothers. She lay the kitten down in a gap between two big boulders and returned for her other kitten.

Although the fire had not yet reached the cave, she was stopped well short of the entrance by huge flames that had engulfed her route to it. She tried to find a way through the flames and the intense heat, frightened and in panic. She knew by now her kitten would be at the entrance looking for her. Its meows would be loud and terrified when it saw the fire. She was beside herself. Helpless. Finally, she had no option but to return to the one she had saved before he wandered off from his new strange surroundings in search of her, or at least familiar, comforting scents.

Sebete was busy trying to decide which of the many rabbits fleeing the fire he should go after when he heard the kitten's meows. Even though he was a dog not a cat, he recognised the terror in the cries. Instinct made him want to intervene. Why? How could anyone know? Maybe it was just territorial, the fire was an invader? He raced down the channel between the advancing fire and the cave where the kitten was sitting, ears flat with terror, hunched against a big rock. In one movement he stopped, scruffed the kitten, which immediately quieted, and took off again back up the diminishing escape route.

**

As Pat knelt before it, patting Sebete, telling him how clever he was, the kitten got itself to a sitting position looking totally confused and fearful, back to its plaintiff meows. It hissed once as Pat gently picked it up, talking to it in a quiet reassuring voice. Repeating the same comforting words again and again, stroking her hand gently over its ears, still flat against its head. Pat had handled enough kittens to know she had a girl in her hands and noticed one of her ears was the same colour as her body fur. Unusual, as caracals normally have two distinctive black ears. She had a single black ear.

Feeling her warmth and the security of her arms the caracal kitten began to relax, with only the occasional loud meow now. Its ears were no longer flattened. Now upright the little tufts at the tips of the ears, unique to the caracal, made Pat smile.

Sebete, still interested, followed her as she made for her room despite the demands of the guests to see the kitten. It had had enough trauma for one day. She did detour a little nearer to the patio though to briefly hold the kitten up so they could all see it. There many "Aaaahs" from wives and clicking of cameras from everyone who needed photographs to add spice to the reviews they would be writing.

Roger tugged Brad's arm, "Brad, where's your camera buddy?"

Brad shrugged his shoulders, "Lost interest in photography. Too time-consuming."

Pat said, "It's a caracal kitten. Must have got separated from its mother and siblings by the fire. Or worse. I don't know how, but Sebete must have spotted it and saved it from the fire. He's a star," she said, patting him again. Sebete wagged his tail in appreciation, enjoying the accolades he was getting. Ridgeback in tow, Pat made for the quiet of her bedroom and to figure out what to do next with her new charge. "We should try and organise a milk bottle and teat of some kind, shouldn't we?" she said to the kitten in a cooing voice. "Wonder if Marin left any of Annah's old bottles lying around."

Everyone on the patio agreed their time at Caracal Ridge had been riveting so far. What with splendid mountain vistas and a real-life drama, "Dog saves wild cat from fire."

One of the journalists patted Dirk on the back, "You know how to entertain in this place, Dirk. What's next? Ah, of course. Agatha Christie."

Dirk smiled.

It was already dark on the patio and people began to move into the dining area to find a table. All were tables for four, and couples who had been chatting when Dirk and Jon started moving them inside seated themselves together so they could continue their conversations. Brad was intent on grabbing the table near a large open window that looked out onto the patio. "I love the view and the air," he insisted. He had a vague idea what the first action of the mystery night would be from harassing Roger into telling him how the plot would kick off that evening.

"Just tell me what action gets things going. No more. Just interested. Won't share with anyone." He was going to be ahead of the game.

Georgie and Eve grumbled that it would get chilly later. "So, then we can close it," he said.

Much later, whilst the four of them were helping themselves to delicious-looking food from the buffet, that's exactly what the woman at a nearby table did. She was in an off-shoulder dress and feeling the chill. Although the window was a very large sash window of the time, it was perfectly weighted and slid down easily. In the chatty, laughter filled room with a few glasses of wine in them, neither Brad nor his party noticed it was closed when they returned to the table. All four very focused on the food on their plates prepared by Jon's grumpy cousin Thomas.

**

Dirk was in one of the utility rooms nearby making sure Kris was fully prepared.

"Jong why did I agree to do this? I am really nervous now. You owe me a good few beers for this, hey Dirkie."

Dirk tried to calm the nervous novice actor seemingly on the edge of stage fright. "Don't worry. Just a few things to do. Tell you what let's do the blood now then you don't need to worry about it in the dark," Dirk said.

Taking his cue from Dirk, Jon punched Kris on the chest. "Ouch."

"Sorry, now just lie here by the cupboard."

Kris lay on his back, 'starters' gun in his sweaty palm, fake blood spreading across his chest.

Dirk said, "OK, lights go off. You fire the gun. Slide it under the cupboard. Jon will throw the door open and leave you to be found. Easy."

Looking around the room once, Dirk gave Kris, lying on the floor, the thumbs up and closed the door. He patted Jon on the back. "Got your torch for your escape?" Jon nodded, his hands wet with fake blood. "OK, stand by. Action in about two minutes," he whispered walking quickly down the hallway.

Looking like he was no more than a busy resort manager being busy, Dirk hurried across the patio to the main switch box. "Here we go," he said under his breath.

***

When the lights went off, the room was plunged into blackness for the first few seconds. An opaque, eye-blinking blackness. As pupils gradually dilated, the eyes that held them were also suddenly widened in response to a loud gunshot nearby, immediately followed by a sound not unlike the crash of a lightning bolt striking the earth too close for comfort. The crackle you hear before the thunder, when the sound barrier's broken by a speeding downward shaft of static electricity. But this night it was the sound of shattering of glass.

Brad had hurled himself through what he thought was the open window intent on getting to the action as fast as possible. Catching the perpetrator in the act. Or at least seeing him fleeing the scene, for surely the designers of this plot would not have expected someone to take a short cut to the crime scene.

When Dirk switched the lights back on after the planned five-second interruption, the stunned silence signalled the horror of the scene that was unfolding back in his dining room. Dirk and Roger arrived at the window facing the patio as Jon was turning the face down Brad over onto his back. There was little blood. A spike of glass as big as a dagger was buried deep in his chest.

***

Pat had forgotten the plan to switch the lights off for a few seconds, and she was in the middle of feeding the kitten with one of Annah's old bottles when they went off. Then the gun shot.

"Shit," she said, jumping in the darkness. On her bed alongside her, Sebete raised his head, listened for a moment and then lowered it and went back to sleep. Then the lights were on again. Finishing the feed, she eased the kitten alongside Sebete. The plan was to make sure there was more dog smell on the kitten than human smell in case a reuniting with its mother was possible the following day. Sebete raised his head again, sniffed the kitten and lay back down with a yawn. If it meant he could sleep on Pat's bed, he was OK with being a foster parent.

***

It had only taken the ambulance about twenty minutes to get to the farm. It seemed like hours to Dirk. Now standing alongside their ambulance, flashing lights revealing distant onlooking faces masked in fear, the paramedics spoke to an ashen faced Dirk and Roger. As he latched the ambulance's rear doors the senior paramedic said quietly that it was likely Brad was dead before he even hit the concrete floor of the patio. The glass dagger had penetrated his heart like a high calibre bullet.

As the ambulance crunched down the farm track a scream pierced the air. Dirk gasped, "That's Marin." He and Roger raced back to the restaurant.

***

Kris had been lying on his back in the darkness now for about half an hour. Jon had flicked the light off in the room before slipping through the now open door and disappearing. Kris had heard some sounds from time to time. Once, breaking glass he thought? Then footsteps thumping in the passage like someone was running. Were they on the way to find him? But nothing. The fake blood began drying on his warm skin. Making him itch. He waited and waited, growing increasingly uncomfortable and impatient. Finally, he had had enough.

There is only so much Dirk can expect from a mate, he said to himself as he stood up, nearly slipping on the sticky floor. Finding the light switch in the darkness he flicked the light on and scrambled under the cupboard for the starter's gun. The Club would be furious if that wasn't returned, he thought. As Kris arrived on the patio, he saw through the windows to the restaurant that only Marin and a few guests were left. Standing at the bar drinks in hand. "What the hell?" he said to himself.

Hearing the crunch of glass on the patio, Marin and the few guests seeking fortitude in a strong night cap swung around nervously, hoping to see Dirk and Roger returning. A white-faced Kris stood in the doorway, tousled blond hair streaked with red hanging in his eyes, entire shirt front red with blood and gun clenched in hand.

***

Climbing the first hill on the other side of the dam, Pat struggled to keep up with Bonniface and Sebete. She stopped to catch her breath. The kitten was wrapped in a blanket in her arms. It's small, tufted ears the only sign it was there. It was just after midday as she looked back towards the farmhouse. It was the first time she had seen the view from this side of the valley. The mountains behind the farmhouse were quite imposing from here. Dwarfing the farmhouse and its outbuildings. She noticed the last of the weekend guests were driving down the track towards the old sandstone entrance arch. After the traumatic event of the previous evening, nobody had been keen to stay on, preferring to get away from the scene as quickly as possible. The poor woman who had closed the window had needlessly blamed herself. She and Eve sobbed in each other's arms. Roger, stunned, standing alongside them, a consoling hand on Eve's shoulder. Pat was about to turn back to follow Bonniface when she spotted Sergeant Onderbann's police vehicle pulling off to one side of the narrow track to allow a guest's vehicle space to get by. *What's Cor doing back here?* she said to herself. *Thought he asked all the questions he wanted answers to last night. Traumatised some of the guests even more. Maybe he's back to arrest somebody. That's not funny, Pat.* She turned to catch up with Bonniface and Sebete, who were waiting patiently up the path.

***

Sitting now at a table on the patio, Cor took a sip of his coffee and tried to ignore the faint aroma of marijuana. *Poor buggers,* he thought. *Probably need it after last night. There is more to come, guys.* A large brown folder lay on the table between him, Dirk and Roger.

"You are not going to be happy with what I am about to tell you. In fact, I officially don't have to tell you and probably shouldn't, but as you are my friend, Dirk, I thought you should know," he said.

"In situations like last night's unfortunate incident we have to enter the deceased person's details and death certificate reference number into the National Police Database," Cor said. "I thought it would, as normal, just accept the details we got from you about Brad and confirm it was added to the database. In fact, it came back with a high priority flag.

Brad was known to the Drug Enforcement Division and the system referenced a previous file sent to us. It was requested by my station commander at the time of your arrest, Dirk. The system also noted that Brad was on visa probation for defaulting on his visa renewal and being in possession of an illegal substance."

Roger said, "Yes, I remember Brad telling me that he had got into some trouble with his visa, but it was sorted out. He just had to make sure he told Immigration when he travelled interstate and give the address he was staying at. Nothing about drugs."

"Yes, and because Dirk has a previous court appearance, the farm's address was recorded, which Brad gave them as he was compelled to do when travelling interstate, would crossmatch and raise a flag for Drug Enforcement," said Cor. "They contacted Brad immediately, seeing an opportunity to check out whether Dirk had any further involvement with drugs. Brad must have had some kind of obligation to them."

Cor placed his hand on his folder. "This is the file I mentioned," he said, as he flipped it open and took a large black and white photograph from the top of the pile of papers. He placed it in front of Dirk and Roger. "Do you remember this being taken?"

The image showed Dirk, Roger and Jon standing in the vegetable patch alongside the marijuana plants. Cor went on, "You would not have seen it of course because, as instructed, Brad returned the whole camera to the Drug Enforcement people after his weekend here. Your friend was a drug squad informer, hence the arrival of those first two 'guests' of yours, Dirk."

Roger and Dirk were open-mouthed. Stunned.

Roger said, "Well, that explains why Brad became such an avid photographer overnight and gave the hobby up almost immediately."

"Yes, and that explains how my first guests knew where to find the patch so easily."

"I didn't hear that," said Cor. "And now I must get back."

***

Bonniface had known of the cave since he was just a small boy. His father had told him stories about how it had been used as a last resting place for dying elders of the tribe who inhabited this vast mountainous land. In those times it was also home to caracal mothers and their kittens. He had not seen any caracals near the cave recently, but this was where the fire was yesterday, and not far from where the last caracal he had seen had crossed swords with Sebete. It was worth a try, he agreed with Pat. Leave the kitten at the mouth of the lair and move back to a vantage point nearby, downwind of the entrance. Far enough to not be intrusive, but still able to see the kitten and protect it if it was threatened, which was unlikely with Sebete on hand. Left for a while, the kitten, without the security of Pat's arms, would soon start meowing and they would see what happened.

Pat held Sebete by his collar so he could not try and explore the cave. The rocky entrance was about waist high but very narrow. Bonniface made a small impromptu *boma* out of rocks that would stop the kitten from wandering off while they waited.

Satisfied with his handiwork, Bonniface turned, still on his knees, to Pat, "Come Malakabe, we leave your baby now. For the real mother." He took Sebete, who seemed to sense being boisterous would not be popular right now. Pat knelt down beside him and gently placed the kitten in the *boma*. It cowered against one of the small boulders, ears flat.

Quietly they moved back and took up a position hidden by rocks and fire blackened scrub, about a hundred yards away. All that could be heard was the dog's panting but even that was intermittent as boredom got the better of him and he readied for a nap. They waited, eyes fixed on the kitten and the entrance. No movement from either. Five minutes. Ten. Nothing.

Suddenly the first "Meow." Just one. Pat and Bonniface exchanged glances. Sebete pricked up his ears, not bothering to open his eyes.

Another ten minutes. The kitten was meowing constantly now, clearly distressed, having lost the security of Pat. Like Sebete, she was now becoming distressed herself, ready to go to her 'baby's' aid. Bonniface shook his head slowly, looking at her with understanding. Both had their eyes firmly fixed on the kitten when there was a flash of movement at the mouth of the cave. With relief they saw the large tufted ears. It was a caracal. The head moved slowly from left to right. Scanning. Ears twitching. Nostrils raised to the wind. Was it the mother? With two graceful leaps she was in the *boma*, sniffed the kitten, scruffed her and disappeared back into the cave.

Bonniface smiled as Malakabe and Sebete did an impromptu dance.

***

All the national papers had a small piece on the Caracal Ridge Resort incident, with appropriate headline banners. Some even had it featured on their front page, albeit bottom right. Some even had a follow up article buried in the paper with more details on the resort. The name, Caracal Ridge became known countrywide overnight.

END OF PART 1

PART TWO

FOUR YEARS LATER

Chapter 9

The Trap

Malakabe, and what Dirk liked to refer to as her army, were high in the hills on the other side of the valley, mountains towering above them. As she lowered her binoculars, Sebete and her two boys came into view, scrambling over a rocky outcrop. Vula, only just turned eight, lagged behind Sebete and Gaza. Pat never ceased to marvel at how fast they had grown over the years. Devouring farm life and the lessons they learnt in both her community school and walking the hills with Bonniface and Sebete. Herding the cows and learning Sotho.

Behind the boys in the distance, on the other side of the valley, smoke rose lazily from the farmhouse chimney. With electrification via a new overhead powerline to the farm, the coal stove's days were numbered, Pat mused. As were the romantic but very risky oil lamps in the surrounding thatch-rooved guest villas. Whenever she took in this scene, she was struck with how the villas had seemed to spring up so quickly behind and around the main farmhouse buildings. Like asparagus spears around a mother plant. They seemed to have taken just a few days to appear but of course it had taken a lot longer.

They had celebrated the completion of 'Number 20' just last week. The gathering included builders, asparagus packers and workers, Pat's trainee teachers and of course the growing resort staff of cooks and cleaners. As Pat enjoyed the worker's impromptu dancing around the barbecue she thought, *Wow, Dirk's got quite a payroll to handle now. No wonder Jon's angling for an assistant. This community is growing, must be over thirty or so people here.*

High above the villas a single vulture circled in slow motion, held aloft easily by rising thermals in the endless blue sky. It was so high you could not possibly make out any features, but you knew the gliding shadow with massive, unflapping wings was a vulture. If you were in the bush under a vast expanse of blue sky, there was going to be at least one sighting of a vulture during the day. Cruising, needing to eat, waiting for a sighting of some hapless animal below, injured, dying or dead already, the remains of a kill.

Pat watched it, the way its circular soaring flight moved it slowly across the landscape. She imagined its shadow somewhere flitting across the veld, rocks, treetops, blocking the sun from reaching the earth for a fraction of a second. Dirk said that in a day they could cover over a hundred kilometres in search of food, as a result of their ability to fix their wings and soar for hours at a time. *How does he know all this stuff?* she wondered. *A born and bred city boy?*

The wind rustled the tall veld grass around her, and she smelt the long dry blades toasting gently under the sun. *The joyful, impossible to duplicate, scent of Africa*, she thought. How do the people who've left the country, fearing the move to democracy, survive without being able to experience the scent of an African dawn? How *does* Clive do it?

"Man, it's a fix you need regularly," she whispered to herself as she turned back to the binoculars. She re-scanned an area she knew was popular with the cats due to the abundant rabbit population. No matter how much her arms ached with the weight of the glasses, Pat would seldom lower them until she had a sighting. As she did now. *There she is, I think.* She caught the flick of the caracal's head, and then the tufts on her ears came into focus. The single black ear. Pat's heart always skipped a beat when she saw it was *her* cat. *Now, beautiful girl, where are those kittens of yours? They are still too young to have left you.*

Without lowering the binoculars, Pat called to Sebete to come to her. Sometimes she wondered if the caracal she was watching remembered being saved and released by her and Sebete. Probably not. Wishful thinking.

She knew the dog would likely pick up the caracal's scent from this downwind location and might go to investigate. Pat knew also, there was no threat to the mother from the dog, but having kittens *she* might get aggressive. If nothing else she would certainly move off if Sebete stuck his nose into things. Better to avoid a confrontation. The boys followed Sebete to her side. Gaza said, "What's wrong Malakabe?" Without taking her eyes from the glasses, Pat whispered, "Be quiet for a few minutes please, play here near me. Keep Sebete here with you, I'm watching the mother cat."

Ever since Sebete had brought the kitten home after the fire, Pat had become increasingly fascinated with the caracals in the hills. She had had to walk miles over the years, never without Sebete in tow of course, as the cats kept to their far-flung respective territories. The locals had come to consider her the guardian of the caracals. She was certainly acknowledged as the expert on the caracal population in the valley and foothills.

There was a sudden movement in the grass next to the mother, and two kittens raced into view tumbling over each other in a mock fight. Pat's arms ached as she watched them play for several minutes, occasionally jumping on their mother trying to engage her in their game, but she was too intent on scanning the surrounding area for threats to her young. And of course, for prey. *Those two of yours look very healthy, for sure. You're all a lot better off without father around,* Pat thought to herself, glancing away from the eye pieces, checking that Gaza and Vula still had Sebete under control. Gaza was poking at something with a stick, Vula and Sebete excited observers. Pat watched as the caracal moved off slowly, glancing over her shoulder from time to time to make sure her young were following. Pat was just wondering if the mother was taking them hunting when there was a sudden sharp, metallic crack behind her. She spun around to see the boys and the dog reversing back through the grass away from where Gaza's stick stood upright like a dead sapling.

Pat was there in an instant. "*Ba qabeletsoe*, trap, trap!" yelled Gaza, pointing at the trap. It was a fearsome looking device with jagged edges that would have broken the boy's or Sebete's leg had either stood on it. "How do you know about traps?" Pat yelled in panic.

"Bonniface showed us before," Gaza said. "The farmer puts them here to catch the animals that kill his lambs."

"Which farmer?"

The shrug from both boys told her she would have to talk to Bonniface about it. Pat unhooked the trap's chain from the tree it was attached to and marched off down the hillside with it, Gaza's sapling now easily snapped from its jaws. She was fearsomely angry. She tried to put the image of the boys or Sebete or a caracal caught in the trap out of her mind.

"Come on, hurry up. I need to talk to Bonniface," she called back over her shoulder.

Taking her at her word, Sebete burst past her down the hillside at pace before suddenly veering off into the grass, inevitably distracted by a rabbit running for safety.

***

Mountains Roger had not seen for a long time finally began to emerge over the hazy horizon that it seemed to him he had somehow not been able to get any closer to, even after hours of driving. Not really peaks but impressive enough, they signalled he was not far off Brandfort, the last town before the farm. The turn-off from the main road to the farm a short distance thereafter.

Georgie and he had been out of the country for over four years having seized the chance to set up a business in England. The opportunity had come at the right time for them. Roger was keen to distance himself from the consequences of the traumatic incident resulting in Brad's death and the role he was forced to play thereafter. Being Brad's friend as well as employer meant that in the absence of any other close relationship Brad had in South

Africa, Roger had to assume responsibility for contacting Brad's sons and ex-wife in America, assisting with the arrangements for the body and effects to be sent home. All in all, a harrowing few weeks for both he and Georgie, who at the same time was providing constant support to a shattered Eve. Georgie was happy with the move as she had always been keen to try other countries. However, she did not expect she would have to continue to provide support to Eve when she also ended up in England.

Eve had finally moved on from the tragic incident. She fell in love with an English guy she had met at a cookery class. Something she had taken up as a distraction and an opportunity to make new friends. It had initially been an idyllic relationship, producing two baby girls. Her new husband, however, had insisted on returning to the UK as a safer option than South Africa for their family. Roger and Georgie had seen them from time to time, but as the years went by and Eve visited them more and more without her husband and stayed for longer it became obvious to them that things were deteriorating in Eve's marriage. Probably as a result of bringing up kids with little in the way of a support network exacerbated by a strained relationship with her in-laws. Finally, after an acrimonious divorce, Eve and the girls returned to South Africa and Eve's hometown, Durban, where her mother Rita still lived.

Roger and Georgie's time in the UK had seen them not only get to grips with building a new business but also raising a daughter. It had been demanding, especially not having their support network around them either. They had decided, after a particularly hard winter, their little girl Kirsten with constant colds and flu, they were due a break. Time to be at home in the sun for a while. Roger had come out to South Africa to meet a few potential employers a local recruiter was representing, whilst Georgie handled the sale of their business and home, back in England. No small undertaking Roger guiltily conceded.

Georgie had been apprehensive about Roger visiting the farm. They had heard some nasty stories about attacks on farmers whilst they were away, but Dirk had assured them on a call that they were generally related to past ongoing ill treatment of workers which was certainly not the case at Caracal Ridge. Nonetheless, Georgie had insisted he update her regularly, especially the minute he arrived at the farm, no matter what time it was for her in the UK. Roger was staying with Georgie's sister in Johannesburg for a few weeks and had borrowed his bother-in-law's car for the trip to the farm. Having transport had also proved useful for the several trips he had made to his son and daughter who both had partners nowadays. Since their last visit to him and Georgie in England, a lot had changed. They were both at university with part-time jobs and reasonably independent, although Roger and Georgie paid for their fees. The way they spoke, asking him myriads of questions, indicated they were delighted with the addition of Kirsten to the family and seemed to be looking forward to meeting their new sibling. Roger was relieved, having felt some apprehension about, first, the addition of a stepmother and then a baby that was bound to be doted on.

***

They reminded Bonniface of the many times as a boy he and his friends had lain at the edge of this cliff staring over the sandstone ledge down into the valley below. There was no resort back then, just the old farmhouse. They also crawled their way up to it like these three were doing, fearing a stumble and fall, down onto the rocks below. He and his friends always laughed as they got closer and closer to the edge, chanting, "*Mala a kulang, mala a kulang* (sick stomach)."

Either through nervousness due to the sharp drop, or not wanting to be seen against the skyline from below, all three were on their knees as they edged forward. Up here so high above the farmhouse and surrounding villas they could scan the whole area. It was obvious to see there were no security guards in the resort.

Bonniface and the other boys would lie for ages, staring out into the distance and being high above the valley, with the breeze whistling in their ears as thermals rose from the rocks below, imagine they were Black Eagles gliding over the veld seeking out prey. Occasionally they would spot a duiker grazing in the distance and picture themselves in a sharp dive ending with talons outstretched.

Bonniface had come around to the high ground behind the farmhouse searching for cows that had wandered off and were known to end up here sometimes. His father had brought him up here to search for stray cows. He would peer out across the valley and tell Bonniface stories about the hunters in the valley even before *his* father's time. Whenever he was up here, Bonniface would remember his father telling him about how his grandfather spoke of the time when the land below belonged to everyone. *No white farmer Bonni, no owners, the land was all of ours, we shared it with everyone. For hunting, for growing crops for raising families.*

Bonniface had been on his way back down a path hidden by tall grass when he spotted the three men below him. He was close enough to hear their voices but invisible, above them, hidden. They spoke Zulu quietly to each other and any indigenous person from the area would have heard from their dialect they were not local.

"*Ukukhethwa okulula,*" one murmured. The other agreed it 'looked easy', saying there might be plenty of purses and jewellery lying around in the rooms they could see below.

Their leader had their one and only gun stuck in his belt. He eased it around to a more comfortable position behind his back as he lay down on his stomach, turning to look at the others saying they must not be hasty. They should not forget they had all agreed they must always go for the big prize on this trip. There would be lots of cash from payments from guests in a safe in the main house.

Turning back to the view below him, the leader thought how little these two had learnt since they had joined the gang. He remembered so well how he got his first job and how much he had learnt even on his first day of crime as a twelve-year-old,'*small boy*'

They squirmed their way back from the ledge and, stumbling and falling down the rocky slope they had climbed earlier, returned to their battered truck. They were intent on continuing their assessment of available targets in the surrounding farmlands. They had come a long way from Soweto to take advantage of, as they had been told, unsuspecting targets in areas where robberies never occurred. They would take their time to find the best opportunity because after they struck, the alarm would be raised, and they would have to make a hasty exit from the area. There would be no time for a second attempt. Totally focused on their precarious descent they did not see the herdsman observing them as they arrived back at their truck. He had come up around the back of the steep hills that overlooked the farm buildings to look for the cattle, having had no success finding them in all the normal places they tended to wander off to.   Hidden in the tall grass Bonniface watched the rear of the truck as it rattled off. "*Mathata* (problems)," he murmured to himself, no grin on his face.

***

Roger was just congratulating himself on an uneventful drive to the farm when he felt the car lurch and heard the unmistakable 'kluk kluk kluk' of flapping tyre rubber on the road.

"Shit," he said as he pulled over, probably not more than twenty minutes from the farm, a few minutes from the turn-off away from the main tar road through to Fynberg.

He could hear Georgie saying, "It could have been worse Roger. You could have crashed off the road. It could have happened in the dark." How could it happen in the dark when she made him promise, on pain of death, that he would only travel during daylight hours? But then he discovered, yes, it could be worse. There was a spare, slightly flat, tyre but on opening the boot Roger discovered that his brother-in-law had for some strange reason taken out the wheel spanner and not replaced it.

This time he said, "Fuck, now what. Nice one."

Suddenly Roger remembered passing a dilapidated shonky-looking service station not far back. He looked up the road. Yes, there it was, not too far. He locked the car and started towards the garage at a trot, it wasn't that far off sundown.

Roger moved from foot to foot as he waited patiently for the garage owner to finish attending to the customers he was with. He was bent over a tyre on his work bench with three others. Roger could not understand a word of the very loud conversation, but there were some laughs and the odd curse in Afrikaans when the clamp slipped, "*Kak*, man."

They ignored him completely as he waited and reflected on the fact that 'Shit, man' sounded more descriptive said in Afrikaans when suddenly his eyes took in what they were doing.

Using a pair of pliers and the clamp they were literally sewing up the two-inch gash in the burst wall of a tyre with wire. Oh my god, thought Roger. Really? Is avoiding the cost of a tyre and tube worth that type of risk? Never mind the fine. Well maybe, if you have no money and you are trying to complete your trip.

He thought of the anecdotes he had heard about the ten-seater vans black taxi drivers used to ferry twenty or so people around in at a time, including the odd goat sometimes. Those vehicles were occasionally largely held together with wire. Certainly, *some* of the taxis he had seen looked like they were and sounded like it.

Finally, the stitches were complete, and they were ready to put the tube back in before putting the wheel back on their truck and inflating the tyre. As they turned from the work bench and the owner Roger was shocked. All three had the meanest look he had ever seen on a human face. Wretched faces sculptured by excessive drugs, alcohol and intense trauma, probably since they were young boys.

Roger wondered if the individuals he was seeing before him were products of what was claimed by the government to be a 'lost generation'. During his time at the Officer Academy, he had been briefed on findings by leading consultants on behalf of the South African

Defence Force Intelligence Unit. The research was intended to assess what the security forces were likely to encounter in keeping the country secure under an oppressive apartheid regime. It stated the facts as established through one-on-one interviews with political detainees and other offenders. It was intended to equip army officers with knowledge of the mental state of 'the enemy'.

It was a fact that young people who grew up during the apartheid era were in many cases subject to far more intense hardship than adults. A consequence of how families coped under apartheid. Parents, mostly the fathers, who were so exposed to the pain of a hopeless environment sometimes turned to alcohol as their only escape. A week's work, up at 4 am and back home at 8 pm to a one-room shack without light, electricity or water. No future. Rewarded with meagre wages. Wracked with the hopelessness of their situation, some fathers simply drank their pain away. Weekends lost in drunkenness. And their family? No food, beatings, both mother and kids, no school, no future. An endless weekly cycle of hopelessness from when you were old enough to remember. From here could come a 'lost generation'. Scarred. Numbed. Unable to feel. Taking what they needed for survival from anywhere they could get it. It spawned an era of street children, gangs, some living in drains, begging or involved in crime to make money for food. Sexual abuse and violence a way of life. Recent research Roger had seen indicated that they ranged in age from nine to sixteen or so. They mostly felt they were better off on the street with some money in their hand than being abused at home.

They are not Charles Dickens' young 'pickpockets'. They are violent young people who go on to further, more serious adult crime. Roger would never forget the look in the eyes of these three in the garage. Their appraising look as they left the workshop with the wheel.

"Can I help you?" the owner was saying for a third time in an exasperated tone. "Oh, ah yes, sorry." Roger told him what he needed, and he reached under the counter and came up with a universal wheel spanner. "Take this, it fits all. I would run you down, but I need to stay here for them," he said nodding in the truck's direction.

"No problem, I'll bring it back."

***

Having successful changed the wheel Roger turned the car around and drove back to the garage to return the spanner. He needed to have the tyre pumped anyway. He drove up and stopped next to the air pump. The other three he was pleased to note had gone. Then he kind of remembered noticing a vehicle pass him while he was changing the wheel before turning off the main road where he expected he would be turning off eventually as well.

When he walked into the workshop, he found the owner on his hands and knees on the concrete floor holding a bloody, oily rag to his head.

"After all the help I gave them they bashed me and took all the money," he groaned. Roger helped him up and into his desk chair. Picking up the phone the man dialled a number, waited a few seconds and then spoke rapidly in Sotho to whoever answered.

Roger said, "Was that the police?"

He forced a quiet laugh, "No, they are too busy to worry about a black guy and his old garage. Waste of time. It was my son, he will come and get me. I will tell the *mapolesa* tomorrow."

***

Crunching to a stop at the farmhouse Roger was taken aback by the increased number of dwellings and the number of people around. Some obviously resort staff, some clearly guests. Opening the car door, he was greeted by a large, tail wagging ridgeback who was definitely not Sebete. He was a young dog. "Are you one of Sebete's wild oats?" Roger said, as he patted its muscular shoulders.

A young woman came bouncing through the old sandstone gate, greeting him with a wave and a beautiful smile. "Welcome to Caracal Ridge, Roger," she said. Roger thought he recognised her as one of the girls from that day at the polo, considerably grown up. "Do you remember me? Marie. I remember you as a very tall Elvis Presley," she laughed.

Roger grinned, "What a night that was. Of course, you were serving in the restaurant that night, weren't you?"

He followed her through the gate, somewhat put out by the fact that Dirk had sent one of the staff to greet him, but then realised he was being precious. This was a business now and had processes. Part of Marie's job was obviously to know who was arriving and to welcome them.

Instead of crossing the patio into the house, Marie led him to the dining and bar area. It had been expanded to include a reception and lounge room.

Dirk was just finishing a call at reception. Marie touched his shoulder and whispered in his ear before disappearing into the adjoining kitchen. He thanked the caller for their help, cradled the phone and turned around with a grin. "Roger, good to see you. It's been a long while."

To Roger's surprise, Dirk ignored his outstretched hand and put his arms around him in a welcoming hug. "Sorry I had to finish that call. Been trying to speak to customs all morning. What a pedantic bunch. The fact that our asparagus has been sitting on the runway in a hot container, unloaded, seemed to have escaped them."

If Dirk's ebullient greeting wasn't disconcerting enough for Roger, Jon's, "Hey Roger, long time my friend," greeting and one arm hug as he took his bag from him really took him by surprise. Roger was moved by the affection he felt for the two of them. It made the segregated environment he had been brought up in seem ludicrous once again. He remonstrated with himself, *we didn't allow black people to sit on a park bench, had separate shop entrances, made them sit at the back of a bus. What was going on in the minds of white South Africans?*

He was ushered into the bar where Jon and Dirk took up positions behind the bar facing him. Seated on his bar stool, bag stowed under the counter, Roger said, "So what's been going down? Other than the fact you need to get your freighting people to adhere to some processes."

They talked and laughed as all three shared anecdotes from the time Roger had been away. The asparagus project. It had grown significantly with their success in Europe and employed up to thirty workers including packers.

Guests were beginning to drift in for pre-dinner drinks, so they moved the conversation to more general topics in between Jon and Dirk serving the guests.

Dirk said, "I've put you into a spare villa Roger, complimentary of course. With Jon in the house now with me, Pat and her two boys, we have kind of run out of spare rooms."

Roger raised his drink to his lips to help with his attempt at a natural response, saying, "Sounds great. Can't wait to try a villa after all our patio talks about them." In his mind he could see Georgie reaching for a jigsaw piece and placing it with a smile. This reminded him he had not yet contacted her to confirm he had arrived safely so easing himself off his stool said, "Hey Dirk, can I make a quick call to Georgie, let her know I arrived safely?"

***

Arriving back at the farm, Pat sent Vula and Gaza through the gate to the house with instructions to get themselves showered and ready for dinner. She then strode past the cars parked in the guest parking area up to the barn where Bonniface and the other workers kept their gear. He greeted Pat with his normal grin, "*Na u hantle, Malakabe?*"

"I am well, thank you, *ntate* (father), but tell me please what farmer does this?" Pat asked dropping the trap she and the boys had found on the work bench.

The grin faded from Bonniface's face. He beckoned her over to the corner of the barn. There lay a pile of similar bone crunching traps. Bonniface told her he had been collecting the traps for months whenever he came across one during his herding. He slipped into Sotho and as was the custom Pat had to listen patiently to a long, roundabout story about farmers in the area, the threats to their animals over the years and what they did to obviate them, to keep their livelihood safe before, as she knew he would, *ntate* would finally arrive at which particular farmer was using these illegal traps. Pat was patient, she loved the music of the Sotho language and had picked up enough over the years to get the gist of what he was saying. Even if she missed some words there was only one name she wanted anyway and that would come at the end of Bonniface's response to her question.

"So, it's the young farmer? Alan is his name, yes? Are you sure, *ntate*?" Pat asked.

Bonniface's grin had returned when he said that he knew it was that farmer because he was the one always asking him if he had seen anyone taking traps away.

***

Leaving Jon to manage the bar, that evening after dinner Roger, Dirk and Pat retired to the patio to do some catching up. Early in the evening, Roger had sat with Pat at a table in the main house for Gaza and Vula's much earlier dinner. He marvelled at how much they had grown. How articulate they were. Full of interest in everything. Even asking Roger what it was like in this far away country he lived in called England. They could switch between Sotho, Zulu and English at will.

It reminded Roger of his best friend at school who had come from a farming environment. A young white boy cared for on a daily basis by a Zulu woman, he spoke only Zulu, including to his parents, who were both of course fluent in Zulu, until he started school. They had had to give him a crash course in English the weeks before he left for boarding school.

Later, as they sat down with their drinks, Roger delighted to be back in the familiar old patio setting adjacent to the main house, Sebete came sauntering across the lawn towards them. In his wake was the dog that had greeted Roger earlier when he arrived.

"What's this then, Sebete's past caught up with him?" Roger laughed.

Dirk called the dogs to him. Patting them both, or thumping them more accurately, he said, "This is Moriti. It is Sotho for 'shadow' because he is seldom seen far behind Sebete. Follows him everywhere. Except when Pat is out checking on her beloved cats. Still not disciplined enough for caracal tracking, not so Malakabe." Pat, smiling, was about to say something and then stopped.

Dirk went on the explain that their young neighbour had been so taken with Sebete he had got a ridgeback for himself, even though it had been Sebete who had killed one of his father's lambs in the past. Roger remembered arriving at the farm the first time and seeing Sebete tied to the dead lamb.

Unfortunately, once the pup got a bit older, he had started wandering and followed Sebete home one day. After that he was not content unless he was up at Caracal Ridge hanging out with him. The neighbour had been constantly driving over to fetch him.

"Alan gave up in the end, not seeing the point in tying his dog up all day and asked us if we would like to keep him. Hence the arrival of Sebete's protégé whom the people on the farm soon named Moriti."

Pat said, "I was going to ask you, talking of Alan, did you know that he has been setting traps on your farm?" Pat recounted the events of that afternoon. Roger hoped for Dirk's sake that the response he gave Pat was the right one. "What the hell?" Dirk exclaimed.

Alan had complained to Dirk that he was having problems with predators. Another reason for getting the dog. He had said nothing to Dirk about traps though. Dirk said he would call him in the morning to discuss in more detail.

Pat asked that he leave it to her. She would drive over and talk to him one-on-one in the morning. Poor bugger, thought Roger, he will be facing an irate cat mother.

With the emergence of the internet and email in the last year, Georgie and Roger had been able to keep in more regular contact with the farm. However, Dirk was not normally very generous with detail in an email, so now he had the chance, one-on-one, Roger was interested to hear from them what the rest of the family was up to.

Marin and Annah had moved back to the area and were living in Fynberg. Marin had joined Lerryn as a much-needed additional partner in her thriving law practice. Nearly six, Annah had begun spending time at the farm with Dirk, sometimes staying for several days, once nearly a week. She loved the way Gaza and Vula doted on her, treating her like a young sister, insisting she go to their mother's community school with them. Roger was interested to see if Dirk and she had got any closer.

Lerryn had not heard a word from Luigi since the day he absconded with the cash he had skimmed off the restaurant takings, although her mother said she had seen him in Durban once looking rather dishevelled. "Down and out like he always was," she said. Rita had never liked him from the day Lerryn introduced him to her.

Lerryn had become so involved in her practice, she hardly thought of Luigi again. She had been courted by the odd farmer since then but other than dinner at the restaurant she used to manage, not much had happened on the romantic side of her life.

Dirk himself was clearly enjoying what he was building and the progress he had made towards being able to empower the people on the farm. He was obviously proud of Jon and what he had achieved. Firstly, completing a three-year accounting Diploma by correspondence. Secondly, taking on the role of representing the workers in negotiating what benefits they should be reaping for their endeavours on the farm projects. In the last year they had made enough from the asparagus and resort activities to pay a bonus to all the workers over and above their normal wages. It was not a huge amount, but enough for some to buy an additional cow for their allotments or farm implement or just a luxury item they had not dreamed of owning.

"They know they're in a close-knit team now, part of the farm," Dirk smiled. "And, of course, what Pat has built has been the cream on top for us."

Roger could see Pat had thrived. After arriving at the farm feeling she had failed to achieve anything since leaving university, she had seized the opportunities presented to her. She had nurtured the two boys dumped on her by their father and created a community environment on the farm that not only gave an education opportunity to underprivileged young kids, it created teaching jobs for several people in the area. With the help of Tom and his business and government connections, she had applied for and been given an Education Department grant which funded new classrooms and teacher training. The farm school had come a long way from a few kids being taught rudimentary lessons in the old generator shed.

For a few minutes the three of them were quiet, lost in their own thoughts. Roger enjoying the collage of colourful memories: his first rather awkward meeting with Dirk at the dam, being shown the start-up asparagus activities, the dreams of a resort, Pat arriving sad and disappointed with her life. The tragic event at the press promotional weekend seemed a faded memory he had no desire to recall, so he turned the page without a glance at that image and closed the album.

Instead he turned in his seat and raised his glass, "Congratulations you two, your achievements for the people on this farm are becoming quite something, not to mention yours as a mother to those two wonderful boys, Pat." Dirk smiled his thanks. Pat blushed. Roger had never seen her blush before. With her long red hair framing her now crimson face before tumbling down over her shoulders, she really did look a bit like the personification of a flame, he thought.

"To Dirk and Malakabe, and your growing farm community," he said clinking their glasses with his.

***

Allan had heard many stories about Dirk's sister from his workers, the one they called Malakabe. The mother of caracals they said. Much to his amusement they refused point blank to have anything to do with his traps. Malakabe was not only a fearsome protector of the caracals, she had also built a school for the local children. Messing with her was only going to bring retribution they told him. Either from her or from the local community.

Alan had only recently moved onto the farm full-time after completing a degree in agriculture. At his graduation ceremony, he had been told by his parents they were returning to England for their twilight years. *It was all his*. A farm inherited from his parents, as was the respect he got from the workers. He had heard them bemoan the fact that the '*lihoai tse hlomphehang haholo*' (well respected farmers) had retired and left the farm enough times to know he had a way to go to earn the same level of appreciation from them in his own right.

During the time he had been on the farm he had met Dirk regularly, as he used his lands for grazing his cattle and had to pay him each month. In fact, Bonniface was his more regular point of contact being the person who collected the herd in the morning and brought them back in the afternoon for milking. He had never met Dirk's sister, Pat. Anyway, he had had his head down getting to grips with running a farm. Early mornings had meant early to bed, exhausted. Very little socialising or even neighbourly visits.

So, when he opened his front door in response to her loud early morning knocking, he nearly dropped his mug of newly poured coffee. The red hair carelessly falling across her shoulders and steely green eyes dropped his mouth open. It clamped shut when the trap landed at his feet with a clang.

"Good morning. This yours?"

Alan was smitten. He thought he heard himself invite Pat in and offer her a coffee, before he realised that he had sat down at the dining room table and she was still standing. He jumped up as she said she could not stay and wanted his assurance there would be no more traps. He said he had given up with the traps anyway as they got stolen all the time. Bonniface had said he had never seen any strangers on the lands, so had no idea how they were disappearing.

Alan thought he saw a smile touch her lips as she said, "Really? Nothing bad about that. Well, I am telling you that you are lucky that my young boys and the dogs have escaped your traps, never mind the caracals. If you lose a lamb to a cat tell me. If you can prove it was a caracal, I will pay you for the lamb."

Alan still had his mug in his hand, he stood at the door waving as Pat drove off. She didn't wave back even though she saw the gesture in her, skew as always, rear view mirror as she rattled up his driveway in Dirk's truck.

***

As the guests were long since all in bed, Bonniface had switched off the outside spotlights in the car park area. It was part of his routine as night guard each week. Workers volunteered to do one shift per week for which they earned extra wages. Although it meant he was not with his wife for one night, Bonniface quite enjoyed the late-night shift as it meant he could be near his son who now lived in the house. He wondered about that still after more than a year. Him on these nights sleeping with the other workers in the worker's dormitory, and nearby his son in the farmer's house.

Standing in the dark, his torch switched off, he was invisible in the darkness as he looked towards the villas with their night light above each door. Behind them the dark slope rising to a steep cliff lit by the moon towering over them. The golden glow of sandstone in moonlight. Below them the farmhouse mainly dark except for the bar and the kitchen where the cook, his nephew Thomas, was finishing up his cleaning for the night.

Bonniface sighed then grinned. His wife had been right. Jon had done well working with Dirk.

The new training he had done had meant he was given the job of bookkeeper for the farm. It escaped Bonniface though why so much adding and subtracting was necessary in order to know what to pay workers and to know whether your farm was thriving or not. Surely you just looked at your cattle or your crops to know that? If your wife and children were not thin or sick, then you must be getting paid well?

But still no wife or babies for Jon. Bonniface worried about that still. Does Jon not yearn for the warmth of a young woman beside him?

The crunching of tyres on the driveway brought him back to the present. As the truck turned into the parking area, only its small park lights on, Bonniface froze. He could not read but he knew numbers and he could see enough of the only just illuminated front plate to know who was in the truck. They were the same numbers he had seen on the truck up behind the house yesterday. *Batho ba batlang khathatso* (people looking for trouble), he was sure.

He stayed motionless in the trees alongside the car park hewn from the bush. The engine and lights switched off. Even before they opened the doors, he could hear them whispering. The driver was giving instructions it seemed. Bonniface saw the glint of metal in the dark as they emerged from the truck. Knives. They moved silently through the opening in the sandstone wall towards the farm buildings. When the last one had disappeared through the old gate Bonniface moved away from the trees and made for the worker's dormitory as fast as his old legs would carry him.

***

257

Roger and Dirk were sharing anecdotes at the bar. Over Dirk's shoulder Roger's view was through a large window across the newly built patio towards the mountains, majestic against their dark starry backdrop. Behind Roger sat Jon, pouring over a ledger, tapping a calculator, Sebete and Moriti tethered by leads lay next to him. Dirk did not allow them to roam around as they pleased during mealtimes, and although the guests had all left the dining area and bar and gone to bed, no one had got around to unharnessing the sleeping dogs.

Laughing at the description Dirk had given of the events in the charge office when the station Commander had told off Dirk's arresting officers for their incompetence many years ago, Roger leant back sipping his beer. He was suddenly aware of a deep growl coming from Sebete. That's when he saw them. They came from nowhere. Three dark figures, old silent movie silhouettes moving past the window behind Dirk. Roger knew immediately these were the same three he had seen in the old garage on the way to the farm.

They burst through the double doorway leading into the bar and lounge, their faces lit for the first time confirming who they were, one pointing a gun, the others brandishing knives. "Get on the floor, get on the floor," they were yelling simultaneously, faces contorted by murderous expressions. Sebete spun in the air as his leap at them took him to the end of his lead and he was yanked back.

Pushed from his barstool by the one with the gun, Roger fell forward over the snarling Sebete, probably saving him from a being shot as Jon hauled him back towards him and the still unsure, prone Moriti. All three partially under the table.

"Who is the boss farmer here?" the leader shouted. Dirk started to rise from the floor behind the bar saying it was him. "Get on the floor," he shouted as he leant across the bar counter and shoved the gun into Dirk's face smashing his lips against his teeth. The other two were already grabbing money from the cash register on the counter above Dirk. One-handed, never letting go of the large knives they carried and waved at Dirk's now bloody face below them.

"Where is the safe?" the leader yelled again.

Jon said he could take them to the safe. "Must I get up?" he asked.

"Yes, clever black boy with the bookwork. You get up, but you do any funny stuff I shoot you, and your dogs," the leader yelled. Jon sensed what Roger knew, these weren't just thieves. These were young men born of a violent past. Psychopaths. The sooner they were given what they demanded the sooner they would calm down and their own chances of surviving this ordeal would increase. He rose slowly, keeping his hands where they could see them and moved towards the door to the kitchen, hoping Thomas had gone by now. "It's in the kitchen," he said.

Just at that moment, Pat emerged from the door leading to the toilets. "What's all the shouti…" She was grabbed by the knife wielding two and flung screaming to the floor, this time sending both Sebete and Moriti into a combined, snarling outburst of teeth-baring rage, their leashes taut, dragging the table, nails on a blackboard. Roger used all his strength to pull both dogs to him before either of the thugs reacted.

"Go with him to the safe," the leader yelled at them, before either recovered from their stumbling retreat in the face of the two snarling dogs.

Jon knelt before the safe and began to turn the dial. "Faster, faster," one screamed at him. Finally, his trembling fingers found the sequence of numbers and he had the safe door open. Before he could move away the heal of a boot smashed into the side of his face. "Fuck off away, *umfaan*," one yelled as Jon was sent sprawling across the concrete floor of the kitchen. He gave his knife to his accomplice and started scooping money, and valuables left there by guests, from the safe. Leaving the semi-conscious Jon on the floor streaked with his blood, they returned to the bar, the contents of the safe stuffed into a hessian bag they had found lying on Thomas's work top.

Near the door where she had entered the bar, the leader was pointing his gun at the ashen-faced Pat, telling her to get up and to follow him. He said she was to go with them at least to the main road, as hostage in case anyone came after them or they ran into a police patrol. If everyone

260

listened to their instructions, they would find Pat waiting at the turn-off. As he lay there listening to the leader's shouted instructions Roger doubted that would be the case. The chances of Pat surviving unscathed were nil.

Pat was screaming and resisting. She lashed out at one of her attackers catching him squarely on the nose, buckling his knees for a moment. A blow from behind on the back of the head with the handle of one of the knives made her fall to her knees and they dragged her across the patio to the car park.

"If any of you move, we will cut your girl's throat," the leader shouted into the bar, before slamming the sliding bar door shut.

Pat was still trying to resist as the three of them dragged her to their car, barely visible in the darkness. The leader told the other two to get into the car as he dragged Pat around to the driver's side. He shoved his weapon into his belt and reached for the handle of the passenger door as Pat jerked wildly to free her arm from his bruising grip. Gripping the door handle he paused momentarily, hearing a thump in the darkness nearby. A second thump came as he stepped back to yank the door open. The third thump was drowned by his scream of pain as the trap he had stood on snapped shut over his ankle.

Pat was suddenly free as he reached for the side of the truck for support. On the other side of the truck the other two made to rush around the front of the vehicle to see what had happened. They had barely taken a few steps before they both felt the bite of steel traps themselves. Screaming and stumbling around trying to reach and pry open the trap's jagged jaws resulted in them setting off more traps. To add to their painful confusion the regular thump in the blackness surrounding them was growing closer.

It was at this point that Bonniface switched the flood lights back on, illuminating the parking area. Notwithstanding their pain the three thieves were silenced by the spectacle of fifteen or so of the farm workers armed with knobkerries advancing slowly towards them, banging their weapons in unison on the hard ground of the car park as they approached.

As the ring of workers drew closer in a semi-circle around the three, they raised their knobkerries. Not having Pat to contend with, the leader had freed himself from the trap he was in and pointed his weapon at them. The other two members of the gang were not that confident about the usefulness of their knives in the circumstances and continued to try and free themselves from multiple traps.

Roger and Dirk had crept up to the archway opening in the sandstone wall when Pat came flying through and into Dirk's arms, sobbing hysterically. It was at about that instant that Roger felt, for the second time at the farm, the impact of a galloping, larger than life ridgeback released from a tether by Jon, thump past him.

Standing above the other two with his arm stretched out in front of him the leader was always going to be Sebete's target. The dog's jaws clamped on his upper arm breaking it and ripping flesh as the full force of the ridgeback's muscular body crashed into him, knocking him forward onto one of the remaining traps.

Chapter 10

Fighting Fires

What was immediately apparent to Roger when he tentatively approached the now well-lit parking area and poked his head over the sandstone wall, was how things could change in the blink of an eye. The robbers who were their attackers minutes ago were now bruised and bleeding prisoners. After the traps and Sebete had done their part, a few well-aimed blows from the workers with their knobkerries had subdued the thieves.

Trussed with ropes from the barn, they no longer looked the menacing individuals they were. Sebete, still intent on taking revenge was held back by Bonniface who had threaded a rope through his and Moriti's collars for fear of them running into any still armed, leftover traps.

Earlier, after being alerted by Bonniface, the workers had sprung into action. Within minutes, directed by Bonniface and by the light of a few torches, they had set the traps around the car, spreading leaves that were abundant on the edge of the parking area over them. Melting back into the blackness with their weapons at the ready, they awaited the signal to move in from Bonniface. He was just on his way to see what had transpired in the main buildings when he heard the leader shouting at someone not to follow them and Pat's anguished cries. Fearing she might stand on one of the traps as they dragged her to the car but determined nonetheless, he hurried back to his position near the main light switch as planned. The workers, as instructed by Bonniface, would move forward once they heard the traps go off.

Later, as he reflected on the outcome, Roger decided he had seen a community exercise their right to defend what was theirs. In just a few years working with Dirk, they had come to realise the farm was also theirs in some small way. As workers they were now part of it, not just working on it. They were sharing in its prosperity and any threat to it was a threat to them and would not be taken lightly.

**

The following morning, by halfway through breakfast it seemed to Dirk like none of the guests had heard or seen any of the incident. He was going to leave it like that. All the workers had been told to keep quiet about what had happened. Dirk did not want any bad publicity if he could avoid it. It was bound to be distorted and the press would exaggerate the whole thing he was sure. The previous night, after receiving a call from Dirk, Cor had arrived soon after with several of his officers. They seemed almost disappointed that all they had to do was load the battered perpetrators into their police van. Cor had taken a statement from Dirk and, with one of his men driving the impounded robber's car, had returned to Fynberg charge office with his vanload of prisoners, their ropes having been replaced with handcuffs. They were unlikely to be escaping anyway, given their leg wounds from the traps.

"Tell me, Dirk, since when have you had traps on your property? You don't do any trapping." Cor said as he got into the van.

"Haven't got a clue, Cor," Dirk laughed. "And you are right, I definitely don't trap animals. Just robbers it seems!"

Sergeant Onderbann had laughed and waved as he drove away back down the bumpy track, his prisoners moaning in discomfort as the rocking vehicle tossed them around.

Explaining away their wounds as innocently as possible the guests had been told Dirk and Jon had merely come off worst while freeing a buck caught in a paddock fence the night before. Pressed for more details by one excited guest Dirk had mumbled, embarrassed telling a lie, about hooves and horns thrashing in all directions around them in the dark. Pat was staying in bed on the local doctor's orders, so they did not need to cover for her. Dirk was adamant if he could avoid any news reports about a farm attack at Caracal Ridge he was going to.

Roger suggested the media might even like a story about a worker community coming to the rescue, but Dirk did not want to risk it. Roger thought it could be a great message to send to people agonising over the growing threat to those living in the farming areas of South Africa. Maybe promote the strategy of sharing some of one's wealth with the surrounding community, as Dirk had, to create a harmonious environment. Roger imagined an environment where communities grew up around farms and rural towns, where the communal ownership was such that these areas were unattractive to criminals because the likely outcome of invading the community's space would be retribution. He resolved to debate it further with Dirk when things had settled down a bit.

**

Panting up the hill on the other side of the dam a week later Pat felt the trauma of the previous weekend was finally starting to fade. Catching a glimpse of one of the caracals would be just the sort of calming medicine she needed. Sebete was ranging ahead as usual, while Moriti strained on the leash Gaza and Vula both hung on to, arguing who was strongest. Moriti was on his first cat-spotting trip. His test run.

Halfway up the hill, Pat stopped at her regular first lookout spot. Raising her binoculars, she called Sebete to her, instructing him to lie down. Guiding his charge alongside Sebete, Gaza yelled, "*Paqama fatše, Moriti.*"

"That's no good," Pat said. "Tell him in English otherwise you two and Jon will be the only ones able to make him lie down. He will just get confused."

"E Malakabe," Vula said, bowing facetiously. It got him a gentle poke in the ribs from a laughing Pat.

"E Pat, you mean," Gaza said, giving his brother a push. "Did you not hear? Only English to Moriti, small boy."

Pat had thought many times over the last week how the two boys had possibly escaped the consequences of being orphans. If they had found themselves on the street in a township fending for themselves daily, scratching out an existence, would they have ended up like those three? Driven to crime by a life of despair.

Watching them laugh and jostle each other she decided it didn't take much to avoid destitution really. Some love, a guardian, a community around them, a school. The chances of an orphaned child succeeding in life went up considerably with these basic things. Simple nurturing.

She raised the glasses and scanned the veld hoping for a sighting. A pair of black tufted ears above the waving carpet of brown grass. *God it was dry. The grass was like tinder. When would it rain?*

Pat told the boys to let Moriti off his leash so he could roam with Sebete. Like a shadow he would return with Sebete when she whistled him in.

Lifting her gaze above the scene of the boys chasing after the dogs, she scanned the resort buildings on the other side of the valley, nestling below the overhanging sandstone cliffs. Her mind wandered again. She imagined she could see right into the main house. Herself in there with Gaza and Vula. It was evening, she could see the windows lit by candles. And there were Dirk and Jon by the fire with the dogs. On the wall above the fireplace the painting Roger had bought Jon that cherry festival weekend years ago. Of a young boy staring towards the top of a koppie where a group of older boys were gathered, a township spread out behind them, probably Soweto.

Yes, Gaza and Vula's extended family. Secure, cosy even. Her eyes ran over the villas. What if each of them housed a family. What if each was used as accommodation for a foster mother who cared for two orphans or abandoned

269

kids. Twenty villas with twenty foster families. That's forty kids saved, gathering in her school in the morning, instead of gathering on narrow, dirty, dangerous roads dividing thousands of shacks, many housing destitution.

A crow calling in the distance high above her in the mountains brought Pat out of her daydream. Dirk and Jon weren't sitting in front of the fire. Far below she could actually see them down at the dam, near the grass embankment that formed the wall of the dam. They seemed to be busy working on something to do with the large water release pipes embedded in the embankment.

She turned back to the hillside above her, lifted the binoculars to her eyes. *Where are you? Let me see those ears peeking above the grass. A pair of ears, one black and one brown would be best of course.*

After another fruitless ten minutes, Pat decided she would need to move further up the hill. Knowing the boys had already had a long walk she told them they should take Moriti and go down to the dam and see what Dirk and Jon were up to. They were delighted at the chance to do something new and took off immediately they had the dog on his leash. He protested initially, but finally trotted along with them, head turned over shoulder occasionally looking back longingly at Pat and Sebete climbing through the grass.

She called after them, "If Dirk and Jon have already left when you get to the dam don't you dare go near the water, OK?" They waved their acknowledgment in her direction.

Sebete had already started up the hill, knowing instinctively Pat was on the move.

About twenty minutes later, she saw the first of the caracals. It was on the move up the steep sandstone face at the base of the mountain. She scanned the face to her right and left, and it was not long before she saw a second cat leap to a ledge in the vertical face. *This is unusual* she thought to herself. Two in such close proximity. Then she saw the third. It was already some way up the face, looking back at her and Sebete. *It's like they're gathering,* she thought. Something is making them move closer, away from the isolation of their individual territories. Pat felt the anxiety deep down inside her. Do they sense a threatening event of some kind? A large predator? A black eagle? More rival for prey than threat. No, doesn't make sense. *Oh my God, you are so paranoid,* she said to herself. She went back to the glasses. Determined to see her caracal mother and the kittens before she left the hillside.

***

Earlier, back at the farm Dirk had been in the bar hunched over a computer screen. Ever impressed with the benefits of the new technology he had acquired in the last year, he was busy scrolling through the new bookings. Touching his still tender lip gingerly, Dirk scrolled from week to week on the screen. He looked up when he heard Jon roar off down the track to the asparagus fields on the farm motor bike. Roger had borrowed Dirk's truck to take his tyre for repair in Fynberg, leaving Jon to use the battered old cross-country bike. As he had taken off, Jon had thought, *at least Sebete and Moriti are in the hills with Malakabe.* Both dogs hated the bike and tried to bite the tyres whenever the engine roared to life making for perilous balancing when taking off.

Going back to the screen, Dirk did a double take when he saw the resort had been booked for a whole week, including weekend, by the booking system. Previously there had only been one villa booked for the Christmas week. For Tom, who was visiting with Mandy and Kerry from England. They had moved there two years ago due to Tom's deteriorating health, convinced that he could get more progressive treatment overseas. Dirk often wondered if it was also an attempt to be closer to Clive and repair their relationship.

Although he did not recognise the name associated with the multiple bookings it was obviously legitimate as a large deposit had been paid. The system would not confirm any booking without a credit card payment. *Oh well,* he thought to himself, *no Christmas breaks in the hospitality business.*

Sliding off the bar stool in front of the screen, Dirk moved out onto the patio. In the distance he could see Jon and the workers. The long strip of asparagus fields, like a green snake in the dry brown veld, followed the winding course of the stream, all that was left of the river that once flowed through the valley. His gaze rose up into the hills above. He could not see Pat or the boys and their dogs, but he knew they would be up there somewhere.

Dirk looked towards the dam and decided he would walk down and make sure the emergency pipes they had installed in the dam wall in case of fire were unclogged and the stopcocks functioning.

He smiled to himself as he thought how the person who had made him think about this precaution was the same person who had saved them from the robbers a few weeks ago. Good old Bonniface, our guardian angel behind the scenes.

Later, seeing Dirk at the dam wall, Jon waved from where he was in the asparagus fields with the workers. Dirk waved him over and he raised both hands, fingers spread, indicating he would be over in ten minutes.

Alongside Jon, a woman was giving instructions to some of the workers. It was his sister Gombi. She had worked on the asparagus project for two years and Dirk had recently suggested to Jon he give her a chance to be his understudy. As the project expanded, they might need a second supervisor, especially with Jon getting involved on the bookkeeping side of things. Bonniface's grin was even broader than usual when his wife teased him that the family business was getting bigger.

***

On the main street of Fynberg, smiling ruefully as his hand recovered from Koos' vice-like handshake, Roger was getting an update on the goings on in the town. After being away Roger, was enjoying Koos' thick Afrikaans accent.

"You remember that father of Marta's? He forgot it's not the way anymore, you can't *sommer* go around punching people. So, he got charged for assault. Ended up in jail for three months. Couldn't pay his fine. Dirk's sister refused to take his case even after he applied to the Justice Centre in Bloemfontein for legal aid. His wife buggered off as well. Left him for some guy in Jo'burg. Ag, poor Marta, living with such a Pa," Koos said shaking his head. "People say he slaps her around. If he did it in front of me, it would be the last slap he gave anyone. But it's not my business. *Jy weet, ou Roger.*"

Roger suggested she might be better off if she could get a job at the resort. Be with her friend Marie maybe. Dirk had good accommodation for staff, and they got free board. He said he would ask Dirk if he had anything. The next instant he thought his ribs were cracking in the bear hug Koos was giving him.

"Jong Roger, you're a good oke. Always look out for people. That would save the girl. Listen *broer* I must go. Blerry cows will burst if I don't get the milking going. See

274

you again, hey," Koos laughed, slapping him affectionately on the shoulder so hard Roger staggered briefly. He waved as Koos roared off in his bakkie and continued up the main street trying to find Lerryn's office. Typical of a small town, the first person he asked responded, "Yes, the lawyer with the red hair, very good, she'll get you off. The building next to the hotel, up there."

Easing his way through several people with anxious expressions, Roger went up to the reception desk behind which a sign said 'Lenbruikte and Belmorjon, Attorneys'.

He was about to ask for Lerryn, when he heard her behind him, laughing, "Well, look what the cat dragged in. Roger, good to see you after all this time."

They had just sat down in Lerryn's office littered with manila folders, when Marin burst through the door looking distraught. She stopped in her tracks when she saw Roger, and putting on a smile gave him a brief hug. Turning away she said, "Sorry Roger, shit, Lerryn have a look at this. Just arrived from the Justice Centre in Bloemfontein."

"Can it wait a few minutes? Rogers been away for years." Lerryn laughed.

"All the better Roger is present when you see that," Marin said, waving her finger at the folder.

Smiling an apology to Roger, Lerryn reluctantly opened the folder to the first page. It was a request from the

Justice Centre in Bloemfontein, to provide legal aid to three prisoners being held in the local charge office. For an armed robbery, including assault, at Caracal Ridge Resort.

"Fuck," was all she could manage.

"*Yeah,* fuck, I'll say," said Marin.

They both turned on Roger. *This happened over a week ago. Were you already here, Roger? If you were, you are also in trouble.* They were talking at once. *Unlike lawyers surely*, Roger observed as he squirmed uneasily in his chair.

"Two things. Dirk wanted to avoid the guests knowing about it, so we have all been trying to act normally. Maybe too normally. It all ended well so there was no need to worry anybody else about it. I think Pat and Dirk just wanted to get over it, in their own way before having to engage in conversation about it. How am I doing," Roger asked hopefully.

"Not well. We'll see you tonight. Lots of questions," Lerryn said. Picking up the file she handed it to Marin, "Conflict of interest, right?"

"I'll send it back," nodded her practice partner. "See you later, Roger."

Back on the main street on his way to collect his tyre, Roger reflected on his unfortunate timing. He suddenly felt relieved that he was on his way back to Jo'burg in the morning. He wondered what this week's job interviews would bring.

***

Back at the farm, after putting his repaired wheel back into his brother-in-law's trunk, Roger strolled around looking for Dirk. The weekend being well past there were very few guests around, so in the absence of Dirk, or an unsuspecting guest being available for a chat, Roger decided to nosy around the currently deserted asparagus factory to keep himself amused. The workers must all be in the fields with Jon he thought.

Walking slowly through the rows of tables he let his fingers run over several of the newly sealed cardboard cartons. Each box was about six inches high and he guessed they could probably each take about three layers of asparagus trays similar to what one bought in a supermarket. Each was proudly stamped, 'PRODUCT OF CARACAL RIDGE FARM, SOUTH AFRICA', an outline of a mountain range in the background.

At the end of one table he noticed a carton that had not yet been sealed. He flapped the lid open to see if his estimation was correct. Absent-mindedly lifting the top tray of asparagus, he saw a second layer of the same thing below it. Lifting the second as well, he was taken aback at small flat pillow like plastic bag that lay below. Mainly because it was full of what looked like dry, green grass cuttings. Marijuana?

Unable to resist, he did a quick scout around and sure enough he found the large bag of grass stored at the back. Opening it he was smacked in the face by the pungent aroma. Definitely grass.

In the bar, Roger gratefully accepted a coffee offered by Marie and headed out to the patio to sit down and try and absorb what he had discovered. In the distance he could make out what must be Dirk and Jon near the dam. The surface shimmered and shone like it did the day he and Georgie had arrived all those years ago.

Well, I'll be damned, he thought. Who would have guessed? A perfect scheme, if not illegal. The thing you launder your illegal proceeds through, actually rides piggyback with your product. The asparagus payments more or less return your proceeds from the grass to you clean. Then, on top of it, you have the resort right here to launder money through as well. Brilliant.

***

Down at the dam, Dirk and Jon were weighing up what their next move should be concerning fire protection for their crops and buildings.

"Losing these plants in a fire would set us way back, Jon. You have them up to multiple harvests now. It would take at least three years to get back to that point if we lost them. The grass is OK, that grows like weed." They both chuckled. "This next shipment will bring in enough funds to build additional villas and the new school and community centre Malakabe is after."

"Letting some water flow from here and running the sprinklers permanently over the asparagus immediately we see any approaching blaze should work," Jon suggested. "Mind you, the flames can get big. All the embers."

"Yes, you're right," Dirk said. "I think we should make sure. I know it's risky, but if there is no wind tomorrow, we should burn a fire break from the stream about two hundred metres up the hill, all the way along the stream from here. Look who's here to give some ideas." The boys and Moriti came running up the grass embankment of the dam wall.

Jon said, "*Na u ile ua lahleheloa ke Malakabe?* (did you lose Malakabe?)"

"No," Gaza panted. "She told us to come back to you because she was going higher."

Vula said, "*O re tlameha ho tlisa Moriti* (She said we must bring Moriti)"

"Yes, well he is also only a young *umfaan*," Jon teased.

Dirk said they should head off back to the house so he could call Alan and see if he could help with the fire break the following day. As they started up the track, they spotted Roger coming towards them through the asparagus fields. They met with him about halfway up. Roger said he had wanted to let him know Lerryn and Marin were coming over and they were on the war path. He did not mention he had noticed there seemed to be as many marijuana plants in the many acres of asparagus fields as there were asparagus plants.

Instead, looking up to the top of the track he said, "Speak of the devil." Lerryn's car was just turning into the resort car park.

***

Lerryn and Marin were not sure whether they were seeking retribution for being left out of the loop, or reassurance that everyone was alright at the farm. In any event, when they closed the office that evening they headed straight to Caracal Ridge.

Having been pre-warned by Roger of the wrath that awaited them, Pat and Dirk decided to play the sympathy card. This would be backed up by how the growing spirit of the Caracal Ridge community had been highlighted during the incident.

It worked to a certain extent. Lerryn fussed over Pat's scalp, saying she should have had stitches and she would be lucky if she did not have a bald patch in her beautiful red mane. "They will call you *Moriri* (bald) instead of *Malakabe*." Marin had to accept the fact that as Gaza and Vula had no idea anything had even happened, didn't even wake up, it was likely that had Annah been at the farm she would have been safe.

After dinner and farewell hugs for Roger as he was on his way back to Jo'burg, Pat and Dirk walked the two lawyers to their car. They needed to get back to Fynberg as Marin's babysitter was called at the last minute and Lerryn had a case to prepare for in the morning.

"You look pretty down, girl," Lerryn said, hugging her twin sister. "It must have been traumatic."

"Nah, it's not that. Well a bit of that, I suppose. It's more the caracals. I am terrified what will happen if there's a fire. Our mother has two kittens. They are far too small to keep up, to follow her to safety at pace or if she has to climb the mountain to escape the flames," Pat said.

"It probably will never happen," Dirk said. "They have been through similar dry seasons without a fire many times."

"Let's hope so," Marin said, as she waved goodbye to the two boys at their bedroom window. They ducked down when Pat looked around to see who Lerryn was waving at. "Little scamps," she said with a smile.

***

Roger had just settled into his drive home when he saw the burnt-out wreck of a vehicle on the side of the road. There were police and ambulance crew on the scene already and he was waved on by one of the policemen. What did catch his attention though was how the grass was burning and had spread some distance from the wreck already. He estimated they must be about twenty kilometres from the farm as the crow flies. Nonetheless, he resolved to stop in Brandfort and give Dirk a call just in case.

Wow, what a week it had been. Never mind the attack last weekend, now Dirk the 'drug lord'? He threw back his head, thumped the steering wheel with one hand and yelled, "Oh, fuck!"

Georgie's jigsaw puzzle expression suddenly popped into his head. He remembered his thoughts about this when they first visited the farm. She knew Dirk from way back. Her expression, as she listened to him talk about the farm and his plans, during that weekend. Had her intuition been taking her here. To what he had discovered yesterday.

Roger wondered if the idea of sending marijuana with the asparagus had come from Dirk's school mate contact in Holland. For decades, smoking of grass was allowed in cafes in the Netherlands, but not the growing of the plant. His friend already had a brisk business supplying quality produce, including Caracal Ridge asparagus. If the cafés had demand for it, why not grass? Being ex-South African, Dirk's friend knew he would be able to grow it on the farm easily and at low cost, given the abundant cheap labour.

Roger tried putting a positive spin on his discovery. Was Dirk's wrongdoing only one of breaking the law as an illegal grower. He was not a *dealer* was he? And the drug was going to a place where it was legal to use it anyway.

And if the funds arising were being used back here for the good of an under-privileged community? He hadn't seen anyone driving new BMWs on the farm, had he? Wearing Ray-Bans? He laughed out loud at the image of Dirk and Jon alighting from a big, black, shiny BMW in sunglasses.

Roger remembered how insistent Dirk was that marijuana would be legalised in the not too distant future. For both medical and recreational purposes. He wondered how the judge who had nearly convicted Dirk five or so years ago would feel about this argument nowadays? Would he still *commend* Dirk? Roger smiled to himself.

Later, as he cradled the phone in a public call box that clearly doubled as a urinal, Roger was thinking his next call would need to be to Georgie to bring her up to speed. He was not looking forward to that. Probably a big overreaction coming. "Not going back to that country. Too dangerous."

Coming back to the present and his call to Dirk, Roger was still quite surprised at how seriously Dirk seemed to take his message about the fire he had seen. Saying he needed to check a few things he had hung up abruptly. Not even a goodbye.

As he left Brandfort behind and picked up speed, Roger thought, oh well, better start thinking about your job interviews this week. But his mind kept wandering back to the grey-green plastic bag lying snugly below two layers of fresh green asparagus. Travelling companions to Europe. Sharing the same bunk. As his mind finished replaying that scene, he let it play over past events at the farm, those that had been grass-related. Poor old Brad came into his mind. The photographs of Jon and Dirk's marijuana plants near the house he had taken for the drug squad. He remembered how apprehensive Jon seemed that afternoon when Brad insisted they detour to the vegetable garden. Suddenly Roger's heart missed a beat. He found himself gripping the steering wheel really tightly. Jon was the first one on the scene when Brad crashed through the window that night. Roger remembered wondering how Jon had managed to cut his hand just easing Brad from his side onto his back. *Oh boy, Roger, now you are getting seriously paranoid*, he said to himself. *A bit melodramatic don't you think?* But he could not get his mind away from the scene in front of the smashed window, Dirk and Jon exchanging looks over Brad's still body.

***

Following Roger's call, Dirk phoned Cor to see if he had any reports on fires in the area. Nothing. Dirk told him what he had heard from Roger about the accident and Cor said he would keep an eye on any developments there. Later calls from other farmers like Dirk would soon tell him that the out-of-control fire, driven by a strong wind was heading in the direction of Caracal Ridge at pace. Late that evening, he phoned Dirk to warn him.

"Look anything can happen with wind changes but I think you should take precautions. At least send the little ones to town. To your sister." Dirk said good idea, he would talk to Pat right away.

***

It appeared above the mountains a few nights later as the sun went down. A red ominous glow, growing larger and more intense as darkness descended. Light dimming in Caracal Ridge's natural amphitheatre to reveal, centre stage the main actor, fire. This tragedy to be played out against a backdrop of tinder-dry veld grass, the towering mountains curtains already drawn.

Standing on the patio overlooking this unfolding scene, Pat thought that her cats, from their high positions in the mountains, must already be able to see the flames in the distance that were creating the glow. Watching as the flames climbed the hills on the opposite side ready to breach the summit and descend towards the farm. Was her mother cat and her young with them, watching those flames? She folded her arms around her, trying not to let intense anxiety morph into all out panic.

Walking through the door onto the patio Dirk said, "Cor says latest reports indicate it will reach us by tomorrow. Unless a miracle." He put his arm around Pat's shoulder. "Don't worry, sis, these cats have been fending for themselves since the beginning of time. They will find a way."

"With two kittens in tow?" Pat murmured. "They're too big for her to scruff and carry to high ground and too small to jump to a ledge themselves."

Jon came panting through the sandstone gate. He said he had been sending word out all afternoon telling the families who lived on the farm they could come up to the

286

community centre for shelter tomorrow if needed and if they wished. Most were saying no, they knew what to do.

"I just turned the sprinklers on so overnight they can soak as much of the ground as possible, and the foliage. There was a troop of baboons in the asparagus. Moving not eating though. Going to high ground to get away from the fire I think."

***

Dirk and Pat were on the patio early after a sleepless night. The morning's sunrise revealed an intensely blue sky pierced by a huge pyro cumulous cloud rising above the mountains. Normally formed by warm, rising air from a fire that condenses when it gets high enough. Below it, out of sight to the three nervous observers, would be the smoke which they would see as the fire got closer to the mountain skyline, ready to move into the valley through the gullies running down into it.

"Clouds like that have even been known to form storms. That would be my miracle," Dirk said. In the distance the sprinklers shot circulating jets of sparkling water across the asparagus fields. A happy contrast to the dark foreboding cloud rising above them. Beyond the fields, more or less following the winding stream bolstered by the water they had released, was the black fire break that Dirk and Alan had created a week ago.

By mid-morning the smoke could be seen spilling over the tops of some of the mountains. Pat and Dirk had not moved from the patio. Standing, silently transfixed by the unfolding potential catastrophe. Pat had sent the boys into town to stay with Marin. Just in case the fire did jump the firebreak and wet areas they had created along the stream and actually come all the way up and engulf the farmhouse and surrounding buildings.

Pat slumped down onto a chair, shoulders drooping. "What am I going to do. I can't just sit here not knowing." Dirk was surprised. It was second time he had seen tears running down his sister's face in just a few weeks. He could not remember when he had seen her so distraught before.

He put his hand on her shoulder. "It will be OK. She's a survivor that cat." They both turned as they heard the sound of a trail bike pull up the other side of the sandstone wall. Dirk thought it must be Jon. Maybe he had some good news.

To their surprise it was Alan who came running through the opening in the sandstone wall. "Bonniface just came down from the hill. He went to fetch a cow that had wandered off yesterday. It was too dark to find her, so he left it until this morning. He says he saw your mother cat and her cubs at the cave."

Pat sprang up like she had been pricked with a needle. "What?"

"He said you would know the cave. I figure if she has taken them in there to shelter from the fire, all we need to do is cover the entrance so the smoke can't get in and she and the cubs will be safe. They can survive a few hours without food or water."

"We? What do you mean we?" Pat asked looking away to check on the fire. The smoke was visible now.

"I have some old fireproof insulation cladding that was lying around in the barn. Here, in my backpack. We can get there and back on my bike if we get on with it. Let's go, Pat."

Ignoring Dirk's comment that she was taking a big risk, Pat rushed inside to grab a torch. Cave and torch seemed synonymous to Pat in the moment. She found one which she threw into a small backpack left lying on one of the boy's beds. Alan was astride the roaring trail bike waiting. Pat climbed onto the back. "Hang on tight, it's going to be a rough ride," he called out above the sound of the engine.

Descending down the track at breakneck speed they passed the dam, slowing only slightly across the rocky stream and started bouncing and skidding up the slope through the long grass to the cave, Pat shouting directions into Alan's ear. It seemed only the other day she was making him jump to dodge a trap she had thrown in anger at his feet in his doorway. Now here she was, clinging for dear life to him, yelling in his ear, unable to avoid pushing her cheek into his neck and hair. They could smell the smoke now.

When they skidded to a stop near the cave entrance, a troop of chacma baboons watched them, looking agitated. Once Alan switched off the motor, they seemed to calm down and continued on their way, much to Pat's relief. "They're making their way to high ground, Jon says."

Alan tried to see if he could look into the cave. To make sure the cats were in there. He tried to make the entrance bigger, to squeeze through. When he stood back, frustrated, Pat did not waste any time. The smoke smell was getting stronger.

Gripping the sandstone ledge above the cave entrance she supported herself as she slid her legs into the opening of the cave. In years gone by, the entrance must have been much bigger but some of the boulders that had rolled down the hill after plummeting from the side of the mountain above had ended up here, lodged in front of the entrance.

She could barely slide through, there was no way Alan would have made it. Not without some kind of machinery to move a few of the boulders.

Once through, she turned until she was on her knees and able to reverse into the wider opening beyond. As she moved backwards, she noticed the small *boma* she and Bonniface had built out of rocks to keep in one place, at the cave entrance, the very cat she was going into the cave to find. It was still intact after all these years.

"Are you OK?" Alan asked, on his haunches, looking helpless.

"I will be if I see you again in a while." Trying to assuage her growing fear by being facetious Pat said, "If I'm not back in a day, call my mum." With that, she disappeared from view and, as they had planned, Alan began to collect as many small boulders as he could find.

It was very dim in the cave. Limited light came from the small cave entrance. Oh shit, the torch, Pat murmured. She crawled back to the entrance. "Alan, Alan. The torch. In my backpack," she called. She took it from his outstretched hand and turned back towards the cave passage. A few metres in, she could crouch and move slowly forward without crawling.

Pat stopped after every step and listened. She did not use the torch for fear of panicking the caracals, if they were indeed in here. Another step and listen. Nothing. As she completed her third step, she heard the rustle. Maybe pebbles? She listened. Hoping to hear a meow from a kitten in the darkness. Or an angry hiss and spit from a protective mother. That's all she needed to confirm. Then a quick flash of the torch to make sure they were all there and she could go.

Pat listened. Nothing. She took a half step. Nothing. Then she thought she heard something. Impatient to see her cats she switched on the torch. The snake was a metre from her face, half its body vertical, poised to strike. Pat screamed as she fell back on her backside. In the beam of the torch lying next to her she could see the glistening white fangs of the black Mamba buried in the toe of her boot. It seemed like slow motion as it withdrew its fangs, recoiled, ready to repeat the strike. The split second before the second strike seemed like slow motion as Pat, transfixed in terror, saw the snake suddenly disappear from view. Grabbing the torch from where it had fallen alongside her, she waved it around in panic wanting to see where her attacker was readying itself for her. Finally, she saw it. Just it's long black shiny body, thrashing around, throwing ancient bone fragments lying on the cave floor in all directions. She could not see the snake's head. To her delight what Pat saw instead was one black tufted ear and one brown one pointing towards her as the caracal mother growled, head bowed almost into the dirt, her incisors holding the throat of the snake in a suffocating death grip. The snake was still moving when the kittens, now full of bravado, pounced on the body.

"Pat, Pat are you OK? What happened. Shit, answer me." Alan shouted trying to get his head and shoulders into the cave entrance.

"I'm OK," Pat gasped, as she handed Alan the torch. "She saved *my* life this time. Oh, and just so we can avoid the awkwardness when you pull me out of this hole and I am able to burst into tears, I have wet my pants." Pat remembered all those years ago when the boy on the bus wet his pants. Embarrassing, but it was about to get worse.

The only way Alan could get Pat out through the entrance was to get down on his knees and haul her upwards towards and over his chest. This entailed putting his hands under her now very sweaty arms, taking her weight and pulling her gently towards him. By the time she was out they were face on face, Pat astride a prone Alan in her wet pants like she was a jockey urging her horse through a last furlong.

She was shocked at how intense the smoke had become in the few minutes she had been in the cave. There was no time for awkwardness or the tears she had expected. They quickly moved the old fireproof cladding into place over the cave entrance and began piling Alan's collection of boulders and stones over it. In between gasps she gave Alan a synopsis of what had transpired in the cave. "Jesus, Pat. I've seen one those guys, angered by something, probably been stood on, take out two cows in a meadow in as many minutes. Dropped them like stones. You were extremely lucky."

They looked upwards together as the first crackling, snapping of the fire was born on the increasing wind blowing down the hill from the heat to the cooler air below.

Alan got the bike started as Pat grabbed her backpack and jumped on behind him. Holding him tightly from behind as the bike bounced off.

***

Bouncing over rocks in the stream below the embankment
that formed the wall of the dam they saw Dirk and Jon
busy opening the stopcocks to run more water into the
stream. It gushed down towards them, spreading through
the rocks that had been isolated from the river water for a
long time. Alan stopped the bike for a few moments to
shout to Dirk they had been successful at the cave. Sitting
on the back still with arms around Alan, unnecessary as
they were stationery, Pat looked to the side, downstream.
She was amazed to see so many animals making their way
across the stream or just hanging out near the water in the
damp areas. Jackals and dassies, predator and prey, in
close proximity. The desire to survive the fire distracting
them from their normal instincts. Further above the
stream, Pat saw there were more buck than she would ever
have guessed existed in these hills congregating in the
damp, cool asparagus fields. Looking back, they could see
the flames in the gullies now. Alan revved the bike and
they headed up the track to the farmhouse. Dirk and Jon
followed them, some distance back on the farm's old trail
bike, Sebete and Moriti snapping at the tyres.

Back on the patio, they watched the unfolding devastation.
Marie stood arm in arm with Pat. Thomas stood silently,
wringing his hands in his apron. It was calmer in the
valley so the fire had slowed, but nonetheless moved
forward relentlessly. Like an ocean wave in slow motion,
the wall of red with a trail of smoke rising behind it,

294

moved down the hillside towards the firebreak and stream. In its wake, it left a black carpet dotted with the occasional smouldering patch and grey-white sandstone boulders now stark against the dark background. There were also islands of undergrowth that inexplicably had not burnt, small knolls of veld grass that were intact. Pat thought they must be unexpected, welcome havens for some terrified animals. Rabbits most likely.

It was the time of reckoning. All the staff had now stopped work and were spread across the front lawn, Marin's garden, to watch the final act. Even the few midweek guests were on the patio, video cameras held high. Dirk had warned them of the huge risk should the grass on this side of the fire break catch, but they all insisted they would see it through.

Silence fell over the group of observers as the closest line of fire neared the fire break. And then a small cheer as a break appeared for the first time in the solid line of red that had been descending unchecked down the hillside. This first break began to grow wider and other similar breaks appeared as Dirk and Alan's fire break did its job. They were lucky. The wind was not strong enough to blow any burning embers, flaming arrows, across the stream and wet asparagus fields into the dry veld grass on this side.

A large brace of duiker, thrown together by the only escape route from the inferno, were already contentedly nibbling on the lush green leaves of the marijuana plants that grew amongst the asparagus plants. Almost hidden in the ferns they occasionally raised their heads to stare up at the blackened hillside that had once been their home, small tails wagging away flies. Wary, perhaps conscious of the potential for fire to flare up where the remaining pockets of smoke drifted lazily from dying embers of burnt thorn trees that used to dot the hillside.

***

Pat and Alan did not have to wait long. They sat alongside Alan's trail bike, hearing the metallic clicks as the exhaust pipe and engine cooled. They had moved the rocks, still hot from the passing fire, away from the cave's entrance and, for fear of frightening the cats, pushed the bike about two hundred metres away from the cave without starting the engine. Pat watched the entrance through her binoculars in silence. Occasionally, when her arms ached, she lowered them and handed the binoculars to Alan so they would not miss even the briefest sighting.

Pat massaged her arms and folded them around her knees trying not to think the worst. That smoke had seeped into the cave. She gazed up the black slope, nothing moved except smoke still drifting from isolated embers. The blackness made her think of the snake. What if there was another? That got the mother while she was finishing off its mate. That an inexperienced kitten tried to tackle. What if the mother had panicked when she found she couldn't get out of the cave, went deeper with her young and couldn't find her way back? Tears made pathways down her cheeks, black from the sooty dust thrown up by the trail bike.

"Yes!" She jumped at Alan's sudden exclamation.

As he watched, a kitten had appeared at the entrance. Pat, sobbing and laughing now, saw Mother follow shortly after, the second kitten close behind her, *almost touching her,* Alan said, binoculars to his eyes still. They were no good to Pat at that moment, her eyes full of tears.

The caracal seemed bemused by the change that had taken place in her environment. They watched as she sniffed the air, listening intently, trademark swivelling ears turning this way and that. Even from this distance, Pat could see that one black ear she knew so well.

After a few minutes the caracal decided to return to the cave, kittens still close by her side. The one that had come out first was still sniffing at the warm rocks. *Why go back? This is fun, smelling warm rocks*, Pat was thinking when mother reappeared, scruffed her and disappeared from view again.

"I think she's playing it safe. Going to give it a few more hours before making any trips. She knows what she's doing. The main thing is they are all safe. Thank you, Alan."

"I enjoyed the adventure," he laughed. "So, I'm forgiven? You know, my traps."

"Yes, you are."

"I would still love to know where they disappeared to, one after another," he frowned.

Pat smiled to herself, wondering if the day would come when she let him into Bonniface's secret. When it would be considered an amusing incident.

This time the ride back to the farm was slower and more casual, but Pat found she was still holding on to Alan, enjoying the confidence she got from feeling him lean easily with the trail bike as they wound down the fire-blackened hillside. She was happy. Things had turned out well for her cats. She hoped the others had all been safe, with the baboons, in the high areas they both chose.

Chapter 11

Coming Home

The email Georgie received from Tom a few months before Christmas was not a surprise. She and Kirsten had visited him and Mandy to say goodbye before she left to return to South Africa. Kirsten was only eighteen months old so Kerry, now nine, immediately slipped into the role of mother, guiding the toddler around the garden. England was enjoying one of her Indian summers and they were sitting on the patio, which enabled her to keep an eye on her daughter as she stumbled around the garden.

Tom had been telling her how his relationship with Clive had improved since they had moved to the UK. "So much so that I have decided to have everybody together for Christmas. Reunite him with his brother and sisters. Given the weather and the fact that most of the family are in South Africa I have booked out Dirk's place for the week leading up to Christmas." He always called the farm, 'Dirk's place', never by its name. "Dirk knows Mandy and I, and Kerry of course, are going to be there anyway," he said, putting his hand on Mandy's hand. That's new thought Georgie. "But he has no idea who has booked out the entire place yet. Told me as much."

Tom went on to tell Georgie that he would be delighted if she and Roger would come as well as his guests. He felt she was almost one of his daughters, which brought an unexpected, surreptitious dab of a tissue to the corner of Georgie's eye.

Sitting in front of her computer reading now, she had felt a slight twinge. Foreboding, yes, but also excitement at seeing the entire Lenbruikte family again. Clive she had not seen for over ten years. The others? it was at least four years, although she had spent time with Eve in the UK. And Rita? She had been a second mother to her in those days when she was still with Dirk, and regularly in the Lenbruikte home.

Georgie was also looking forward to being in a community environment again. Although she had loved England, she had missed her friends, her network and any chance of building an extended family. By all accounts

Caracal Ridge was becoming just *that,* and Georgie looked forward to experiencing it. Being part of a community was something that played on her mind more and more lately. She had tried to discuss it with Roger a few times, but he seemed nonplussed at being in anything but a private environment. Georgie thought he must picture it as being back in his army days when he huffed about *living with a whole lot of strangers.*

Georgie had been back in South Africa two months when the email from Tom arrived. Of course, it immediately took her back to the day she visited them in England. For a while her thoughts stayed with England and her home there. It had been a good summer that final year, but she could imagine how winter must be closing in, being just a few months before Christmas. The betting shops would already be giving odds on it snowing on Christmas day. It never did. Just grey and gloomy and cold.

***

Kirsten had loved the warm sunny days of Jo'burg since they had arrived. Their rented house did not have a pool, but Roger had set up a small plastic splash pool for her which was more than adequate. She loved it. She still refused to wear anything but her Wellingtons though, unless she was actually in the water. *Old habits die hard,*

Roger laughed. *They got her through some cold wet days in England.*

Their neighbours loved seeing her in her tiny swimming costume and gumboots. The black maids in the area called her their gumboot girl.

"Show us your *umdanso wami*, gumboot girl," they called to her when they passed her playing in the front garden.

Roger knew this was in reference to the legacy of gumboot dancing, a popular Sunday recreation in the various mine compounds. It was the one highlight in a miserable, grimy backbreaking week for the poorly paid mineworkers on the one day they did not have to disappear into the bowels of the earth to get the 'white man's gold'. Exciting, warlike dancing, always done in mineworkers gumboots, decorated for the occasion. Over the years, gumboot dancing found its way out of the mines and into mainstream culture. *In the darkest hour, rhythm and joy found a way,* Roger reflected.

Sometimes when they passed by, the maids would break into an impromtu mine dance for Kirsten, raising their knees high and stamping them down whilst singing a rythmic chant. Kirsten would wriggle around and stamp her feet completely out of time and uncordinated, sending them into howls of laughter followed by affectionate hand clapping which the little girl joined in with.

Tom's children, his brothers, his ex-wife Rita and Marin received the same email. It arrived the same day Georgie got hers. It invited each of them and their partners to join Tom and Mandy for a week of relaxed catching up and Christmas celebration at Caracal Ridge. To join in the first complete family gathering since the siblings had all grown up and gone their separate ways. It was to be a celebration of the family and extended family's close ties and their diverse richness.

The email was also not a total surprise for Dirk who wondered who'd made the reservation for Tom.

After the fire, Dirk had decided he was going to capitalise on their lucky break and organise some fire insurance in case it happened again. Jumping into the old farm bakkie he headed into Fynberg to chat with Marin and Lerryn about what the best approach should be and to find out who a good insurance broker was in the town. He had agreed with Marin he would collect Annah at the same time for a visit to the farm. Now the fire threat was over she could enjoy time with the boys and the dogs. Dirk was beginning to enjoy his time with her as well, now that she was older and curious about everything she saw, especially on their farm walks. His relationship with Marin was much better too, and there was the odd time their eyes met for longer than was natural for friends. *Who knows what's down the line*? he thought.

It had been a while since he had visited the town, but his truck was recognised by many of the locals who waved as he drove up the main street. Stopping near the one decent café in town, he parked and strolled across the road. Entering the café, he waved at the owner behind the counter. "Hey Pete, what's up?"

"Not a lot Dirkie, it's Fynberg you know," Pete shrugged. "And you? Fire missed you we heard. Great result."

"News travels fast."

"Oh yeah. Well Marta is Marie's buddy remember. She told us all about it," Pete said throwing his thumb over his shoulder at a young waiter serving a table behind him.

Dirk recognised Marta although he had not seen her for years. She had recently come up in a conversation with Roger after he had visited Fynberg to fix his tyre just before the fire. She apparently lived in a very unhappy environment with her father. He had told Roger he would talk to Marie about it, but then the fire had distracted him, and he had forgotten all about it.

Marta came across with a smile, "Hello, Dirk. How are you? Do you remember me? Marta. Marie's friend. What can I get you?'

Roger was shocked. She looked drained. What happened to the sparkling eyes and the cheeky, flirtatious smile?

"Of course, I do, Marta. Just a black coffee, thanks."

"Sure thing," she smiled and turned away.

Dirk was just about to drive off in the direction of Lerryn's offices when he heard a tap on his passenger window. It was Marta. As he leant across and wound the window down, she said, "Dirk, sorry, would you mind very much if I asked you something?"

"No, jump in," he said, opening the passenger door.

Marta only got half a word out before she burst into tears. Dirk patted her arm gently, "OK, take it slowly. Just tell me how I can help."

It was much as Roger had said. A nightmare situation at home with her father. No one to turn to, nowhere to go. No money other than what she earned as a waiter.

"Do you not have a job, any job, for me at the farm? Like Marie? She says I could share her room," Marta finished with a laugh. "I have to get away, Dirk."

Dirk had been thinking about taking on a junior for reception work and general marketing stuff but had intended to offer the role to one of the farm locals.

"OK, I will talk to Marie and Jon about where we could use you. But it will only be a low salary to start. Free board and lodging though. What about your Dad? Will he agree?"

"I'm twenty-one now, I can do as I please. I don't need a lot if I have free board. Just money for clothes."

"OK, call Marie and organise it with her. Tell her what I said."

Marta burst into tears again, this time she had a smile on her face as she gave Dirk an awkward sideways hug in the cramped cab of the truck. "Thanks so much, Dirk. I will phone Marie right now. I'm so happy," she said, as she closed the door and ran back to the café.

Boy, am I going to be enemy number one with her father and Pete, Dirk thought, *as he drove off in the direction of his sister's legal practice.*

The young woman sitting in front of the 'Lenbruikte and Belmorjon Attorneys' sign in reception beamed when she saw Dirk. "Hello, Dirk. *U phela joang* my friend." She was Jon's cousin and a great fan of what was transpiring at Caracal Ridge. How is Malakabe?"

"We are both well, Jean. How are you?"

"I am very happy now I hear the fire did not get you. My Uncle Bonniface, I think, saved you with his warnings?"

"Yes, Jean, maybe he did. Maybe he did," Dirk smiled, shaking his head with both hands raised in salute.

"I will tell them the other lawyer is here," she flung over her shoulder with a laugh, as she bounced down the hall to the offices. She doesn't miss a trick, that one, Dirk smiled to himself.

***

Driving back to the farm Dirk was thinking what a success Lerryn and Marin had made of their legal practice. They were well thought of and their reputation had spread far and wide.

"Car coming, Daddy," brought him back from his thoughts, bringing a smile to his face.

He slowed and pulled off the road slightly to allow the oncoming taxi to pass. On this road it was prudent to give a taxi as much space as possible. The black taxi drivers were famous for their extremes. Often courteous, often reckless. Unusual he thought. Can't remember the last time we had a *taxi* bring anyone up to the farm.

***

The boys were in the parking area with the dogs when the taxi pulled up. They were excited to see the minivan with its white chequered stripes running down the sides and over the roof. The driver waved them over with a big grin. "Are those your horses young ones? Can you ride?" he asked them in Sotho, pointing at the paddock that housed the polo ponies.

"We are learning," Gaza said. Vula chimed in with, "I am better than him. Even Jon says so."

"Ah, so Jon's your teacher. I have seen him play polo. He must be a good teacher." With that he took off, tyres spinning in the loose dirt of the parking area. "*Tsamaea hantle bacha* (Go well young ones)," he waved.

As the taxi moved away, it revealed a woman standing with a small bag and a smile on her face.

"I am Zulu and I understood most of what you were saying, but maybe we should try English which I am sure you can speak," she said.

The boys liked her immediately, the way she spoke to them as if they were older than they were. Sebete and Moriti also liked her, wagging their tales, sniffing at her bag. She seemed nervous of the dogs though.

"*Tloo lintja, Sebete, Moriti, no* (Come away dogs)," the boys yelled in unison.

"My name is Timbi," the woman said. "Can you sit with me a while and tell me about yourselves and all the exciting things you do on the farm?"

"Let's sit down at the dam. It's nice down there for talking," Gaza said.

"Dam," was all Sebete needed to hear and he was on his way, Moriti right behind. The woman walked slowly, Gaza and Vula taking up positions either side of her, pointing and chatting non-stop. She laughed out loud once or twice at their comments.

***

When Dirk pulled up at the farmhouse the boys and their new friend were already some way down the track to the dam, and he did not notice them walking with the dogs. Lifting Annah out of the bakkie and the top-of-the-range child seat Marin had insisted on before allowing Dirk to take her in the vehicle, he said, "OK, darling, let's get you settled and have something to eat and drink before we find the boys."

"Yes, let's find Vula and Gaza," she laughed.

Pat walked into the big farmhouse kitchen as Dirk was tidying up after Annah's meal.

"Have you seen the boys anywhere. Can't find them or the dogs which means they have probably gone off somewhere out of voice range."

Picking Annah up, kissing her on the cheeks, Pat said, "And without permission, aren't they naughty boys, Annah. What do you think?" Annah smiled and held Pat's hair in her hand, examining a long red lock closely.

Looking through the window up towards the back gardens and the villas, Dirk said, "Annah and I were about to look for them ourselves."

After another ten minutes of calling and whistling, the boys and the dogs were still nowhere to be found. "They must be a long way away or Sebete would have come running at my whistle," Dirk said with a frown.

"Shit. The dam, of course. Let's go. They can't resist that dam," Pat said.

Within a few minutes they were rattling down the track to the dam, Pat wedged between Dirk and Annah in her car seat.

"There they are. Who the hell is that woman?" Pat said, much louder than necessary with the bouncing of the bakkie and a little panic still in her.

"I have no idea," Dirk said. "We did not have any guests scheduled to arrive today?"

The boys and their new friend were sitting at the top of the grassy embankment waving down at them when Dirk brought the bakkie to a stop below them.

"Annah, Annah," Gaza called. "Yay, you came to visit."

"Bring her up here," Vula called.

Pat, now out of the cab with her hands on her hips, said, "What do you two think you are doing leaving the house without permission? And at the dam?"

"You said the dam was OK if we came with an adult," Gaza protested. "This is our new friend Timbi, she's an adult."

"I'm sorry it is my fault," the tall, well-dressed woman said. She did not stand up.

"I asked them to sit with me and tell me about the farm. They said the dam was a nice place to sit, so I said please take me there then," Timbi said quietly.

The boys loved the way Timbi changed things just a little bit to protect them from Pat's wrath. "Sorry Malakabe," they chimed together.

"You only call me that when you are in trouble, right? Well you are. Come down and play with Annah for a bit so we can talk to Timbi."

Climbing up the grassy slope, Pat said, "Sorry, Timbi, I'm Pat and this is my brother Dirk. We did not expect any guests today otherwise someone would have been there to welcome you."

"No, don't worry, I did not have a need for a room. I am not staying, just visiting for a short time," Timbi said.

"Oh, I see," Pat said, exchanging glances with her brother. Dirk looked as perplexed as she. "What makes you want to visit us? For such a short time, when we don't know each other?"

Timbi smiled. "So, you are the famous Malakabe I heard about in the town. And from the taxi driver. You do know me, Pat. Or knew of me I suppose, although we never met."

Holding her hand out in the direction of the boys, now busy helping Annah back down the embankment she had tried to climb, Timbi said, "Vula and Gaza, they are the reason I am visiting."

Looking back to Pat, she said, "They are my sons."

Pat sat down on the grass alongside Timbi in a way that was only slightly less ungainly than a fall. As Timbi began her explanation, Pat's mind was racing. *She's come for her kids, as is her legal right, of course. I never thought of this. What could I have done? I should have asked Lerryn for advice. Too late.*

312

Dirk had sat down as well, looking out over the asparagus fields, quietly rolling a smoke without saying anything.

***

Timbi had brought the kids to Pat and Gus years ago because she was destitute. Gus was getting payments from social services but giving nothing to her. Had it not been for her hardworking parents, they would have starved. Finally, she decided she had to take responsibility and change things for her and her boys.

The first part was to make sure the boys were looked after while she found a way to train and get a job. Hence Gaza and Vula being left at Pat and Gus's doorstep. There was huge unemployment in the country, even with affirmative action. After years of job reservation, when white people got first shot at jobs, black women were now at the top of the priority list to employ, followed by black males and then white people. But you nonetheless needed a skill to get a job.

After months of rejection, Timbi had finally stumbled upon a charity organisation that funded people training as teachers, a desperate need in a country catching up on decades of lost education for so many of its young people. She studied every night by the light of a candle for the entrance exam and made it. After being accepted at a teacher training college, which included accommodation, Timbi began her training and graduated after three years. "It was always my promise to myself," she told them, "that I would give up my boys if it was a sacrifice that would benefit them eventually. Once I achieved independence, I could go back and find them, able to look after them properly forever. Since graduating I have worked for a year now. I even have some money saved."

***

Below them on the track, the boys were holding Annah on Sebete's back like he was her pony. He didn't seem to mind, but kept walking off leaving her suspended in mid-air, screeching with laughter.

Timbi said, looking intently at Pat, "Two hours ago I got out of that taxi to collect my two sons. I told the taxi to come back at 7 o'clock. Now I will be leaving without them."

Pat's head, down as she picked blades of grass and let them blow away in the breeze, shot up. She looked directly into Timbi's eyes, which had not left her the whole time.

"Ah Malakabe, you have done a wonderful job as a mother. They have become two fine boys, loved and

314

disciplined. Look at them, how happy they are. They have told me all the things they do here, all the things they learn, all their friends. The dogs, the horses. Walking in the hills looking after your caracals. What mother would take them away from this to a township?"

"Dusty, polluted streets instead of hills and fields. Gangs instead of friends. People crammed into shanties. The electricity the ANC government has given us just helps to shed light on the squalor people live in. It will be a long time before my boys will be able to live like they live here."

Pat said, "You must tell them you are their mother. What you have done for them. That one day you will have your own house. I am sure. Let them decide."

"I will think about that tonight. I will decide before I come back tomorrow. I want to spend some more time with them, maybe I will tell them. Perhaps the time is not right?"

Dirk spoke for the first time. "You won't be 'coming back' Timbi, because tonight you stay here with us, as our guest. You can have one of the bigger villas and maybe the boys can stay with you. They will want Annah to be with them of course, so it might be a bit crowded," he laughed. "See you up at the house."

Tears were streaming down the cheeks of both Timbi and Pat. God, not again, Dirk smiled to himself as he jogged down against the slope of the dam embankment to load the kids and dogs onto the back of the truck. He thought the two women would enjoy a walk up the track together without him and the kids.

***

It was just after midnight when it came to Pat. The ideal solution, if she could just pull it off. She had been tossing and turning since going to bed. Walking back to the house that afternoon she and Timbi had concurred they should not tell the boys until they had agreed the best way forward. They would sleep on it and talk in the morning.

Over dinner they shared a few laughs over some Gus anecdotes, before Timbi took all three kids to her villa to tell them old Zulu folklore stories. Gaza knew he was Zulu, so his interest was piqued when she told him earlier, after the taxi had left, that she was Zulu. He wanted to know more Zulu people, and taking his lead from his older brother, so did Vula.   Annah was just happy to be included, to be with her two heroes.

The idea that had come to Pat needed Tom's help. It was only about ten in the evening in London, she would call him. Pat wanted to be confident in her proposed solution by tomorrow.

Tom was delighted to hear Pat's voice and, knowing his daughter, he was not surprised she dispensed with the pleasantries in rapid fire and launched into the reason for her call.

As he knew, she had started an informal school for Gaza and Vula that had grown into a much bigger 'informal' school that included kids from all around, and two untrained but very passionate teachers from the community of local mothers. If she had a formally trained teacher in place, and the right facilities, could she apply for a government grant? More importantly, could he leverage his contacts to make it happen?

Tom told Pat the best avenue was through the Schools Investment Fund which was supported not only by the government but several of the country's biggest companies. The biggest of which was People Mutual whose CEO was a very good friend of Tom's. Given the dire need for schools, and the fact that she had already had a working prototype, so to speak, Tom thought the Fund would fall over themselves to help. It was exactly what the Fund was formed to achieve, and they already had many independent schools under their wing. Tom said his friend was always waxing lyrical about what they had achieved. He would call him in the morning.

Pat was so excited she couldn't contain herself and a flood of words came out about her thoughts around building a community of foster homes alongside the school.

"Sounds interesting Pat, but first things first my girl. Let's see what tomorrow brings, hey?"

"Thanks Dad. Look forward to seeing you guys at Christmas."

Sleep came slowly to Pat that night as her mind raced ahead. She suddenly remembered Allan was coming over in the evening. With no sleep she would look a fright.

***

The following morning, she told Dirk about her idea, her late-night call to their father and his response. "I have no objection and if my other shareholder doesn't mind then go for it," Dirk said. "It will make the resort that much more newsworthy as far as I'm concerned. You could kill two birds with one stone."

It came out of the blue for Timbi, but Pat could see she was getting more excited by the minute as Pat explained her proposal. Over the next few months, Pat would attempt to bring the plan to fruition. Two or three months after Christmas it was planned Timbi would be living at Caracal Ridge with her sons. She would be the focal point of the new school. They resolved not to tell the boys that Timbi was their mother until everything was confirmed one way or the other. Having said that, they both suspected Gaza was already putting two and two together, although he had not said anything.

**

Pat was still surprised when the formal-looking letter with a Schools Investment Fund logo arrived, even though Tom had told her weeks ago the response from his friend at People Mutual had been positive. Maybe she just could not believe she might pull this off. She held her breath as she tore open the envelope and scanned the contents.

Yes, the Fund was interested in what she was doing and would be sending one of their investment analysts to visit her school. Was the 15th of November acceptable?

Pat was dizzy with excitement. Her mind raced over what had to be done. What the presentation of their school should look like. She needed help. Dirk was far too busy, but Alan responded to her call with enthusiasm. He had done a course at Uni that related directly to handling investment funding. He thought he would have a few ideas on what they might be looking for in a potential investment opportunity. The following day they started putting together a plan.

Chapter 12

Christmas at Caracal Ridge

Georgie looked over her shoulder at Kirsten strapped tightly in her car seat. She was fast asleep, her head to one side, blond hair dangling. Leaning into the back, Georgie propped a small pillow under her head, enjoying the smile that appeared for just a brief second before she continued her deep breathing. Putting her hand on Roger's shoulder for support she brought him back from one of his 'driving through endless maize fields' daydreams he had when he drove to the farm, and she said, "I know we have discussed this at length but given the circumstances and the timing, I think we should just let this drug thing of Dirk's and your other suspicions slip away, or at least park them until after this Christmas week at the farm. Is it really any of our business, anyway?"

"The drugs, maybe not, but Brad was my friend. Don't you think the honourable thing would be to at least share my thoughts with Dirk? Get some answers. Were Brad's accident and the drugs related? Was it an *accident*?"

"OK, OK, I understand your dilemma. But I know Dirk. He might be a lot of things, but he is not a crook. He is a pretty honourable guy. Seek an *explanation*, rather than seeming to ask him to vindicate himself and Jon for what appears to have transpired. Let him see your concern for *them* as well, not just Brad."

"You're right, as always. I will tread softly," Roger sighed.

The grass was green with regrowth, Roger noticed, as he passed the point where he had seen the fire he reported to Dirk many months ago. Helped by the spring rains, no doubt.

"This was where the fire started," he said to Georgie. "Remember the accident I mentioned I saw on my way back to Jo'burg after the farm?"

"Wow, it certainly covered a fair distance to the farm."

"Yes, and in just a few days," he replied.

He did not say anything when, further on, they drove past the garage just before the turn-off to Caracal Ridge. Georgie had freaked out when he had told her about the robbery. A diluted version down the telephone line to the UK. She was still sending him *I told you so* responses as he had tried to downplay the traumatic event with exaggerated descriptions of the robbers jumping around attached to the traps.

He put a strong positive spin on it, saying it showed why these things never happened where there was a happy community spirit between white owners and black communities, because it never ended well for the bad guys. This had been a one-off, an anomaly. *They had come all the way from Soweto for goodness sakes!*

Fortunately, Georgie had been distracted with the sale of the house and business in England and, as always happens, by the time she arrived back in South Africa, time had dulled things a bit.

The news of his drug find had also helped to distract her when it came to the subject of Caracal Ridge. Nonetheless, Sebete and Moriti would be sleeping outside their villa for the duration of their stay, their kennels having been moved there by an accommodating Dirk and Jon.

Kirsten was wide awake and pointing with glee at the polo ponies as they drove the last few hundred metres of the driveway up to the farmhouse. As they came to a stop in the parking area, Marta and Marie appeared with welcoming smiles.

"Oh, you've doubled up on the welcoming party, have you?" Roger laughed as he hauled Kirsten out of her car seat.

"I remember you two lovely ladies. The Cherry Festival dinner, at the restaurant," Georgie said.

"Marie and Marta," Marie said grinning, pointing at herself and then Marta. "Or as Pat says, 'the M&Ms'."

"Of course," Georgie gave each a hug.

***

Notwithstanding the warm greetings Roger and Georgie exchanged with Dirk and Jon, Roger found himself unconsciously on the lookout for signs of anything sinister. He teased himself for his paranoia, but it would not leave him.

They had arrived earlier than the rest of the family, so that first evening they were still part of a normal resort guest crowd. Kirsten stomped around the dining room in her gumboots much to the amusement of the guests before being tempted away by Gaza and Vula who took her to see the chickens. "Hope they don't tell her we'll probably

323

have eaten a few of them before we leave," Roger murmured to Georgie over their candle. She for her part was finding it difficult, in these congenial surroundings, to imagine the attempted robbery that had taken place in this very room, let alone any thoughts about a chicken's risky life. *That* night, Roger might have been under the very table they were sitting at. She unconsciously looked under it, bringing a look of puzzlement to Rogers face.

The following morning, leaning on the wooden rails of the polo pony paddock watching Jon give the boys their riding lesson, Roger decided it was time to raise his apprehensions with Dirk.

"Do you mind if I ask you something Dirk? It may make you laugh, or it may piss you off and if you want to, feel free to tell me to piss off and mind my own business."

"Wow, Roger, now you have me intrigued. Go for it, buddy, I'm not easily offended," Dirk said patting him on the shoulder.

Roger told him how he had stumbled on the neatly packed carton of asparagus with a bottom layer of marijuana in the packing room, and how it looked like mainstream export of drugs.

Roger said he guessed it was on its way to Amsterdam, to his mate, and that since it was legal there it might not look that bad?

"But still? Really, exporting drugs? Doesn't sound like you, Dirk," Roger almost pleaded.

Dirk sighed. "We kind of got sucked in. A bit of mother nature and a bit of serendipity," he said.

He explained how, after moving their patch of weed down to the asparagus fields as a result of the 'drug bust' fail at the farm all those years ago, Jon and he found that the plants were self-sowing throughout the asparagus field due to the ideal conditions. Plenty of fertilizer and irrigation.

"We just laughed it off, thinking we would get around to bringing it under control one day. You guessed right though. Out of the blue my buddy in Holland contacted me to say he would take any marijuana he could get his hands on. At premium prices. We had just finished the last of the villas and were skint. Pat was desperate to put up some buildings for her community centre and proper classrooms for her school. I thought, what the hell, it's legal there, it's for a good cause here, let's just do it."

"The rest is history," he said, grinning and pointing to the buildings where workers were just completing the finishing touches. "Beautiful new facilities for the community."

"And now you're involved you're going to carry on, I guess," Roger said.

Dirk laughed, "No. The duikers put a stop to it. The fire drove a whole stack of them into the asparagus fields where they discovered that marijuana leaves were far tastier than fern. There were no spears coming up at the time. They cleaned out every single plant. By the time they had finished, the veld grass was shooting up on their old hill, so they slowly started moving back leaving the asparagus intact. A good result for all probably, as we may have been tempted. Jon and I were thinking about getting a big black BMW each," he said punching Roger on the arm gently.

"Well I am glad you are not a drug lord, I must say," Roger grinned. "The duikers get stoned?"

"Not really, there were no flowers at that time and that good stuff we all enjoy is very low in the foliage. They looked pretty relaxed though. Gaza and Vula could walk right up close to them before they moved off. Had Sebete and Moriti totally confused as well."

Roger took a deep breath and decided to settle his biggest concern. "The night of Brad's accident, when we arrived on the patio, outside the window. Jon was already there, turning Brad over onto his back. Did you not wonder, if, as the paramedic said, Brad's death was instant and supposedly there was therefore very little blood, why Jon's hand was cut and he was covered in blood?"

"No, not at all. To speed up things we decided *he* not Kris, who was panicking, should smash the glass capsule under Kris' shirt. The fake blood you bought for Kris' shirt, remember? Jon was a little over-zealous, and in addition to getting the stuff all over his hand and arm, cut his fingers as well."

Dirk laughed, "Roger, Jon liked Brad. Why on earth would he stab him with a piece of glass?"

Roger looked sheepish. "Of course. Sure. I guess the drug thing made me a bit paranoid. Can we just forget it? I'm sorry."

Trotting past where they were standing Vula yelled, "Look at me, Roger. Am I better than Gaza?" Dirk said, "Hey, Roger, go and get Kirsten. I'll take her on a horse with me."

"She would love that," Roger said, hurrying back to the house to find his daughter.

***

Pat and Alan's relationship had progressed since the fire. Alan's standing had leaped in the eyes of his workers when they realised he and Malakabe were together. *Would one day be in their farmer's house,* they hoped. *Soon there would be little ones with red hair.*

Pat was happier than she had ever been. There were exciting things on the horizon, she enjoyed her life on the farm and Alan was providing her with what she had missed for so many years. He, for his part, was deeply in love. Pat could do no wrong. His only concern at the moment was this Christmas clan gathering. How would he fit in? The family were so close. Pat just hugged him and said, "Don't worry, you're with me, therefore you're part of the family."

***

Roger was totally enthralled by the scene unfolding on the patio the morning of the great family arrival. How things had changed. By eleven that morning, everyone invited was there, ensconced on the patio under the watchful eye of the distant rolling hills and mountains. Crisp blue sky, cooling breeze and crows calling in the distance made up the setting.

Below, in the gardens Marta and Marie were orchestrating games for all the kids. They had insisted they were staying at the farm over the Christmas period, it was their home now. In return for Dirk's past kindness, they were adamant they would babysit all the kids that week and weekend giving him and the rest of his family the opportunity to enjoy what was probably a once in a lifetime family gathering, without stressing over their children.

Roger observed the group with fascination. Pat and Allen, who would have guessed when earlier that year Pat took off to confront him over the traps? Marin and Lerryn, legal champions of the under-privileged who, until Lerryn opened her practice, assumed they weren't included in the entitled world. Eve and her partner, Moira, who fussed over Eve's daughters more than she did. There she was at the edge of the patio right now to check on the girls one more time. Clive who arrived stoic, quiet, but was thawing rapidly, now in an animated conversation with Jon, resting his thin white hand, skin translucent, near Jon's black muscular arm. Roger was examining his own arm and hands to see if he had got his tan back since returning from his years in England, when he heard Jon say, "Clive, you are the whitest person I have ever met."

Dirk and his mother Rita in heated, whispered conversation. Her companion sitting quietly beside her, making a point of not listening, staring into the distance. He seemed more like a butler than a partner. He was like someone who had wondered into the wrong party and decided to act like he *was* in the right place, hoping that if he said as little as possible nobody would realise he was uninvited, he could get through the evening and leave without being embarrassed.

And, of course, Tom and Mandy. Tom enjoying being the appreciated benefactor, paying for everyone's holiday. But looking older, and for the first time that Roger had seen, vulnerable. Like something had stolen his mojo. Mandy, even more attentive than Roger remembered, watching him like a hawk, moving his cup closer so he did not have to stretch, pushing a cushion down behind his back.

Tom was in deep conversation with Pat and she was getting progressively animated, grabbing Alan's hand and then letting it go to grab Tom's. Firstly, Tom's CEO mate had called him to say the Trust was going to invest in Pat's school. The report that had got back from the visit to Caracal Ridge was accepted, and they would be contacting her in the new year, but she should proceed with appointing her senior teacher.

Also, he had sat next to someone on the plane who turned out to be very interested in Tom's account of what Pat and Dirk had been doing with their local community. He and his wife had built a community initiative from the ground up that was now a substantial organisation located north of Durban, in a rural environment similar to Caracal Ridge. In summary, it was built around providing opportunities for orphaned kids. They had an infrastructure of foster mothers based in a village of small cottages. Each looked after a few kids, so they were able to enjoy a normal family home environment in their own homes, even a garden. They had a large school with considerable extramural activities available for development of the children.

"Their work has caught the attention of the government and the couple have established a good relationship with key department heads," Tom continued. They were so enthused with what he and his wife had achieved, they had asked him to help them create similar initiatives around the country. He was thus very interested in what Pat was doing and the potential to grow it through government funding. To become part of a greater community initiative.

Tom said he had given him her email address and he would be contacting her to invite her down to look over what they were doing on the Durban north coast.

Roger watched Pat's face morph from surprise, to disbelief to rapture as Tom spoke. He thought to himself, *this woman is the tortoise and her siblings all hares, she has caught up and moved ahead as the years have passed.*

***

The days and evenings passed by in relative harmony. If some of the new relationships their offspring had were a surprise to Tom and Rita, they did not show it. As they were preparing for bed one evening, Roger, thinking of Clive whispered, "He seems to be a bit *out there*? Is that how you remember him?" Georgie was paranoid about someone walking past their villa and hearing their conversation so she had insisted on what she called muted conversation, but Roger having a naturally loud voice could only manage normal or whispering.

"He was always a bit of an introvert." she responded, as she busied herself with makeup remover over the hand basin in the open-plan villa.

"Well, he and John have been very close the last few days, that's for sure. Is Jon gay?"

"Oh God, Roger. How many times have you not seen a demonstration of that fact since we first came down here?" she said, getting into bed and switching off the light.

Lying in the darkness Roger could hear Kirsten snoring quietly in her cot in the corner. One of the dogs scratched himself outside their door, his leg banging on the wooden kennel wall. Sounded like he was knocking on their door to come in. They seemed to be quite happy being on guard dog duty. Kirsten kept finding them snacks so what more could they want, mused Roger.

He thought about Georgie's fear of someone walking past and hearing their conversation. He grinned in the dark. Maybe *I* should do a walk around in the dark and see if there are any 'goings on'. Do a 'sneak by' of the villas. Would the dogs bark? *Oh God, Roger, just go to sleep,* he admonished himself, but could not keep the smile from his face. Georgie was starting to snore as well now.

***

Christmas Eve was the penultimate gathering and the most complete. Kids were included in this event, of course. With their help, using all sizes of shiny, coloured baubles, Marie and Marta set up a huge, beautiful tree. The dogs were put on their leads after Sebete's tail, wagging furiously with excitement, smacked a bauble off the tree across the room and Moriti pounced on it like he had been thrown a ball. He still had a red splinter or two stuck in his whiskers.

Georgie had brought Christmas tree candles and insisted they use them on the tree rather than electric Christmas lights, and in the darkness of the dining area, light from each individual flickering flame was reflected by hanging baubles resting against dark pine needles. They reminded Roger of planets orbiting in some dark universe.

Watching the extended family milling around the tree, laughing, teasing, pointing out wrapped presents piled under the tree he thought that this particular week they were indeed all like planets, drawn to the farm, *their* sun, to orbit around. Tom the magnet, the gravity that was holding them close for a week. *When he left, they would disband,* Roger observed.

***

On boxing day, after breakfast, Tom asked his five children, Rita and Mandy to join him in the bar. A family-only discussion which excluded his youngest, Kerry. After some confusion where partners who assumed they were included were asked politely to leave, they sat down facing him.

"This has been a wonderful week," Tom began. "To all be together after so long. I've wanted to be together with you all for ages. Like we used to be in the big house in Durban. It's a memory I have always cherished. One I wanted to refresh this Christmas, so I could take it back with me."

Tears were running down Mandy's cheeks. His children were frozen in their chairs. Their expressions fearful. Faces turning pale. Pat instinctively reached for her Mother's hand.

"You all know I have not been well for the last few years. It turns out that what looked like a curable, or at least controllable, condition is not. I only have a few months to live." Tom paused for what seemed to those watching his face, an eternity. Finally, managing to get his emotions under control, he continued. "I don't want to drag these next few months out. You guys knowing I am deteriorating, wishing it was over. I wanted to say goodbye in as happy an environment as possible. I think we came close to that this week. I have made arrangements to go into a special nursing home when I return to England. Not a hospice. I will be looked after and comfortable until my time comes. I won't be lonely so don't worry. The drugs will see to that."

Rita was stoic, her girls crying quietly around her. Dirk looked down at his trembling hands. Behind him, now standing, Clive stared out of the window towards the mountains. Dirk could hear him involuntarily gulping, quietly catching each choke that tried to escape.

"Mandy and I have agreed what should be divided up equally amongst you from my estate. The rest goes to her and Kerry. Dirk, I would like my share in Caracal Ridge to go to Pat and Lerryn." Dirk nodded.

"So today will be sad, but try and remember the happy part of our gathering this week. I love you all. I am going to rest in my room now. If you would like to come and say goodbye on your own, I will be there. We leave this afternoon, I don't want to drag our departure out."

***

Roger was stunned when Georgie informed him what Dirk had just told her about Tom. He shook his head. You have to give it to him. In control. The family father figure to the end to the end.

"And courageously pragmatic. Leave on a bittersweet note rather than put everybody, including himself, through a slow, painful departure. Took guts. Still, going to be hard for everyone but possibly hardest for Mandy and Kerry," Georgie said quietly.

Looking down into the garden where Kirsten was holding Marta's hand as the older kids played a game of tag, Georgie continued, "If that was a surprise, you better sit down for the next one. Dirk also said Tom wanted me to go and see him as he had something he needed to tell me."

***

Georgie tapped gently on Tom and Mandy's villa door. Mandy opened it with a smile. "Come in, Georgie, Tom is just having his tea. Would you like some? Have a seat, I am not sure about these 'rustic' chairs of Dirk's?"

"It's the open-plan toilets that worry me, not the chairs," Georgie laughed.

Letting the smile slowly leave her face, Georgie turned to Tom. "Oh, Tom, I am so sad to hear your news. Dirk just told me. You are very brave. So sorry, Mandy."

"Georgie thank you, but as I have told the others, please don't feel sad. I have long reconciled with my next few months. I had, even when you came to say goodbye in England that afternoon," Tom said patting Georgie's hand. She placed her other hand over his before having to grab for a tissue.

"I am very happy with what God has allowed me to enjoy. Even today, my caring Mandy and our loving daughter keep me secure. In a small way it has also allowed me to influence the directions life has taken for Dirk, Pat and

Lerryn. Even Clive, although in what might be seen as a negative way initially.

My wealth is not mine really, it was provided by the universe. I have used it to the best of my ability and with my departure, need to leave it behind to be used for the best purpose. Dirk and Pat have a wonderful opportunity to build something great here at Caracal Ridge."

Not 'Dirk's farm' anymore, thought Georgie.

"Which is the segue I was looking for. Let me share some thoughts with you, Georgie," Tom continued.

Tom relayed his two-hour discussion with the guy in the plane he had told Pat about on the first day on the patio. Tom saw initiative North Coast Haven, or NCH as it was known, a perfect match with what Pat and Dirk were doing. Although they sought funding, the husband and wife team from Durban did what they could to make their community initiative self-funding. Much like Dirk was already doing with the farm, with proceeds from the asparagus and grazing going to the community buildings, Pat's school and wages in general.

Georgie smiled to herself as she wondered whether Tom knew it was actually Dirk's drug initiative that had built the new community centre.

Tom went on to say it seemed that this couple was a savvy business couple who had conceived the idea and then brought people in to manage the operating side of NCH. Tom proposed a reverse of this.

"Dirk and Pat are wonderful at what they do. Totally involved, passionate. They will be responsible for the actual execution of what Caracal Ridge does, farming, resort and school community. But Caracal Ridge is going to be, whether you like it or not, an enterprise if it is to prosper. It will need formal business and financial management processes. That, Georgie, is where I believe you and Roger come in," Tom smiled.

Georgie's mouth dropped open. She was about to say something, she was not sure what, when Tom raised his hand slowly, requesting a chance to finish what he was saying.

"I know you loved your time in our family environment when you and Dirk were together, Georgie. You are a community-minded person. That's probably what brought you and Dirk together. I also know you and Roger have proved you can run a business. You two would do a wonderful job here, Dirk and Pat think so too, so here is what we propose."

Tom said he had told Dirk and Pat that in return for Roger and her committing to a two-year tenure, he would put an amount in trust that would guarantee Roger's salary for two years, pay for the construction of a suitable family cottage for them and cover their relocation costs to Caracal Ridge. Her salary would be paid out of the farm's revenue and of course their food would be free. She and

Roger would make the decisions on the day-to-day running of Caracal Ridge as a business operation, but more strategic stuff would need to be agreed by the four of them. "If you can't agree you can have a vote," he finished. "You'll find a way I am sure."

After bidding Tom a tearful farewell and promising to make contact with Mandy, asking her to call if she needed anything, no matter what, Georgie made her way back down the grassy slope to the patio where she had left Roger. Her mind racing, trying to absorb and assimilate what had been offered. She did not even notice the vista of mountains and hills as she normally did from the raised area the villas were located in. She felt a growing excitement at the thought of not only being part of a community but helping to grow it. It was a way of life she had thought about a lot lately. But what about Roger? His new job. He loved big city life. Going to the bar with his friends. Taking clients to big sports games.

***

"Well. Are you going to tell me or not?" Roger asked Georgie, who it appeared was lost somewhere in her thoughts. Jigsaw puzzle? he wondered.

"Sorry, got distracted there." She went on to relay her conversation earlier with Tom. She watched as Roger's face went from incredulous, to surprise, to mind racing. The sparkle that was growing in his eyes told her that a move to Caracal Ridge was likely.

***

Roger, as he was prone to do in these situations, initially tried *oh God I feel so awkward* and then *it's really a family thing isn't it?* but Georgie was having none of it.

"You owe it to him. And Dirk, Roger. Show your respect. You're just saying goodbye."

"Yeah, but forever."

"Well, treat it as your first *final* goodbye. You had to have one sooner or later," Georgie snapped, growing increasingly impatient. "How do you think I feel?"

Once he got to the parking area where Tom and his family were loading their car, Roger found his courage. The family were standing around the car trying to be happy, as Tom had requested, or at least impassive.

Excusing himself for barging in, he said, "Tom, I just wanted to say goodbye. It was a privilege knowing you." Roger swallowed, that sounded so final, oh shit. But Tom smiled and said, "Likewise Roger. Please consider my proposal favourably. It's important to me."

Roger surprised himself by stepping forward and hugging Tom, "I will. We will." And then Mandy, before escaping back through the archway to the house.

Chapter 13

Rolling Stones

It was the second time in the past year that someone lay at Bonniface's cliff ledge looking down on the resort. Like the previous occupants of this lofty position, this observer did not necessarily wish Caracal Ridge or the people in it any good either. Marta's father had decided in the bar at lunchtime he should sort out this problem with his daughter running away to the hippy's farm. Now he tried to focus the very old pair of binoculars he had found hanging up in his garage earlier. His elbows ached from being pressed into the uneven rock surface, but he was determined. The Protection Order that red-head bitch lawyer had got Cor to serve him, with a smirk on his face, was not going to stop him making sure his daughter was not molested in this devil's place below. He had heard the rumours of drugs and black people living in the farmhouse with white people. "*Sies, jong*," he said, spitting in the dirt alongside him.

Far beyond the roofs of the resort buildings below, the new green grass that had appeared on the distant hillside after the fire was already beginning to return to the faded gold of veld grass. A flash of light caught his eye as sunlight reflected off the windscreen of Alan's truck bouncing down the hill towards the dam.

Up here, Marta's Father was certainly more than three hundred metres from where she lived so no problem, he knew. Already having a conviction, he could take no chances being arrested again. He would be back in *tjoekie* quick time. He moved slightly to get more comfortable and farted loudly. "*Whoa jong, Oudemeester wat se jy? brandy and coke, seker*," he chuckled to himself.

If he could just catch them up to something down below, he could report them at the charge office in town. He was the girl's father, they would have to listen. Take it seriously. Especially if there were drugs involved. "Pity it does not matter to the cops what these blerry blacks do nowadays," he growled to himself.

***

343

Their weekly routine soon became a daily one, as time passed. Jon would wait until he was more or less alone with his books before calling Clive. The reception area was quiet in the late morning which was ideal for Jon to do his farm bookkeeping. It was late evening in the UK so Clive would be at home. Jon would let the phone ring three times, as they had arranged, and then replace the receiver so Clive could call back. Their conversations were lengthy and taken up largely with Clive answering questions that Jon had about England. The more he heard the more he longed to experience this country where you could find the centuries-old homes of authors he had read, where in winter it was dark at four in the afternoon and not light again until nine in the morning, where one could still see where the Romans had bathed, see their roads.

***

Marta's father had arrived at the farm drunk, a few days after she moved to Caracal Ridge even though she had explained that it was a great job opportunity she had been offered, a chance to learn new skills and how happy she was to get away from being a waiter. As she was to stay in the same living quarters as her friend, Marie, she believed she had allayed his fears of her being molested by any man.

344

He had nodded grudgingly and gone off to meet his mates for lunchtime drinks at the pub. She suspected he still believed she had been lured to an establishment of ill repute where drugs and wild parties were the norm. That was the belief of his drinking mates, and she expected him to come home surly and angry after a few hours with them.

Marta was right and during the yelling argument between them later he had lashed out at her but stumbled in his inebriated state, missing her and landing on the floor where he stayed for the rest of the evening.

It was only Dirk's intervention that day he came to the farm, threatening to call the police, that got him to leave, yelling over his shoulder that if she didn't come home there would be trouble. Cursing and swearing at Sebete who barked a continuous warning at the intruder, he fell into his bakkie before driving off in a cloud of dust.

At Dirk's insistence, Marta had contacted Lerryn asking her for a restraining order against her father.

***

Down below, most guests were in the bar or having dinner. Dirk, Jon and Pat were winding their way up the grassy slope through the villas on their way to give Marta a surprise party. They struggled under a load of drinks and food for an impromptu barbecue. Marta had been with them three months already and her whole demeanour had changed. She was back to her old self, and they wanted to reinforce her growing confidence. Recently, having Georgie to guide her now, she had already completed her first email marketing project and Caracal Ridge was on the books of several new travel agents.

Dirk had set up a barbecue facility near each staff villa so they could have a private meal from time to time. A break from the normal mealtime interaction with other staff and guests when they felt like some 'me' time. They were equipped with gas bottles and burners only, to avoid any accidental sparks from wood or charcoal being blown into the thatched roofs. This evening, though, they decided to use one of the nearby guest barbecues so Marta would not realise anything was being organised for her.

***

From his perch above, Marta's father spotted the trio and closing one eye, to block out a broken lens, trained the binoculars on them. "Ja, it's that hippy and the same black. Where are they going?" he grunted, as he raised himself unsteadily to his feet. He crouched and moved through the brambles and grass to his left in order to position himself above where they were. He nearly fell as he slipped on loose stones, having had a good few beers earlier over lunch and then sipping from his bottle of brandy and coke on the way to the farm. His stumble launched a few rocks which rolled downward before being lost from sight over the ledge.

Slowly but surely, he moved along the ledge until he reached a point where the ledge fell away and became more of a ravine strewn with all sizes of weathered sandstone rocks, some almost round like soccer balls. Some smaller like golf balls.

He was now directly in line with and way above where Dirk and Jon were unloading their stuff onto a table next to the barbecue. He was on a slope, so he had to sit and lean his back against a boulder, heels wedged into the stones to stop himself sliding down. He could not be seen, but had to keep moving his head to see through the bush that hid him from view.

***

Down below, while the other two set up the table, Pat went across to knock on Marie and Marta's door. "Come on out M&Ms, we know you're in there. *Braai* time," she called.

A face came to the window, Marta, wet hair plastered onto her cheeks. "Malakabe? I was showering, what's up?"

"Wow, Marie *can* keep a secret. It's your surprise party, dummy. For being here three months and being such a pain in the arse," Pat laughed.

"What?"

Marie appeared through the doorway and said. "Thank God, you are here at last. I have been so sick of lying to her all day. Telling her she could not shower would have been weird. Sorry. She won't be long. *Will she Marta?"* Marie said tapping on the glass in front of Marta's face that was still staring out at them, towel clutched around her.

***

Up above, Marta's Father changed his position slightly to see past a branch in the bush. His boot, moving forward, sent a small rock rolling off down the slope. He watched with detached interest as it picked up speed before it bounced into a crevice and came to a stop.

***

Pat went back to where Jon and Dirk were getting the barbecue organised. Pat said, "It's been great having Roger and Georgie here, don't you think? This place is getting very efficient. It's been a while since the three of us knocked off together at five o'clock, hey?"

"Oh yeah," Dirk grinned. "And he has the patience to handle all our government buddies and their bureaucratic processes. I could never have done that for you. He even has the customs guys eating out of his hand. He's even got them emailing us confirmation at the completion of each stage of the export process. My mate in Holland thinks he's the best."

Opening beers for each of them and herself, Pat said, "And Georgie has taught Marta so much about marketing, so quickly, it's hard to believe she arrived here a nervous young girl just a few months ago. I think I will involve them in my final funding submission to the NPO now that Roger has sorted out all the Trust Deed stuff they require for the application." She sipped her beer, "If Marta can wind your cynical travel journalists around her finger, I am sure she could build some good relationships with these government guys too. And, of course, she speaks fluent Afrikaans. That has to be a help."

"I am going down to Durban next week again to meet with the NCH guys on this application, by the way. I will also go and see if Mom is OK," Pat continued.

Dirk shook his head as he loaded sausages onto the braai. "Yes, Dad's passing was a shock. No matter how much we knew it was coming. She must be a bit shaken. They were close, no matter what their history."

Jon put his arms around both of them. "Sorry, guys,"

***

Marta's father, seeing this going on below, moved the eyepieces away from his face so he could shake his head in disgust. "*Blerry swart boeties*," he growled.

***

There was someone else shaking his head as well. Bonniface watched in wonder as his son stood with his arms around two white people. And one a boss? He had never seen a black person hug a white person. Is this not disrespectful? "Whoa, *bohle baa lumela*, (they are all embracing)" he moaned, but he could not resist grinning as it became a group hug.

Bonniface had come across this scene before him just as he started his weekly guard duty shift. One of his first tasks was to check all the fire extinguishers were in place outside each villa. Since the fire, Dirk had become very strict about checking that they were in place every night in case a guest had moved one. Seeing the group at the braai he decided to hang back for the moment, he would check the extinguishers there later when everyone had gone. Instead he moved up the slope to check the other villas.

***

"Here she is, the party girl," Pat called as the two girls made their way across from their villa. Behind the two arriving at the braai, high above them was another girl Pat would have been pleased to see had she not been hidden behind the thorn trees and odd clumps of veld grass that somehow survived on the rocky face above them. She led two others up the steep rock face, leaping from one rock to the next, one ledge to the next. The three looked identical, could have been sisters, except their leader was distinct due to only one of her tufted ears being black.

The caracals moved with grace as they made their ascent. They looked like seals as their silky bodies stretched and slid gracefully through the evening shadows upward, ledge after ledge. Only stopping when one of them spotted something, or heard, or smelt something that sparked their insatiable curiosity. The sisters would gather momentarily before losing interest or their mother moved off upward.

Her kittens were nearly fully grown now, and she expected them to be moving away and leaving her at any time. They had made their first few kills some time ago and were relying on her less and less. With her two girls still around, her territory was under pressure hunting-wise. The rabbit population was still recovering from the fire on the other side of the valley, so she had brought them across here to see what was on offer. She also knew they might spot something that would attract them, motivate them to make their inevitable move into their own territories.

***

Now, knowing what was up, Marta had with Marie's help got ready quickly and was looking stunning. Pat smiled to herself as she saw Dirk do a double take when he turned from his work at the grill to find her standing behind him.

As the evening progressed and alcohol took off the edge, they shared amusing anecdotes which took place prior to Marta's arrival at Caracal Ridge. There were a few though from that first Cherry Festival, and her giggling recollections and descriptions of Roger's entrance to the restaurant, half-stoned, as the tallest Elvis ever, reduced them all to fits of laughter.

She was at the summit now, her two 'kitten adults' behind her. She sat motionless, ears rotating as normal. Nose up sniffing. Her girls busied themselves looking into crevices for anything that might be considered worthwhile for chasing and catching. As she moved off again, they followed her. Until they left her and went off on their own for good, it would be an involuntary response to her moving forward.

Suddenly she froze and dropped down onto her belly. The girls did the same. They knew instinctively they needed to follow her every move now, there was either danger or prey about. It was not playtime for the moment.

She had picked up his scent and had been waiting for sound or movement. As Marta's father lowered the binoculars, she had him pinpointed. He was downwind of them, so they were already very close by the time the caracal mother had caught his scent. All three were on a ledge slightly above him, motionless, watching. He was too big to be prey, probably, but they would observe him for a time, before deciding on a course of action.

***

353

Down below Dirk had just made a little impromptu speech. He complimented Marta on her good work and said how they were all so impressed with her tenacity and determination to learn as much as she could as fast as she could. After a toast to her, Dirk then said he had another announcement to make.

"Jon is leaving the farm to go and live in England." The girls were stunned. Dirk went on to tell them Clive had invited him to stay with him and to get some A-levels before going to Uni, all of which he had offered to pay for. "So, the next time we see Jon he might be a professor," Dirk laughed.

Putting his arm around Jon's shoulder and hugging him, he said, "His sister, Bongi, is going to have big shoes to fill, but he's trained her well."

Marta stepped forward and hugged Jon saying, "Oh I am really going to miss you."

High above, seeing this embrace, Marta's father dropped his binoculars, jumped up, turning to make for his car and the farm where he would 'finish off that black once and for all'.

As he turned, raising his arms, he let out a bellow of rage so loud they even heard it down below, faces turning up to the summit of the sandstone cliff. The cats as one, jumped up, ears flat with fear, bodies curved, arched to their full height, spitting and growling in defiance. Faced with the sudden appearance of this fearsome feline trio, Marta's father took an involuntary step back, his howl of rage dying on his lips, and then another as his weight transferred and he lost his centre of gravity. He felt himself slowly falling backwards, knowing the steep slope falling away from him meant it would be some time before his body actually made contact with the ground again. His scrambling boots set off several boulders on a downward trajectory under him.

The partying group below, faces turned up, still could not make out anything or see anyone above, but kept staring up anyway which was just as well. Dirk saw them first. Several boulders the size of footballs rolling and bouncing down the steep rocky ravine. As they gained momentum, some bounced several metres into the air, whilst smaller ones rolled below them like a mini avalanche.

"Get behind the villa. *Now,*" Dirk shouted. Faces pale with fear, Marie and Marta seemed frozen to the ground. "*Now!*" Dirk yelled again, as he grabbed them both by their wrists, pulling them with him as he stumbled backwards, eyes glued to the tumbling boulders. Jon and Pat were already behind the villa they had been barbecuing next to.

The young girls were screaming as the first boulder thudded into the wall of the villa and several others rolled past. Pat was looking down the slope praying that the kids or dogs were not playing nearby. One rock bounced just before it reached the villa they had sought refuge behind, and rising, crashed through the thatched roof above them, landing on the floor inside with a thud and shattering of glass.

Just as it seemed the procession of descending boulders had stopped, there was a loud clang as one of the final missiles smashed into the barbecue and gas cylinder they had been using, taking the valve clean off. There was an ominous hiss for a few seconds before the released gas, spurting upward, caught alight. Ignited by the still red-hot grill and unattended, now flaming sausages. The column of flame shot skyward like an erupting volcano, setting the thatch roof alight instantaneously.

Throwing caution aside, Dirk jumped up and grabbed the fire extinguisher from its bracket, but it was too late for just one extinguisher. The roof was well alight and sending embers flying in the strong breeze towards the other thatched roofs. A second was already showing flames and a third smouldering, ready to go. Just as an ashen-faced Dirk stared into the face of looming disaster, he was suddenly surrounded by workers carrying extinguishers. Under instruction from Bonniface, who had narrowly escaped the rock fall himself and expecting the worst, they had been sent scurrying for the spare extinguishers in the storeroom. They tackled the big fire and start-up thatch fires with the precision of a well-drilled army.

**

Surveying the doused, smouldering thatch around them, Dirk, Jon and the girls were surrounded by alarmed guests including the two who were the occupants of the villa that had lost most of its roof and internal furnishings. Fortunately, they had arrived at the resort late so had just dropped their bags inside the door to their villa, unopened, and headed for dinner. When Jon smashed the door open to make sure there was nobody inside the burning villa, he had yanked the two cases standing at the door out and thrown them outside onto the lawn.

The other villas looked intact, apart from needing some repair work to the thatch. They had been lucky.

Pat had fetched her binoculars and was looking up at the rocky ravine trying to see what might have caused the sudden rock fall. She let out a gasp, "Oh my God, there is someone lying up there." After a few seconds she said. "It does not look good. Not at all. Someone call emergency." Jon ran off to the office.

Pat handed the glasses to Dirk, suggesting that if he was at all squeamish he give it a miss. He took her advice and handed them back.

***

357

The following morning, Dirk and Roger were standing alongside the burnt-out villa staring up at the cliffs, marvelling at how the emergency chopper pilot had managed to get his aircraft into position and keep it steady alongside the sheer rock face in order to lift out the victim of the rockfall. It was surreal. The helicopter, black cable below it disappearing in a slight arch into the shadows, was high enough to catch the last rays of the setting sun while down below at the villas the intrigued people staring up were already in the fading evening light. The blades seemed to rotate almost in slow motion, slashing through the sunlight and every so often, depending on the craft's position, reflected light down towards the watching crowd below, like someone using a mirror in the sunlight to send a Morse code message to them. The engine's thudding, echoing off the sandstone face, gave the impression there were two helicopters, one invisible. Suddenly the metal stretcher being winched up from below appeared above the trees into the sunlight. A paramedic clung to the framework busying himself with the shape strapped onto the stretcher.

Roger said, "I think you dodged a bullet. The whole lot could have gone up. Still, it was bad though, what with the paramedics discovering it was Marta's father up there." Dirk brought his eyes back down from the ravine above. "Yes. It could have been worse, were it not for Bonniface. We are going to have to give him some kind of recognition." *Commend* him, Roger smiled to himself. He put his arm around Dirk's shoulder, "A bit of good news, buddy. It was only the day before yesterday that Lerryn and I signed off the amended Insurance Policy for the

Caracal Ridge Resort. You not only get paid out for the damage, you are now also covered for loss of revenue."

Dirk slapped him on the back. "Well, that's why Dad wanted you, thanks." Looking back up the ravine, Dirk said, "I need to go and see how Marta is."

Climbing a short way up the rocky slope he found her sitting on a rock some way below where her father had fallen to his death the evening before. Landing on his head as he fell backwards, before taking the full force of several falling boulders. Dirk sat down beside her. She was crying quietly. He reached into his pocket and handed her the pile of crumpled but clean napkins he had grabbed from the bar counter. He took the soaked bunch of old tissues she had been clenching in her hand from her gently and stuffed them in his pocket.

He put his arm around her shoulders, and she laid her head against him, beginning to sob. "It's OK, it's OK. We're your family, you're with us. It's OK."

Gradually the sobs subsided, and she was able to say, "I know you all thought he was a bad man. But he was my father. I did love him."

Dirk said, "Well, whatever his problems, he's at peace now."

Marta didn't say anything, but she was calmer.

Dirk continued to gaze out over the burnt thatch roof and the farm. To the asparagus fields and mountains beyond. Morning fog was hanging in the gullies, cloud topped the highest mountains. It was quiet and peaceful. Despite the traumatic events of yesterday he felt content. The boys and barking dogs broke the silence.

"*Li-taxis li fihlile, Li-taxis li fihlile*," they called, as a taxi pulled into the parking area alongside the sandstone wall.

Running towards the parking area, Sebete and Moriti barking behind them, Gaza and Vula were calling, "Malakabe, Malakabe."

"*Mosuoe e mocha o tlile* (the new teacher has come)," Gaza yelled over his shoulder.

Vula sang loudly, dancing doing a toyi-toyi, "Hello, hello, *Zulu* teacher."

Dirk saw Pat hurry across the patio to where the taxi had stopped.

THE END

9 781912 964291